AF101743

Scallywag!
being the True-Life Adventures of "Mad" Molly McCormick
PYRATE

Also by K. L. Mitchell

Kalazad Series
The Road to Kalazad
Villains
Blazing Centaurs

Helen Highwater and the Burning Eye

====

Scallywag!

being the True-Life Adventures of

"Mad" Molly McCormick, Pyrate

Wherein is to be found a great many Wonders, &c,
Including Cursed Islands, Great Underwater Beasts, Ghost Colonies,
the Kingdom of the Merpeople, and Divers Others

As Written by Herself

Printed Exclusv'ly by Launch Point Press & Print-Jobbing
At the sign of the Desert Palm, LONDON

====

A Desert Palm Press Trade Paperback Original

Scallywag! is a work of fiction. Names, characters, places, and incidents are either the product of the author's imagination or are used in a fictitious manner. Any resemblance to actual persons living or dead, business establishments, events, or locales is entirely coincidental. Internet references contained in this work are current at the time of publication, but Desert Palm Press cannot guarantee that a specific reference will continue or be maintained in any respect.

All other rights are reserved. Desert Palm Press supports copyright which enables creativity, free speech, and fairness. Thank you for buying the authorized version of this book and for following copyright laws by not using or reproducing any part of this book in any manner whatsoever, including Internet usage, without written permission from Desert Palm Press, except in the form of brief quotations embodied in critical reviews and articles. Your cooperation and respect support authors and allow Desert Palm Press to continue to publish the books you want to read.

For permission requests, write to the publisher at publisher@desertpalmpress.com or "Attention: Permissions Coordinator" at

Desert Palm Press
4804 NW Bethany Blvd, Suite I-2, #148
Portland, OR 97229

www.desertpalmpress.com

Copyright © 2026 by K. L. Mitchell

ISBN: 978-1-63304-082-3
E-Book: 978-1-63304-083-0

Editing: Raven's Eye Editing
Formatting: Anne Battis
Cover Design: Lilia Dormichev

Printed in the United States of America
First Edition April 2026

Dedication

According to Noam Chomsky, a captured pirate was brought before Alexander the Great.

"How dare you molest the sea," said Alexander.

"How dare you molest the whole world," the pirate replied. "Because I do it with a little ship only, I am called a thief. You, doing it with a great navy, are called an emperor."

It is to that unknown pirate that this epistle is respectfully dedicated.

Epigraph

"A merry life and a short one shall be my motto."
-Bartholomew Roberts

Chapter One

Fort St. Ambrose, Denwick Island
May 3rd, 1680

I AM A CHILD OF the sea, born in sight of her. All through my childhood, she provided for my family and my home. Later, when I struck out into the world, she gave me everything I needed. She gave me purpose, grand companions, and such sights as I should never have thought to see. But more than anything, she gave me freedom.

I fear she will not do so again.

My crew is scattered, my ship gone, and I sit locked up in this d—d cell. Awaiting only the pleasure of His Grace, the governor, to be hanged by my neck until dead. Yet she is here with me. I know not whether 'tis kindness or cruelty that moved them to hold me in a cell right by the water. By day, I look out the lone, barred window at the waves. By night, I am lulled to sleep by the sound of them lapping the shore. To see and hear it thus, ever separated by a wall of stone, is an agony not easy to express.

I sometimes wish I could slip between this window's bars and let the waves take me...where? There's no land to be seen for miles. The fortress wherein I am confined covers the whole of this island, it being small and bereft of vegetation. There is nowhere I could hide, and nowhere else I could go. The sea, which once nurtured me and freed me, has become my gaoler.

To pass the time, I have resolved to put pen to paper and write my memoirs. The chaplain of the fort, a decent fellow for all he is a Protestant, was able to procure the materials whereby I am writing this ms. I told him I wished to make a full and frank confession, there being no priest to hear it. In a way 'tis true, this being as close to a proper confession as ever I am likely to offer. Let it be my testimony then, and know, whoever reads this, that herein is to be found naught but G—d's Own Truth.

I, Molly Donnelly McCormick, was born in April, in the year of our Lord,1653. Of my family I shall not speak much, save to say that we lived in one of the many small port towns around Bantry Bay, Éire. Papa was a shopkeeper, selling to the pilchard fishermen who frequented our tiny town. I have to say, in all honesty, he was not naturally inclined toward commerce, being more suited to passing the time of day with his customers while Mam tended to the store. As the eldest child, it generally fell to me to help with the running of the shop, and it was in this way that I learned my letters and numbers. My brothers, taking after our father, displayed no inclination toward trade, preferring to hunt the woods inland of our village.

Few girls were near my age, and I was generally busy helping out in the store or chasing after my brothers. There were occasions when I could go about on my own and call upon one of the few friends I had, but these times were, at best, irregular. I never cultivated the art of deep and lasting friendships 'til much later in life. I do not hold this against my parents, for we were all busy with one thing and another. But sometimes I could not help comparing my lot to that of other, more fortunate girls.

As must needs happen with us all, some of the other girls began the process of leaving childhood behind. At the advent of my thirteenth year, I had yet to see any sign of this transformation in my own life. Other women will understand when I say I had been initiated into the sisterhood of women but had yet to witness the physical manifestations one expects at that time. I found myself, once more, envying my friends, many of whom had begun to attract the attention of the village boys. Now mind, I did not particularly desire courtship in itself. I just felt that I was being left behind again.

Everything changed in late summer. Business was slow, and it was becoming clear that the store was no longer able to support us all. It had been a bad year for fishing, and those who (like us) depended on the fishermen for their income were likewise affected. Mam and Papa did their best to shield us, but children being more perceptive than adults know, we could all see there were simply too many mouths to feed.

Papa had borrowed money from Mr. Hennessy, an older man whose family had created the town's fish market and, as a result, became tremendously well-off. I remember Mr. Hennessy came to call on Mam and Papa more often than usual. My brothers and I were sent outside or told to mind the store while the adults talked upstairs. We assumed, of course, that he was coming about the money owed, but he greeted us kindly and sometimes brought little treats for us. Naturally, being inquisitive, we tried to eavesdrop on the grown-ups' conversation, but they spoke quietly behind closed doors. We could never discover what they were talking about.

Scallywag!

One Sunday, we came home from church and had our dinner. Stew again: as times got leaner, we ate more and more stew. There was something in the air, I recall. After Mam and I had done the washing up, it was clear our parents had something on their minds. None of us had any clue what it might be. My brothers were sent out to play, but I was told to wait in the kitchen. I daresay, anyone who remembers their childhood knows the sensation of the stomach knotting up when something like this happens. You sit there, wondering if you're in trouble and if so, for what? My mind was busy running through anything and everything I might have done, but for my life, I could not think of anything that would justify the seriousness that overshadowed that entire day.

After an agony of waiting, Mam and Papa came and sat down at the table facing me. How strange were their facial expressions. The seriousness I expected was certainly there, but of anger or disappointment, there was no sign. If anything, they seemed…nervous. This alarmed me even more. Seeing one's parents distressed is a worrying thing for a child. After all, grown-ups are supposed to be in control and know what to do. That afternoon, at the dining table, they seemed quite small and vulnerable. This was my first inkling that something could be more serious than merely being in trouble.

Papa cleared his throat. "Well," he said, "Molly-girl, we—that is to say, your mother and I—we have been talking, and…well, I need hardly tell you as how we've not been doing as well as we might, lately. The fact is, things are rather lean enough that it's becoming difficult to support everyone under this roof. Now, we know you're a hardworking girl, always earned your keep, looking after your brothers and that. We're proud of you and always will be. But the thing is, well…" he trailed off and turned to Mam.

"What we mean is, you're not a little girl anymore, dear. You're fast becoming a woman, and that means you'll be taking your place in the world. Do you see?"

I nodded.

"Good girl," said Papa. He hesitated, then leaned forward. "You know that Mr. Hennessy has been by a lot lately, yes? A very respectable person, he is. Good family, got that nice house at the top of the hill and all that. He's a good man by all accounts…" he faltered and looked away.

I felt a wave of relief wash over me. Now I understood. "And I'm to go work for him, then?"

They didn't answer straight away. Mam reached across the table and laid a hand on mine. "That's not quite it, love. The fact is, he has taken quite a shine to you. He asked for your hand. In marriage. Isn't that nice?"

The look on my face must have said it all. Mind, he was a nice enough person, and he did live better than we ever would, but I hadn't even begun to give a thought to love and romance, let alone marriage. And to be married off to some wretched old man who walked with a stoop and had hardly a tooth in his head, a man who was more like a dotty old grandfather than a husband, well!

Mam squeezed my hand. "I know he's not...handsome. Or young. But he will be able to take such good care of you. He has that lovely big house, and you'll have servants of your own. No more minding the store or running after those brothers of yours, eh?" She forced a smile.

"Besides," said Papa, "if we're kin to him, then that will take care of the money we owe him, won't it? He's getting on in years, as your mam said, and I reckon even if you don't fancy him, you won't have to worry too long. You'll be a wealthy widow before you know it. Take your pick then, eh?"

"I think it is the best thing," Mam said. "It will give you a life better than we ever could and will benefit the rest of us as well. You've always been such a good, hardworking girl. Now you will be a lady of quality. Imagine all the fine dresses and things you shall have!" There was a wistful look in her eyes. It occurred to me that Mam, who had few enough fine things herself, was imagining herself in my place.

"Anyhow," said Papa, "it's all settled. He's agreed to cancel our debt and even throw in a little extra as a wedding gift. The wedding will be in the autumn, probably around Michaelmas. Plenty of time to make all the arrangements. He's even spoken to Mrs. Geary about getting you up a proper wedding dress. What do you think of that, my girl?"

"*No!*" The word was out of my mouth before I ever realized. I think I was as surprised as they were, honestly. Mam let go of my hand, and Papa just gawped at me.

"No? What do you mean, no?" he finally asked.

"I'm not marrying him."

Now, at that age, I didn't have what you would call a complete knowledge of wives and husbands and that, only a hodge-podge of things Mam had hinted at and what the other girls had pieced together. I wasn't entirely sure what would happen on our wedding night, but I already knew I wanted no part of it. "He's so...*old!* He's got big ears and spots. Also, he smells of ointment."

Papa's face hardened. "Now see here, girl. That's no way to be talkin' about your future husband. I already said it's been arranged. Now I don't want any more brass out of you, hear me? You'll be a married woman soon, but while you're under my roof, you're not too old for the switch. I've had my say, and that's the end of it."

"But Papa—"

"No more!" Papa grabbed me by the wrist. "I'm the head of this family, and you'll do as you're damn well told. Now run along with you, and I don't want to hear another word about this. You hear me?"

I pulled away as he let go. "You're horrid!" I shouted. "I hate you!" I turned, ran upstairs to my room, and threw myself on the bed, sobbing. I couldn't believe what had happened. Being forced to marry some smelly old man because he was rich? Maybe Papa should marry him and see how he liked it. The vision of Papa's portly frame squeezed into a wedding gown gave me a momentary giggle, but reality returned and sank my spirits as quickly as they had risen.

Sometime later, Mam knocked on the door and asked if I wanted to talk. I told her to go away, something I never would have dreamed of saying to her before. Somewhat to my surprise, they left me alone for the rest of the night. From time to time, I could hear them talking in low voices downstairs. They must have had a word with my brothers, who gave me a wide berth when they came back that evening.

I don't believe I slept at all that night. I kept turning the thing over and over in my head. Married! And to a man I hardly knew. I mean, he seemed nice enough, but that was hardly enough to get married on. I'd heard the other girls go on about true love and handsome princes, but my interest in such things had been desultory at best. Still, I couldn't help but feel that I was being robbed of something that should have been mine by right. And all without so much as a by-your-leave. It all seemed so unfair.

And yet, all my life (so much as it was) had been in service to the family. When cooking and cleaning were to be done, I cooked and cleaned. When an extra pair of hands was needed around the shop, I was there. Obedience had been impressed upon me from birth. My duty was to obey my parents, to serve the family's needs. Everything in my life said that I must marry Mr. Hennessy. And yet, I could not for a moment accept this fate. It felt like I had two choices, and both were impossible.

I don't know how long I lay there, turning it over and over in my head, but by the time the sun came up, I had made up my mind, for better or worse.

I was going to run away.

Chapter Two

TWO WEEKS LATER, I stood before the tiny looking glass in my room and regarded my handiwork. I'd been, more or less, in charge of the family sewing since I was old enough to handle a needle and had even taken in some outside work from bachelor fishermen who couldn't do their own mending. Consequently, I had accumulated a fair amount of scraps I could make use of whenever I needed to. I had spent more and more time in my room of late, working on my sewing. Nothing unusual, as far as my parents were concerned, though I daresay they'd have something to say if they saw what I'd made. The trousers were...odd. I wasn't used to having my legs enclosed so, but I could see the practical side. I had some good linen, dyed green, and made a shirt that fit well, if a bit baggy. Mam had taught me to make clothing a wee bit on the large side so that we kids might grow into them. At least my torso was adequately covered. Not that there was much *to* cover, mind. If Mam was anything to go by, I could expect a bit of a change by the time I was sixteen. By then I wouldn't be pretending to be a boy anymore.

    The idea had come to me in the small hours of that first awful night. Running away as a girl was not what you would call rich with possibilities. Where would a girl go off to? I honestly had no idea. About the only option I knew of was to be like those poor women down the dock, the ones Mam said were "no better than they should be." Compared to that, I would rather marry Mr. Hennessy and have done with it. But a boy...well! A boy could be almost anything. Of course, living as we did in a harbor town usually meant going off to sea. I have said that mostly fishing boats came into our part of the bay, but there were trading ships as well. And so one would hear, for example, that the youngest O'Malley boy had disappeared the very day a schooner headed out for the Indies. Most of the boys loved to play at sailors, and there were always a few who went out to see the world.

    Ever since the night of the argument, I had been very careful not to arouse any suspicion. The next morning, I came down early, apologized to my parents for my outburst, and assured them that I would not question their judgment further. This seemed to satisfy them all right, and I was able to keep my head down and start putting my plan into action.

The next task was to find a ship. As I said, they did tend to come in with fair regularity. It was just a matter of finding a likely prospect. Fortunately, I had a bit of an advantage.

"Morning, Nora." I smiled as Nora Sweetham came through the door of our store. She was one of our regulars, always coming in on errands for her folks. Her father was the Master Attendant of our port, and Nora always knew what was happening. She was mostly interested with which boats had the most handsome young sailors, but if you wanted to know about the comings and goings of ships down the port, there was no better source.

"Hello, Molly. Got a list for you, as usual." She handed it over with a smile. "And Da says we'll be wanting more linen soon, so you'll be wanting to put some by."

"Oh, ta." I took the list and began to get her items together. "So, any new ships coming in lately?"

Nora shrugged. "Not really, no. Been a bit quiet. Mind, we're expecting a couple next week. Dutch, I think. Da says it's going to be a panic getting them in and out with all the fishing boats running about."

I stacked the goods on the counter, trying not to sound too interested. "Big crews on those, I should think."

Nora shrugged. "Pretty big, yeah. Lot of foreigners on 'em though. Don't much care for 'em. They always smell a bit off, don't you find?"

"Can't say I've ever been around them that much." I brought the last goods to the counter and totaled the order. "Right, then. See you soon."

Dutch merchantmen, eh? That sounded like just the thing. They tended to go everywhere. I could get hitched on, work my passage to England or somewhere, then go off and get a job cooking or sewing. It wouldn't be the easiest life, but it would do. Later, I could save up some money and send it back home. Yes. That would be the right thing to do.

The following week, I went down to the docks to hand-deliver a bundle of linens and have a look at the two ships that had come, big three-masted galleons of the kind the Dutch call fluyt. The first one's name I do not recall, having not paid it much attention. If you live in a port town as we did, you soon learn to tell a well-kept ship from a poor one. I wasn't going to waste my time on a vessel the captain couldn't be bothered to keep in trim.

The other one, now...the other one was the *Cecilia*, and she was a beauty. Freshly scrubbed, hull free of barnacles, and a trim red stripe down the hull, gleaming in the morning light.

Scallywag!

"Nice ship, that *Cecilia*," I said to Nora when I got to her home. "Don't think I've seen 'em here before."

"Aye, came in last night." Nora took the bundle and fingered the linen. "Very nice. Da says they're taking a load of wool down south."

"Interesting." I leaned closer and smiled at her. "Did any of the crew catch your eye?"

She snorted. "No fear! Just a bunch of shuffling old men. The captain's one of those Puritans, you know them? Very religious. Runs a tight ship, Da says. So tight nobody ever stays with 'em long." She giggled. "You'll never guess his name!"

"Piety? Praise-Ye-Mightily?"

"Fly Fornication!" She colored a little, covering her mouth in embarrassment.

"Get away."

"G—d's truth! Fly-Fornication-And-The-Flesh Sykes. And he looks like it too. I mean, I don't think he's cruel or anything, just very down on sins of the flesh. Oh—and drinking."

"Zounds," I said. "No wonder he has trouble keeping crew."

Nora laughed. "Too right!" She leaned forward. "Poor fellow. He's off at the Brass Anchor, trying to hire some men now."

"What, from that lot?"

"Well, it's not like he's got much choice."

"I suppose not." I smiled and looked out the window. The sun was high in the sky. There was a long day ahead. "Well, I need to get back to the shop. Talk to you later, eh?"

On the way back, I turned the thing over in my head. A religious captain, eh? Well, it probably wouldn't be a very fun trip, but then I wasn't expecting it to be. He would probably stomp down hard on any shenanigans, so that was worth considering. One heard things about young boys going off on their first voyages to sea. On the other hand, if he found out about me, well, that would count as a pretty major shenanigan.

Still, the ship was in good shape. Even if he wasn't the most charming person, he would probably be relatively safe. There was only one way to find out.

That evening, after supper, I got through the washing up as quickly as I could. I told Mam I was going to bring some of my old cloth scraps to a friend. And thus it was that a little before sunset, I made my way back down to the docks, a bundle slung over my shoulder. The docks were a maze of alleys and side passages, with boxes and barrels crowded everywhere. I made my way to the alley behind the chandler's, where several old crates stacked near the back made a perfect little hiding place, and there I proceeded to prepare.

I quickly changed into my shirt and trousers, and one of my father's old caps that he no longer wore. It was a bit big, which meant I could tie my hair up and hide it underneath. A cap full of hair wouldn't fool anyone in broad daylight. I hoped I could get away with it at dusk.

Though it embarrasses me to admit, I'd also stitched up a special undergarment with a little bit of cotton batting rolled up in the right place. I took a little mud from the ground and rubbed it here and there on my face and arms. Not too much. I wanted to look fairly well-scrubbed, but I never met a boy my age who didn't have a little dirt on him.

These preparations done, I stowed my normal clothes and headed to the Brass Anchor. It was one of the more popular dockside taverns, a place for sailors and fishermen to unwind after a long day. I peeked through the side window to see if I could spot the captain.

He wasn't hard to find. For one thing, he was dressed better than nearly everyone there. He was also the only patron sipping a glass of water with his supper and looking like even that was a bit much for him. I've since come to know some other nonconformists, Friends and that. Some of them are rather jolly people. But Captain Sykes looked like he had been born with a lemon in his mouth. Of course, if I had gone through life with a name like his, I dare say I'd have looked the same.

About half an hour later, with dusk falling on the city, Captain Sykes finished eating and rose to leave. I stationed myself by the door, waiting until he came out. I touched my cap respectfully and approached him.

"Pardon me, sir, might you be Captain Sykes of the *Cecilia?*"

I recall I tried to sound like my brother Sean, whose voice had dropped over the summer. The sound didn't come out at all like I imagined. It came out like a boy whose voice was breaking while trying to sound older than he was. In retrospect, I suppose that was for the best.

He turned and eyed me suspiciously. "That I am, lad. Is there something you'll be wanting?"

"Beg pardon, sir. But I heard as you might be looking for crew?"

"Aye, I might be." He looked me over. "Have any experience, do you, lad?"

"No sir, but I've lived around ships all me life, and I'm a hard worker, turn my hand to anything."

"Pious boy, are you? Say your prayers every night?"

"Oh, of course, sir."

"Not in any sort of trouble, are you?" He leaned closer. "You haven't gone and got some poor girl in trouble or anything like that?"

"Oh, no, sir! Getting a girl in trouble is the last thing I want to do!" Well, that was true at least.

"Hm." He considered me for a moment. "What's your name, boy?"

You know, you can plan and plan and have every little detail lined up all in a row, and there will always, *always* be something you forgot until it's too late. My voice caught in my throat. Had I really neglected to come up with a new name for myself? Lord help me, I was such a dunce. I heard "Mol—" escape my lips before I was able to bite it back. My mind raced as the old man looked askance at me.

"Mol... My name is Mallory, sir."

This seemed to satisfy him. "Well now, Mallory, you seem like an upstanding young lad. I could use you, right enough. But understand this: I won't have any degenerates or layabouts on my ship. You're to do your work with a thankful heart, and I won't tolerate any drinkin' or fornicatin' with women of the night. I pay my men well. In return, I expect them to earn their keep and be a credit to the *Cecilia.* I plan to be shoving off with the tide, the day after tomorrow. You'll need to be here before dawn. D'ye think you can do that?"

"Oh yes, sir. Absolutely."

He nodded gravely. "Very well, my lad. I shall look for you then. You're allowed a bag of personal items, not that I suspect you have much. You do well, and I'll see you all right. Do we have an agreement?"

"Aye, si—I mean, Captain, sir."

"Just Captain will do. Now off you go. See you then."

By the time I got back to the alley where my clothes were hidden, my heart had calmed down a little bit. Still, my head swam with the realization of what I had done. In a day and a half, I would be on the high seas, with a new name and a new life. It hardly seemed credible. I allowed myself a moment to sit and let my mind settle before changing. There was so much to do between now and then. One day to make preparations and sail off to sea forever. For a moment I considered if, perhaps, it would be best to just hang the whole thing and go on with the marriage as my parents wanted. Then I remembered the old man and his horrible, old, leering face. No. It could never be worse than that.

That night, when everyone else was asleep, I sat up by candlelight writing a note for the family to find. Not an easy process, my being unsure of quite what to say. I tossed several failed attempts to the fire before settling on something short and to the point.

To everyone,

I am sorry I must leave, but I cannot marry Mr. Hennessy. I do not wish to be a burden on you any longer. I shall send some money home when I can. Forgive me.

Molly

Chapter Three

THE SUN HAD NOT yet begun to rise above the hills as I made my way down to the docks. Getting out of the house had been a bit tricky, not wanting to awaken anyone. Fortunately, the window in my room faced the back, where we kept some boxes and other things. The day before, I had moved one of the larger ones right under my window and thrown an old blanket over it to muffle the sound. It wasn't much fun climbing out of the window and dropping down, but given the fact that I was about to run off to sea while pretending to be a boy, it was the least reckless part of the whole enterprise.

The cool morning air felt unfamiliar on my bare neck. I've always had nice hair—from Ma's side of the family, everyone said—and it seemed a bit of a pity to cut it off. But once it was gone, I felt strangely indifferent. I had wondered if I might cry or feel regret. As it happened, I was too absorbed by how different I felt with short hair. My head felt lighter, less...enclosed. I'd cut my brothers' hair with the tried-and-true bowl technique often enough that doing it to myself had been rather easy. The result was not particularly stylish but looked enough like an average boy of the village.

I didn't go right down to the ship, taking a small diversion to a dock I knew would be empty. It was there that I took the hair which I had carefully collected and turned it out into the sea. I had originally planned to dump it down the privy, but that felt wrong. Consigning it to the same sea to which I was now consigning my fate seemed more right.

The crew was already up and making ready to sail by the time I got to the *Cecilia*. I trotted up on deck, the small bag that held the few things worth bringing along slung over my shoulder as I'd always seen sailors do. Captain Sykes stood on the quarterdeck, supervising. I quickly saw that there were few enough sailors for a ship of this size. Nora hadn't been wrong.

The captain spotted me as I came aboard. "Ah, good. Mallory, wasn't it?"

"Yes, sir."

"Right." He turned to the man next to him, a younger, bespectacled fellow inspecting a handful of papers. "Nevis, get the lad's belongings stowed and set him to work, will you?"

"Yes, sir. Right away, sir." The captain's mate, for such he was, saluted smartly and hurried down to me. "All right, lad. Follow me."

He led me belowdecks and took me abaft to a crowded area near the cargo hold. A long table with benches and various bits and pieces hinted at human habitation. "This is the crew's quarters," he said. "You'll be sleeping here with the others. They'll get you set up with a hammock tonight. In the meantime, stow your kit there." He pointed to a corner where several sacks were piled behind some netting.

That done, he beckoned me over to the table. "Now, to make it all nice and official, my lad, I shall need you to sign on. I'll write your name for you if you can't do it yourself."

"Oh, I can read and write, sir," I said. "Count, too, if the numbers don't get too high. And I know what o'clock it is besides."

Mate Nevis raised an eyebrow. "You don't say? Quite the scholar."

I shrugged. "I had to help Papa in the shop. He weren't so good with figures, you know."

"Indeed." He smiled. "Well, we may have to put you to work with talents like that. For now you can put your name right here...That's the way. And now you're one of us, shall I give you some advice?"

"I should be grateful if you did, sir."

"Mr. Nevis will do. I take it this is your first time at sea?"

"Yes, sir."

"Right. Old Fornication isn't a bad old stick as long as you mind yourself. Always be polite. If he's around, make sure you're busy at something. Anything will do. No swearin' where he can hear it. No complaining. He doesn't like a moaner, and neither do I. When you're given a task, do it just as you're told and keep at it 'til you're done. He can have a bit of a free hand with the lash if he decides you're a-needing of it, but if you're smart and get on the right side of him straight away, you should be all right. Most of the crew have been at sea a good long time now, so if you've any questions, don't be afraid to pipe up. You got all that?"

"Aye, sir. I mean, Mr. Nevis."

"A fast learner. Good lad." He smiled and put the register away. "Now, let's put some of that education of yours to use, shall we?"

"As you wish, Mr. Nevis, sir."

"Right." He led me back up to the deck. "First thing we do," he said, "we're going to introduce you to a vital piece of seafaring equipment. Get the mastery of this, my lad, and you'll be well on your way to being a regular seaman."

"Really? What is it?"

"It's a mop." He handed it over to me. "An' that there is a bucket of water, and this what we're standing on is a deck. Any questions? Thought not. I knew you were bright."

Of the voyage, I shall not speak overmuch. Suffice to say that I spent the following weeks learning my craft. The work was hard. Being, by far, the youngest and most nimble of the crew, I was often given work that the others were less inclined to tackle. As a result, I learned my way around every inch of the ship, from climbing out onto the bowsprit to check the forestays, to wiping down the windows of the captain's cabin—from the outside. Looking back, I spent an awful lot of time either climbing or scrubbing or both. With some ruefulness, I considered how I had chosen to cast my lot with the *Cecilia* because it was so well maintained. I hadn't bothered to ask myself who would be keeping it that way. For all it was hard work, I learned the importance of keeping a tight ship and a well-disciplined crew, lessons which were to stand me in good stead.

We were about three days out to sea when I learned our destination was Barbados, in the West Indies. The New World! I admit it was a bit of a shock. I had assumed we'd go across to England or down along the continent. Holland perhaps, *Cecilia* being a Dutch-made ship and all. Once I got over the initial surprise, I began to see the advantage of a long sea journey. This was a world where people went to start over, to leave their old lives behind, and to make their fortunes. Many was the time Papa would regale us with tales of the sailors he met down at the docks, and many of their tales were about the New World and the wonders to be found. We children had always loved those stories, though in my private mind I often wondered how many of them, if any, were true.

It seemed I was going to find out.

The crew, as Mate Nevis had said, were mostly older and more experienced sailors. Some had sailed with the captain for years, others signed on looking for a quiet berth to finish out their careers.

The cook, Rogers, was a fat old man with a grizzled beard and a bald head. He liked to joke that he "still had all his hair, only it's slipped a bit."

The good-spirited fellow was something of a father figure to the others. Even the captain treated him with respect. I suspect this was because the cook was older by a fair margin.

I was often tasked to work with Sullivan, the ship's carpenter, what with me knowing my numbers and all. I learned a lot under his tutelage. He was middle-aged, thin, and wiry. He kept to himself and could be impatient when someone did not understand something he thought obvious. But he knew his craft right enough. Even if he was a bit standoffish, everyone acknowledged he was a good man.

Then there was Mr. Cheeves, the bosun. He was...well, he was an ass. Mr. Cheeves was one of those people one occasionally meets in life who, given a pinch of authority over others, becomes a perfect tyrant, taking full advantage of his pitiful scrap of power to lord it over everyone else. Nothing delighted Cheese (as he was called behind his back) more than finding fault. The further down the hierarchy you were, the more he delighted in flaying you with words that stung as much as the whip. I will leave it to you, reader, to imagine his delight in having a frail, young "boy" to practice his torments upon.

One of his favorite tactics was to wait until you were finished scouring the deck, then sidle up to you unannounced. He'd take a long, hard look at your work. Inevitably, he would find something at fault, be it ever so minuscule, and demand to know why it was in such a state. Before you could answer, he'd tip out the slop bucket right there and make you do the work again. I suppose he told himself he was teaching me to take meticulous care with my work or some such thing. But, and I tell you this as a condemned woman making her confession before G—d, he was an ass.

The days aboard the *Cecelia* passed into weeks, the weeks into months. I do not know if my reader has undertaken the trip across the Atlantic, but it is a good dozen weeks, assuming fair winds and the ship in good trim. The first few days, I spent my precious few free moments gazing out at the majesty of the sea. When we lost sight of land, I volunteered for watch duty in the crow's nest so that I could see the ocean spread out around me, before and aft. Early on in the voyage, we saw the occasional ship in the distance and would sometimes hail each other if we got close enough. As the journey progressed, sightings became rare.

And so began a period of monotony, with nothing to look at but the endless emptiness all around us. It was, frankly, not a view that inspired.

Scallywag!

By the time we made the crossing and were in the waters of the Caribbean, I resolved that I had had enough of the Atlantic to last me a lifetime. I began to make plans for when we would land. I expected I would be able to find work on the island, somewhere, and could start sending money home like I had promised. If worse came to worst, I could always sign on with another ship, provided they weren't heading back east.

Just about a week out from Bridgetown, everything went sour. I had become a fairly competent sailor. There had been mistakes and lashings to go with them, but they were few enough. The captain regarded me well, when he did regard me at all. I kept busy and made certain not to call attention to myself. Cheeves had been worse than his usual awful self, perhaps guessing that I would not be signing on for the return trip, and he'd therefore better get his licks in while he could. It even got to the point where Mate Nevis took him aside and told him to ease off. That worked for a couple of days, but it wasn't long before he was back to his ways again.

I should explain, incidentally, that from the beginning he had noticed the delicacy of my features and used it as another means with which to torment me. His pet name for me was "Miss Molly." He constantly insulted and belittled me by calling me a girl. I have always found this puzzling, for all men seem to do it with such constancy. It is as if they can imagine no greater humiliation than having the misfortune to be born a female. In my seven-and-twenty years upon this earth, it has seemed to me that women are by any measure the stronger of the two sexes, doing most of the work, having the fewest opportunities outside the home, and having to deal with a world of men. Sometimes I think about asking such a man if he feels that way about his mother. Would he tell her so to her face? Let the reader take what wisdom from this they can.

We were nearing the end of our voyage, and everyone was eager to sight land again. For all a sailor acclaims the virtues of the sea, nothing quite so lightens the heart as stepping ashore after a long voyage. I think we were all starting to get impatient. The crew was getting snappish, and discipline began to flag. If you have ever seen a schoolboy near the end of a long day, you will understand. Twelve weeks is a d—d long time to spend holed up with the same several faces and no chance to get away. That, however, does not excuse my losing control of my tongue and nearly bringing disaster upon myself.

It came about this way. I had been swabbing the deck, as per usual. Cheese was lurking nearby, eating one of the last apples from the barrel and watching me with an insolent eye. I knew his game and was only waiting for him to make a new mess for me. Still, I did a thorough job. If he was intent on finding fault, I would not make it easy. As I was finishing off, he leaned forward with little ceremony and spat a mouthful of half-chewed apple onto the deck.

I ought to have held my tongue, I really ought. But the sheer impudence of the move filled me with ire. "What is *wrong* with you?" I snapped, glaring at him. "That's disgusting, that is!"

He sneered. "Got a problem, Little Miss Molly? Offended your delicate sensibilities, have I? Clean it up."

"Shan't."

His face darkened. "What did you say?"

I knew I was in for it now, but there was no going back. "You made the mess." I tried to keep the fear out of my voice. "You clean it."

"Why you little s—t." He jumped up and threw the remains of the apple overboard. "How *dare* you talk to me that way?" His fists clenched. I remember the last remnants of apple juice sliding down his chin as he came toward me. "I'll teach ye to speak so to your betters!" He drew back a leg and kicked, planting it squarely in my groin.

I stumbled back and fell over, more from surprise than anything. We stared at each other for a long second. His expression changed. He seemed puzzled, somehow, as if something unexpected had happened. Too late, I realized I was supposed to be in pain. I had seen my brother, Sean, take such a kick once during a fight. He had spent the next several minutes curled up in a tight ball on the ground, writhing in agony. Cheese was waiting for me to do likewise. And I hadn't.

He came closer. "Hang on," he said with a growl. "How's a little snip like you able to take a kick like that?" He peered closer at me. "Are you some sort of eunuch or something?" His hand darted out and grabbed me at the crotch. I could see the confusion grow on his face as he felt only the soft padding of my reinforced undergarment. "What's your game, Mol?" His voice was low now, his eyes narrow. I was about to be discovered, and there was not a thing I could do. No doubt, he saw the fear on my face. I tried to think of something, anything, but there was no escape. If I were very lucky, I might be put in irons and turned over to the authorities when we landed. If I weren't lucky…

Scallywag!

    For a moment, I considered jumping overboard. My back was against the bulwark. Perhaps I could shove him away and dive into the sea. I wasn't likely to survive, but the sea seemed kinder than whatever his evil mind might conjure. I felt I could see the suspicion growing in his eyes. Another moment and my life would end.
    All in all, it was rather a relief when the pyrates attacked.

Chapter Four

"SHIP AHOY!" CAME THE cry from the crow's nest above. The bells were clanging. "Straight ahead!"

Cheese glared at me but turned to have a look himself. "What is she?" he shouted. "Get eyes on 'er!"

Everyone stood still, waiting as the lookout fixed his looking glass on the approaching ship. There was a tension I had not felt on board before. Captain Sykes and Mate Nevis appeared on deck, the latter visibly worried. Something was clearly wrong. I almost forgot my own troubles.

"She's a frigate," the lookout called down. "She's riding low but moving bloody fast!"

"The flag, man!" called Nevis. "What flag has she?"

"Looks to be Spanish, sir. I'll...oh."

There was a dreadful silence. "What?" shouted Nevis. "What do you see?"

"The flag, sir. They be running it down."

"Blast!" Nevis thumped his fist on the helm. Captain Sykes stepped forward. "Hard a-starboard! Get them sheets up! Lively, now!" The crew dropped whatever they were doing and scrambled for the masts. Cheese glanced at me, then at the still-distant ship. "Later for you," he snarled and hurried off.

"You too, boy!" Mate Nevis called down to me. "Go up and help with the foremast! If they catch us, we're for it!"

Pyrates! At last I understood. I staggered to my feet and ran, weak-kneed, to the foremast and began to climb.

Of the chase that followed, there is not much to say. We had hoped to get in front of the wind and outmaneuver the larger ship, but the simple fact was that she ran far too fast. A new flag was waving from the approaching ship, a black one. We got the sails up as quickly as we could and held on as the *Cecilia* surged ahead. But the larger ship had, no doubt, guessed our stratagem, and was already moving to intercept. It didn't appear a fast ship, but the speed at which it caught us up was astonishing. It soon became clear that we had no chance.

Captain Sykes stood on the quarterdeck. "Furl sheets," he cried. "Furl all sheets and fall in!" We scrambled to bind back the sails we had so recently let loose, securing them before hurrying back to the deck. The

Scallywag!

captain surveyed us with the same firm, unsmiling expression that had accompanied him since that night in the tavern so many weeks ago. "Right. Gentlemen, we are about to be boarded. Some of you have been through this before, some have not. You are to cooperate fully with them. You will offer them no resistance. Let them have what they want, and we shall be on our way. It's unfortunate, but that is the way of things in these waters. If they decide to leave us dead, well, do what you can to save yourself. Otherwise, I'll not have any bloodshed on this ship. They'll be alongside us in a moment, so if you wish to make your peace with G—d, now would be the time." He turned and strode back into his cabin.

I felt someone nudge me. Rogers, the old cook, bent down and whispered in my ear. "Get below decks, boy. Get yourself hid and don't come out until you hear the all clear."

He didn't need to tell me twice. I was down in the hold in a trice and scurrying about for a place to hide. The cargo hold was a tangle of crates and barrels. I had to climb over most of it until I found a spot among some barrels. I crouched down in the darkness and strained my ears to listen.

It wasn't long before I heard shouting above. The aggressive ship must have pulled to. I heard a series of thumps as the pyrate crew boarded us. I was quite sure they must be getting crowded up there. I could just hear Captain Sykes's voice, calm and level as always. There was another voice, the nature of which puzzled me, as it sounded wrong somehow. Someone shouted a command, and down they came, at least a dozen by the sound of them. They wasted no time but set to hauling up our cargo as quickly as they could. As soon as one box was hauled away, another would be claimed. I later learned that they'd formed a sort of bucket brigade, that being the quickest way to offload a ship. It was clear they'd had a lot of practice.

It occurred to me, rather belatedly, that hiding amongst the cargo was perhaps not the wisest move. In my defense, I would point out that there were precious few alternatives. Our ship was not large, and the number of hiding places was severely limited. The pyrates had finished the crates and were coming for the barrels. I cast about for somewhere better to hide, but there was nowhere else to go. I was cornered behind the last few barrels, squeezed against the hold.

It was only a matter of time. I remember that I prayed, hoping I might be spared. Perhaps they might decide they had got enough, or the rest of our crew might show fight, or—

"Here!" A voice rang out right above me. I glanced up to see a large, bald pyrate with a short beard and golden hoop earrings grinning down at me. "What have we got here, lad? Up ya come! Don't make Black Jack fetch ye!" That was it. I was caught, and there was no resisting. He must have seen the fear on my face. "Don't worry, lad! Ol' Jack won't harm ye, less'n you give him a reason to. Now up you come."

A moment later, I was back on deck, the pyrate having dragged me along by the arm. The deck was quite crowded by this point, with the chain of pyrates offloading our cargo as another group held our captain and crew at bay with their pistols. It seemed like no one had been hurt, but I was far from assured this would continue to be the case. Black Jack dragged me across the deck to a tall, lean figure in a dusty frock coat and tricorn hat with a peacock feather in it. They had their back to us, supervising the transfer of the cargo.

Black Jack cleared his throat. "Beggin' your pardon, Cap'n, but I found a wee rat in the cargo hold." He laughed and shoved me forward. I nearly cried out as the captain turned around. A woman!

Sarah Cunningham, captain of the *Bonnie Mary*. This woman would set me on the course I have followed for a lifetime.

I don't know if I can make you understand quite the impression she made upon me. All the women I had known 'til that point were the quiet, homespun sort. Most were plain, modest, hardworking, and churchgoing. You couldn't imagine Captain Cunningham spinning at a wheel or sewing by the fire. And if she ever set foot in a church, it would be to steal the silver. She was dressed head to toe in the finest clothes, her jet-black hair cascading in ringlets around her face. She could swagger while standing still. Most of all, she had a self-assured radiance that I'd never seen on a woman before. Though the poor girls down at the docks had tried to mimic her glamour in their way.

She strode over to me quickly, a sardonic grin on her face. "Well, now, lad," she said. "Would you mind telling I what you were doing hiding away down there?"

I opened my mouth but was too terrified to answer. I wanted to explain that it wasn't my idea, but what if I got the crew in trouble? Would it be better to take the blame? I tried desperately to work out which would be the lesser of two evils but was unable to build a coherent answer.

The captain knelt down and looked me square in the eye. "Now look here, lad..." She stopped and peered closer, looking me dead in the eyes.

Scallywag!

The expression on her face was strangely unreadable. I braced myself, certain she'd run me through at any moment.

Suddenly, she stood up. She took hold of my shoulder and turned me aft. "Carry on, you lot," she called over her shoulder, as she steered me toward Captain Syke's cabin. "Me an' the lad here are gonna have a little chat."

"Now then," she said as the cabin door closed behind us. "Girlfriend, wife, or daughter?"

I looked at her in confusion. "Pardon, Miss?"

She rolled her eyes. "Oh come on, 'my lad.' You may have those old goats out there fooled, but you're talkin' to Captain Sarah Cunningham, and she's got eyes, ain't she? So I'll ask you again, girlfriend, wife, or daughter?"

There was nothing for it. She knew. I shook my head. "Oh, no, ma'am. None of those. I just...I...it was our family, business not going well, and so many mouths to feed. They wanted to marry me off to this old man. I know it was wrong to run, but I just couldn't. And then the ship was there, and I..." I gestured vaguely at myself. In a way, it was a relief, really. After bottling up the truth and carrying it with me, I rather needed to unburden myself, even if it was to a pyrate.

She threw her head back and laughed. "Well, I'll be!" She slapped me on the back, a move which quite startled me. "How d'ye like that? Don't feel bad, me girlie. You're not the first to run off to seek her fortune on t'other side of the world." She leaned nonchalantly against Captain Sykes's desk, looking me over. "Did a fair job, too, to my eye. Tell me, is it going well for ye?"

I hesitated. It was so bizarre, standing in my captain's cabin, having a friendly conversation with a pyrate. Somehow, strange as it sounds, I felt I could trust her. Something about her demeanor told me it was best to be perfectly frank with her. "Well, we've almost made it to our destination, but I don't think I shall sign on again. Going across the ocean is awfully boring, and...well, there's one of the crew who suspects. In fact, I think I very nearly got caught just before we spied your ship."

"Mm." She studied me some more. "Like it, though? Life at sea? Or looking forward to being a landsman again?"

"It's all right," I said. "To tell the truth, if it weren't for having to hide and all that, I could keep doing it."

"Well, me girlie, just so happens we're always on the lookout for likely lads and the occasional lass of unusual qualities. You'll be all right on the *Bonnie Mary*. You can even carry on as a lad if it takes yer fancy. Either way, I can promise no one will bother you." She leaned forward, smiling like a shark. "I will make sure of that. Me, I look after my people, I do. Everybody gets a share of the loot. We're all outcasts and runaways, you know. That's how it is, gen'rally."

"That sounds very nice, but...I mean, you're criminals. I'm not sure if I—"

"Criminals? Us? Nah, my dear! We're entirely legitimate. The *Mary* sails under letters of marque, I'll have ya know! Authorized to seize cargo and ships of enemy nations. All nice and legal like."

"Really? But which nation?"

"Well, that's the beauty part, innit?" She leaned forward confidingly. "Every country is scrambling to get a slice of the pie down here in the Caribbe, so they're pretty much all at each other's throats. Turns out a girl can collect enough letters of marque that damn near anyone is legitimate prey." She chuckled. "If Peter sends me to rob Paul, and Paul to rob Peter, then I'm all too happy to oblige 'em both!" She grinned. "So what do you say, me girlie? Care to join our jolly band? Or shall I leave you with that group of sour persimmons outside?"

And thus it was that, a minute later, Captain Cunningham kicked open the cabin door and dragged me out with her, a pistol planted firmly against my temple.

"All right, lads," she cried. "Are we about done?"

A tall, black man with a mustache saluted. "Just about, Cap'n. Reckon we've got everything worth taking anyhow."

"Fine. Let's be on our way." She turned to the crew of the *Cecilia*. "Now, gentlemen, we'll be takin' our leave of ya. I've taken a liking to young master Mallory here, and I'll be taking him with me." She leered at them. "I'm sure you wouldn't want anything bad to happen to him, eh?"

Captain Sykes scowled. "Taking hostages on top of everything else, eh?" he sneered. "Is there no end to your ignominy?"

"Ain't found one yet." She began to drag me to the gangplank that connected our ships. "Now keep those hands where I can see 'em, that's the way."

"Wait!"

Scallywag!

Everyone turned. Rogers the cook had stepped forward, holding his old, flat cap in front of him. "Listen, ma'am," he said. "Don't be takin' the lad. You can have me in his place, if'n you like. I'm a da—a very fine cook, me, and I'll go quietly, won't make no fuss."

Captain Cunningham chuckled. "Well, now. Aren't you the saintly one? Tempted I am, but I really don't think so. I've made me choice, though I'm sure the lad here appreciates the gesture." She nudged me with the barrel of her gun. "Say thank'ee," she said.

I gulped. "Thank'ee."

"Right. Now that's done." She backed her way along the gangplank, with me in tow. A moment later, the plank was retracted, the sails unfurled, and the *Bonnie Mary* was underway.

Captain Cunningham waited until we were well away, then twirled her pistol and tucked it away in her belt. "Right, that went well." She smiled. "You all right?"

I nodded. "I feel a bit sorry though. Do you think they suspect?"

She shook her head. "Shouldn't think so. You did a bloody good job."

Yes, reader, it had been my idea to have her take me as a hostage against my will. As much as I disliked the notion of finding myself among a crew of brigands, I didn't dare stay on the *Cecila* any longer, not with Cheese's suspicions aroused. On the other hand, I had a delicacy about jumping ship with a hearty "so long, boys, I'm off to join the people who just robbed you." This way, it seemed that I had gone unwillingly. It was a bit silly, but the truth is that most of the crew were all right, and I didn't want to hurt them if I could avoid it.

As the ship turned into the wind and picked up speed, the captain led me up to the quarterdeck. "Right, you lot!" she shouted. "Everyone, meet our newest crew member!" She turned to me. "Go on. Introduce yourself."

"I..." I glanced up at her, unsure of what to say.

She leaned down so only I could hear. "Whichever name you like, my dearie. It's up to you."

I looked out at the crew. They were a rough lot, to be sure, but they didn't seem hostile. If anything, they exuded a camaraderie that beat anything I'd felt aboard the *Cecilia*. In time, I would come to understand that a pyrate crew is like a family, of sorts, a family lashed together from various broken bits and pieces, but a family all the same. Just then, though, what I knew was that I did not want to lie to these people.

"Molly," I said. "My name is Molly."

"Give 'er a proper welcome!" The captain raised her cutlass high. The crew cheered, raising their fists in the air. It was as boisterous and wholehearted a welcome as any I've known before or since. Captain Cunningham slapped a hand on my shoulder. "Welcome aboard, lassie," she said. "You're one of us now."

As the crew cheered, I began to feel the full import of what I had done. Yes, I was out of danger—one kind of danger, at any rate—but had I just dropped myself into something deeper? They seemed ready to accept me as one of them, but I wasn't a pyrate, not really. No, best to just keep busy and work my passage until the next time we hit land. Then off I'd go, with a little money in my pocket, as like as not, to find some suitable trade in the New World. It was a sensible plan, and I saw no reason why it wouldn't work.

That would soon change.

Chapter Five

IN THE DAYS THAT followed, I became acquainted with the crew and life aboard a pyrate ship. It was surprisingly different from what I (in my admittedly limited experience) was used to. Of course, the same sort of jobs needed doing. Thanks to my time aboard the *Cecilia,* I could do everything that was expected of a younger crew member. There was the usual array of ship's offices: cook, carpenter, and so on. But the atmosphere on the ship, if I may put it that way, was entirely different than that aboard my previous berth. We were not so much a group of workers signed on to an employer, more members of a brotherhood, a group of equals. I later discovered that every member of the crew in good standing was considered a member of their 'company,' with a share due to them of any treasures they took. I tried to imagine old Captain Sykes divvying up the takings of a voyage with his crew and just couldn't see it happening.

On that note, the hierarchy of the ship was very different. The *Cecilia* had been run with a firm hand. The captain gave orders to the mate, the mate gave orders to the bosun, and the bosun gave orders to everybody. On the *Bonnie Mary*, these same titles were observed, but there was a very different attitude toward the crew and officers. It seemed that the regular crewmen had a say in who led. Any full member of the crew, for example, being in good standing and sufficiently well-thought-of by his crewmates, could stand for bosun if he so desired. A vote would be called via secret ballot. If he got enough votes, then the new bosun he'd be. Others in the crew assured me that even the captain could be replaced if enough of the crew desired. In truth, I did not believe them at first, though later, I would see it with my own eyes.

The crew was as motley an assortment as ever I could have imagined. Black Jack, who had discovered me in the hold, took a shine to me, taking me under his wing as a sort of protégé. In the evenings, when day's work was done and neither of us was on watch, he would teach me how to fight with swords and with pistols. I may confess, I was not very good with either at first. Over time, I got quite comfortable with a short rapier from the ship's stores. At night, Black Jack would tell me tales of the places he'd been and things he'd seen and done.

The first mate was Mr. Sanyang, a tall African man with a bald head and a smartly trimmed mustache. He didn't talk much, but when he did, it was with a voice as deep as thunder. Truth be told, I was rather afraid of him at first. Not only was he the first black man I had seen in person, he was by nature a rather intimidating individual in his size and bearing. I eventually came to understand I had nothing to fear from him, but it did take a while.

There weren't many women in the crew. We few bunked together in a small section of the hold. Maggie, the cook, was the widow of a captain who had sailed many years before being done in by the Spaniards. Anna and Dutch were regular members of the crew. Two more different people you could not imagine.

Anna, a prim and proper Englishwoman, obviously had some education beyond what little I had received. She came of high-born stock and had been raised from birth to be a proper lady. Even when working the sails or swabbing down the deck, there was something elegant about her. It was in the way she carried herself. Black Jack once commented, on seeing her working down in the galley with Maggie, "Anna could make mucking out pigs look glamorous."

Dutch, on the other hand, was as rough and crude as any man on the ship. She loved nothing more than to get her hands dirty and was regarded as one of the fiercest fighters, always among the first to jump into the fray. She was perpetually rumpled, with her hair cut short and her boyish frame in a doublet and trousers. Everywhere she went, she walked with a roguish swagger, and the crooked smile of a true scoundrel was never far from her lips.

As different as the two were, they were quite inseparable. They seemed to spend every free moment they could together, whether it was eating or resting, or even on occasion, standing watch together. I remember my surprise when I saw they only had one bunk. I thought then, in my naïveté, that they must be very close friends indeed.

The bosun, James (he went by his first name only), was a thin, quiet man, bespectacled and very tidy. He was a scholarly type, soft-spoken, but quietly efficient at his job. He was, to my immediate relief, about as far as one could get from Mr. Cheeves. Besides seeing to the boat and crew, he was also in charge of keeping track of the minutiae of the daily operations of the ship: freshwater stores, treasure shares owed, and so on. Once he discovered that I could work sums, he enlisted me to assist him in these tasks. They were not the most exciting jobs, to be sure, but it was easy work and out of the sun.

In the fullness of time, when I found myself in charge of a ship of my own, the lessons I learned from James would stand me in good stead.

Overall, they were a good bunch of people, and I found myself quite enjoying the company of these corsairs. Mind, I still planned to keep my head down and make myself a useful member of the crew until we reached land, whereupon I would see to securing some legitimate work. When I confided this to Anna, she seemed somewhat surprised but not upset. "Well, it's not a life to everyone's taste, to be sure," she told me. "But I'm sure you're welcome as long as you make yourself useful. You seem an industrious *gel*, and we need as many ladies on here as we can get." She chuckled. "Still, it's always down to you either way. Just so you know, there's not a one of us here who hasn't chosen this life freely. Whether you do or not yourself is entirely up to you."

I had been sailing with them for about two and a half weeks when the thing happened. The stocks of the *Cecilia* were holding us in good stead as far as supplies, but the crew had been out at sea for a fair stretch and were ready to feel land beneath their feet. The captain gave orders that we should turn and head for Port Royal, in Jamaica. This order met with considerable approval, that town being something of a gathering spot for privateers to relax and find ways to spend their treasure. As such, we brought her due west and headed that way.

It was day three of our return trip when we sighted a large ship on the horizon, flying a Spanish flag. A quick muster of the crew followed, and the captain put the question to us. "All right, my lads and lassies, that fat, Spanish galleon coming up from the west 'tis a navy job if I'm any judge. You know what that means."

I nudged Black Jack, who was standing next to me. "What *does* it mean?" I whispered.

"Means lots of weapons and that, and lots of people usin' 'em," he replied.

The captain continued. "Now, I daresay we can take 'em if you're so inclined, but 'tis up to you. What say ye?"

There was silence for a moment, then one of the crew spoke up. "I'd rather just get on, me. We've got plenty of booty already." Around him, there were murmurings of assent.

Captain Cunningham looked around at the rest of us. "Anyone else?" She stood on the quarterdeck, waiting.

I nudged Black Jack again. "What's happening?"

"Well, we're trying to decide whether to attack the ship, aren't we?"

"But...doesn't the captain decide that?"

"Nah, girl, 'tis up to the company, you see. Every one of us what is in good standing gets a vote. I mean, the captain, she can override if she wants to, but she'd better have a d—d good reason."

This was about the most surprising thing I had ever heard. "All right," I said. "So what do we do?"

"Well, in a minute, she'll call for a vote. You not bein' a full member yet, you don't get a vote, but the rest of us can have our shout. Hang on, here she goes."

"All right, you lot," cried the captain, "Who's for taking her? Holler aye."

There were a few scattered ayes from the crew, but fewer than I expected.

The captain nodded. "Mm, about what I thought. And opposed?"

The chorus of nays was much louder.

"All right, then. Mr. Sanyang, let's give 'em a wide berth." The mate nodded and began to shout orders. We tacked away from the oncoming ship, looking to go around it.

We proceeded forward, trying to shift out of the other ship's way. As I worked the ropes up on the mizzen, it seemed to me that she wasn't getting any further away. If anything, she was getting closer. Others of the crew saw this as well, and soon came mutterings of the ship coming right for us. By the time a quarter of an hour had passed, it was more than obvious that this was indeed the case. We were called back down again and reassembled on the deck. Around me, the crew muttered and glared at the oncoming ship. I will admit I was frightened, but the others seemed more cross than anything. Captain Cunningham stepped up to the quarterdeck and raised her hands for attention.

"It appears, gentlemen an' ladies, that this lot haven't got the good sense to leave well enough alone. If it's a fight they want, then I say it's a fight they shall have. To your stations!" The crew, as one, gave a mighty shout and dispersed in all directions.

As I stood on the deck wondering what to do, I felt a hand on my arm. It was Black Jack. "Come on, me girl. You ever worked a cannon before?"

My eyes widened. "A what? No!"

Scallywag!

He smiled grimly. "Never mind, you'll pick it up. We need another powder monkey. Off you come."

A powder monkey, I discovered, was one tasked with running charges of powder from the magazine belowdecks up to the cannons. It's a job that calls for small, nimble crew members with a good turn of speed. Scrambling through the crowded confines of a ship carrying a parcel of gunpowder without dropping or spilling any (or G—d forbid, letting it near a flame) is a job that calls for particular dexterity. As such, the task is generally given to the younger members of the crew. It is a hectic practice. All the more so when one is actively under attack. I hadn't been down to the powder magazine before and surely would have gotten lost if it weren't for the fact that several others were making the selfsame trip back and forth. I was able to follow in their path, dashing up and down the steps and weaving through cargo and other supplies as fast as I could.

I had rather wanted to see the cannons fire, despite my fear, but there was no time to hang about. As soon as a charge was handed over to the gun crew, it was hard about and back to the magazine again. As we ran back and forth, I could hear the shouts of the gun captains followed by a tremendous roar as each gun was fired. Too soon, I began to hear the whistling splash of the Spaniards' cannonballs sailing toward us.

Exactly how long we were at it, I could not say. I only remember endlessly running back and forth, relaying the powder up to the gun crews, sweating and panting for breath as I hurried nonstop through the darkened ship's interior. One trip melded into another until I lost track of time. I no longer needed to pay attention to the route, my feet running it of their own accord. And still the cannons fired.

The sounds of the Spanish cannonballs were coming closer, often landing close enough to spray our hull and send water splashing in through the portholes. I confess, I had paid little heed to them as I continued running the powder charges.

The impact, when it came, gave me quite a shock. Our ship lurched with a shuddering crash, and the crew's shouts followed the sound of splintering timber.

I was running another charge up to the guns when it happened, and the impact nearly knocked me off my feet. I clutched the paper wrapped around the powder close to my chest and staggered against a support beam. Thankfully, I hadn't spilled any. It took me a moment to get my bearings back, but once I did, I charged up to the guns.

On the gun deck, things had gone strangely quiet. The gun crews, who had been going nonstop 'til then, had ceased their labors and were clustered together, catching their breath and looking grim. I approached a sailor named Benson, who had been working as a loader, and proffered the charge.

He only shook his head. "Nah, lassie. We're done wit' cannons. They got us where they want us."

"Hit to the mainmast," the gun captain said. "We won't outmaneuver her now. They'll be boarding us soon."

It felt like someone reached into my chest and squeezed my heart. Boarded? I looked from face to face of the gun crew, but their expressions told me that there was no doubt about it. Strange though it may sound, I found myself more fearful now than I had been when this same crew had boarded the *Cecilia*.

The gun captain was the first to snap to. "Right," he said. "Get those guns secured and prepare to be boarded. I want every one of you waiting for the bastards and ready to show 'em what they're dealing with." This galvanized the men into action. In a trice, the cannons were all back in place and the crew scrambling to get their weapons. I followed along, running down to retrieve the short sword I had been practicing with. The sword seemed such a small, harmless thing. I remember feeling I must be mad to believe it would make for any kind of defense. Still, it was what I had, and that was all there was to it. I steeled myself, got a good grip on the sword, and hurried onto the deck.

Chapter Six

BY THE TIME I got to the deck, the battle had already begun. Soldiers with muskets lined the deck of the opposing ship, taking potshots at us as we prepared to engage. Of course, given the time it takes to load and fire a musket, only a couple of volleys could be gotten off by either side before it turned to close-quarters fighting. Several of our crew had muskets, as well, not to mention pistols. These latter were held in reserve. The reasoning may seem obvious to the reader, but my young and inexperienced self had yet to learn a pistol's short range.

I joined a cluster of pyrates preparing for the attack. They had the look of those who had been in many a grisly battle indeed. A lanky, ginger-headed fellow with a large chin and a patch over one eye scowled at the oncoming ship. "Bloody liberty," he said with a growl. "Didn't even give us a chance to surrender."

"What? Sorry, do we usually surrender?"

"Well, no. But there's such a thing as observin' the niceties." He brandished his cutlass, glaring at the rapidly closing ship. "Guess we'll have to teach 'em some manners."

Our two ships had hardly got within range of each other when our crew, almost as one, swarmed aboard the galleon, swinging on the *Bonnie Mary*'s ropes and running across planks dropped between the two ships. The speed with which it happened was quite astonishing. Even if a pyrate crew does not start a conflict, once it has begun, they immediately go on the offensive. A quick, all-out attack can win a battle quickly, even against superior forces. Some captains prefer to take a cautious approach, wearing the enemy down until they are sure of themselves, but the aggressive approach has consistently served me in good stead.

Thus it was that the battle turned into a pitched melee almost faster than it takes to say the words. Certainly, the Spanish forces were not prepared. Many dropped the muskets they were still trying to reload and scrambled for their swords. The pyrates attacked nonstop, moving with the practiced viciousness of longtime veterans of the fray. It soon became clear that, soldiers though they were, the Spaniards were not used to this level of resistance. Captain Cunningham's crew was a much fiercer opponent than natives of the West Indies, whose rudimentary weapons were no match for gunpowder and Spanish steel. Our crew had no intention of being "pacified." The Spaniards were in a real fight now. Even to my inexpert eye, they were clearly out of their depth.

It shames me to say I did not cross over with the others. I remained on the *Bonnie Mary*, holding my short sword uncertainly before me and watching the battle with a nervous eye. I told myself I was guarding the ship, should any of the enemy attempt to cross over. Of course, had one of them thought to try, they would have found me no very great threat.

The Spaniard's commanders shouted, whipping their men to a vigorous fight they surely knew they would lose. While I still regarded myself as a neutral observer in the proceedings, I took pleasure in seeing that the aggressors were being put down most effectively.

A movement caught my eye. Up on the galleon's quarterdeck, protected by a half dozen or so heavily armed guards, the ship's officers watched the battle, obviously displeased. There was some sort of hurried conference going on. Someone—a junior officer by the look of him—hastened away into what I thought could be the captain's cabin. The young officer returned with a wooden box he presented to the captain. Even from a distance, I could see the gleam of the silver workings on the two pistols the captain drew out. I didn't know they were fine flintlock pistols and had little time to appreciate them. As I watched in horror, he took careful aim with one of them and fired.

Down in the crowd of fighting men, somebody cried out. One of our men clutched the flowering red spot on his chest and collapsed. I felt the bile rise in me at the sight. Fighting was one thing, to be sure, but standing safely out of the fray, taking shots when no one else could do the same? That was wrong. No, more than wrong. It was a low, dishonorable thing that no man who called himself a captain should ever stoop to. From where I stood, I could see Captain Cunningham in the middle of the fray, leading her crew in the attack. And here was her counterpart, staying safe behind his guards and striking men down from a distance. My blood boiled.

Without thinking, I scrambled up to our quarterdeck, keeping low so as not to attract their attention. From there, I had a clear shot to the captain and his men, but of course, nothing to shoot them with. I had nothing but the short sword in my hand, and that was hardly a threat. I looked around for something else, anything really, but it was a waste. Nothing was up there, save a few crates and such, the captain's cabin, and the ship's wheel, none of which were any use as a projectile. Much as I hated it, my sword was best out of one. As I drew back, it occurred to me that throwing my sword at the enemy would leave me unarmed. Then I reminded myself that they had muskets and pistols, against which a short sword, inexpertly wielded, was marginally worse than nothing at all. Thus comforted, I took the sword as one might a javelin, aimed as best I could and, just as he aimed for Captain Cunningham, let it fly.

As much as I would love to report that the blade struck home, my adherence to the full and frank truth in this epistle demands I report that the blade came up short, only managing to graze the captain's thigh before tumbling uselessly to the deck. At least I had the presence of mind to throw myself behind some crates as he turned his attention toward me. The wooden crates splintered around me, no match for the musket fire from his guards. I threw myself down as low as I could and crawled forward at speed, expecting at any moment to feel a ball of hot lead tear through me.

Once the initial volley had concluded, I risked a peek over the top of a barrel to see what was happening. I had certainly stirred up the hornet's nest. The captain's guards had moved away from the steps and were hastily reloading their muskets as they surveyed the deck for me. The captain, himself, was invisible behind a crowd of attendants. Even from my hiding spot I could hear him crying out like an animal in its death throes. Surely, I hadn't hit him that hard?

One of the attendants moved away, and I saw their captain seated on the deck, clutching his legs and howling like the damned. If I squinted, I could just see a slight red mark blossoming on his hose. It seemed my clumsy throw had been just enough to break skin. I had injured myself far worse making dinner, but he was acting like it was the final judgment.

Others began to take notice. There was a gradual winding-down of the fight as both crews stopped and stared at the captain's histrionics. Even his own men seemed surprised. I could hear murmurs from the soldiers. It seemed they did not overmuch favor seeing their commander behaving this way.

To everyone's surprise, Captain Cunningham herself jumped up on a capstan and addressed the combatants. "Look at him!" she cried, pointing her blood-stained cutlass in the other captain's direction. "Hiding up there out of the fray, surrounded by guards, while you put life and limb on the line! Listen to him, bawlin' like a babby over naught more than a wee cut to his leg!" Beside her, Mr. Sanyang cupped his hands and repeated her words in Spanish.

The effect was...well, I will not say it was immediate, but it was clear she had their attention. I could see the soldiers from where I was. Many of them had thoughtful expressions and kept casting eyes toward their captain. He had ceased his mewling but was still whimpering a bit and muttering to himself.

Captain Cunningham called out, "And ye would take orders from such as him? Truly? That would never happen under the freemen of the Caribbe! D'ye know what we call a pyrate captain what hides behind his men and yowls at the slightest injury? We calls 'em a castaway, that's what!" As Mr. Sanyang's translation rang out over the deck, the Spaniards laughed.

The captain and his guards had forgotten all about me. They turned to listen to Captain Cunningham, their expressions growing darker with every word she said. They said nothing at first, but when their soldiers began to laugh, that seemed to be too much for them. The captain staggered to his feet and shouted something. I thought it was a challenge to Captain Cunningham, then realized he was addressing his own crew.

Cunningham shook her head and tutted. "Dear oh dear, sending others to do your dirty work for ya, then? Also, did I just hear you call your own men a bunch of rats? This is no way to lead your men." This sentiment seemed to be striking true with the Spaniards. Their laughter gave way to grumbling and resentful glances at the captain and his officers. Young and inexperienced though I was, it was well plain to me that the Spanish officers had done little to endear themselves to their crew.

"But I'll tell'ee what," she said. "Bring yourself down here, and we'll have a proper fight, captain to captain. Winner takes command of both ships, what d'ye say? I'll even let ya take first swing at me seein' as you've been gravely wounded and all." At Mr. Sanyang's translation, the Spanish crew laughed again. Up on the quarterdeck, the mood was less jovial. There seemed to be an argument among the officers as to what they should do. It seemed to me that the captain was not at all enamoured of the idea.

It occurred to me that he was in a situation he could not win. If he chose to fight, he would very likely be defeated. An inexcusable humiliation, all the more so given it was coming at the hands of a woman. If he refused, he would (quite rightly) be regarded as a coward by his men, and that would not end well. I have to admit I felt a certain amount of gleeful satisfaction watching him squirm.

Scallywag!

The captain beckoned his officers tight around him, and there was a quick discussion of sorts. When they separated, the captain stepped forward from the others and gave Captain Cunningham a curt nod. She jumped off the capstan and sauntered toward him, both crews making a path for her. A few of the Spanish captain's men stood behind him. I couldn't quite see what was going on, so I crept along aft to get a better view. By this time, they had forgotten all about me, so I was able to get back with little difficulty.

As Captain Cunningham mounted the steps to the quarterdeck, I saw the Spanish captain remove his topcoat. One of his officers stepped behind him and did something I couldn't quite see. Cunningham gestured at the officers to move back, to give her and their captain room. As they did, I saw a pistol tucked into the back of the captain's belt. So *that* was his game.

I scrambled up on the rail, hanging onto one of the backstays and shouted as loud as I could. "Pistol!" I pointed at the captain, trying desperately to catch Captain Cunningham's eye. "Behind his back! Captain!"

Thank heavens she heard me, for she was able to duck down just before he fired. She charged forward and cannoned into him headfirst, sending him sprawling. In a trice, her sword was at his throat. "Well, well," she said, a sneer on her face, "a coward and a cheat as well. I see 'tis no point in dealing honorably with you, bilge rat that ye are."

I couldn't hear what he said in reply, but I saw Captain Cunningham pull back, raising her sword arm high. I wanted to look away, but…No, that's not true. I thought that I should look away, that it wasn't right to watch. I confess, reader, that while I am by no wise bloodthirsty (my record notwithstanding), some part of me craved to see the opposing captain get his castigation. I held my breath, my eyes locked on the scene, as she made ready to strike.

I heard a muffled shout come from below deck on the galleon. A Benedictine friar came running up on its deck, waving his hands and shouting, "Pax! Pax!" He was somewhat short and pudgy, rather young as such men go, as much as I was any judge. Both crews moved out of his way, more out of surprise than deference. He scrambled up to the quarterdeck and placed himself before Captain Cunningham. "Stop, stop!" he cried. "In the name of G—d I beg you, do not do this!"

Captain Cunningham hesitated, eyeing the holy man with suspicion. "And why should I not?"

"It is a damnation on your soul to kill a man in cold blood."

"Is it, now? That's dead interesting, that is." She leaned to one side, glaring at the Spanish captain who still lay prone on the deck. "You should get the word out on that. I think some people would be interested to hear it."

"You leave him alone!" The young friar stood his ground. I have to give him credit. He was scared as anything but kept right at her. "This ship and its crew are under the protection of the Spanish crown and the mother church! We are on our way to the New World to civilize the savage tribes!"

This did not seem to impress Captain Cunningham much. "Oh, are ye now? Gonna show 'em how civilized y'are?"

He did not rise to it. "I have been sent to bring the heathens to the true light of G—d. If you interfere with us, you interfere in holy business."

I heard the captain snort. "Oh well, can't have that, can we? I will point out we sought no battle with ye, but that you pursued us. An odd sort of thing for a mission of holiness? Or were ye planning on civilizing us as well?"

I didn't hear the friar's response. In any case, the captain decided she'd had enough. She sheathed her sword, never breaking eye contact with the holy man. "I'll have my lads fall back," she said, "an' we'll be on our way. Your lot will let us go in peace. If you try firing on us as we go, by G—d's blood, I'll send this ship straight down to Davey Jones, holy orders or no. You hear me?"

"You have my word."

"Well, I suppose that will have to do." She nodded back to her crew. "Fall back, you lot. We're heading out. Step lively now. Parson, grab some lads and see what you can do about that mast." The crew began to move away as a body, streaming back across the gangplank that bridged our two ships. The entertainment (for lack of a better word) being over, I hurried down to the crew to see if anyone was hurt.

Several were wounded, though none critically, I am pleased to say. Parson, the carpenter, rounded up some men, and they set to work bracing the mainmast. The gangplank was pulled away, several of us were sent aloft to unfurl the sails, and we were away.

As I came down from the rigging, I noticed a tense gathering on deck. Two of the Spanish soldiers had come aboard with the rest of our crew. They stood in the middle of a circle of swords, looking quite forlorn and helpless. I hurried over to see what the fuss was about.

Scallywag!

Captain Cunningham came swaggering up, Mr. Sanyang in tow. "What's this then, eh? Got some uninvited guests, have we?"

One of the soldiers spoke up, firing out a rapid stream of Spanish. I've since gotten rather good with the language, but at the time, I could only tell that the poor man was afraid for his life, and rightly so. I looked around at the others. Despite brandishing their swords, most of them didn't seem particularly worried. In fact, the majority of them shared a sort of knowing smile.

When the soldiers stopped babbling, Captain Cunningham raised an eyebrow at Mr. Sanyang. He didn't say a word, only nodded. The captain sized up the two men, moving in close to look them over. Having made her decision, she turned to Mr. Sanyang and nodded back.

"All right, you two," he said. "You come with me, hah? *Vamonos*. Let's go." He gestured toward the hatch. The crew moved out of the way, and the two men immediately fell in behind the mate.

I nudged the pyrate next to me. "Excuse me," I whispered, "what's going on?"

"Oh, this?" He grinned. "Yeah, we don't always get 'em, but more often than not, someone will decide they want to throw their lot in with us. Guess these two decided they'd rather work for a real captain." He chuckled and glanced over his shoulder to the Spanish galleon, which was rapidly disappearing from view. "I have a feeling that lot is going to have a rough time of it. Might even be a change of leadership in the offing, after today."

"You think?"

"Oh, sure. You didn't see the faces of his crew? Seeing his humiliation today...well, him and his officers better be careful about passing any deserted islands any time soon, that's all." He laughed.

All around us, business was getting back to usual aboard the *Bonnie Mary*. As I returned to my duties, I found myself wondering how many of the people around me had joined in this way, jumping ship and casting their lot with a group of brigands. Intriguing.

A few days later, we made landfall in a safe place the crew knew of. The ship was run aground at high tide, and the crew set to work giving her a full refit from top to bottom. I spent most of my time scraping barnacles off the hull, a noisome task if ever there was one. In the hive of activity, I quite forgot about the incident with the Spanish galleon and my (admittedly small) part in it.

But its part in my tale wasn't finished yet.

Chapter Seven

WE SPENT SEVERAL DAYS refitting the ship, the officers having decided that since we had her aground, we might as well see to several minor matters that had gone too long neglected. It was tiring work in the hot Caribbean sun. As each evening set in, I was well worn out. The men of the crew doffed their shirts against the heat, and I envied them having the option. Anna showed me how the women handled the heat by tying a strip of cloth around their breasts, allowing some semblance of modesty. Not that this was a great worry, mind. Some women, like Dutch, didn't bother with covering themselves and went bare-chested. I was shocked at first, but nobody else seemed to take the slightest notice. Over time, neither did I.

During this time, we all got to know the two Spaniards we had brought with us. Two people more different in character than Domingo and Ramirez would be hard to imagine. Large, hairy, and bearded, Domingo was instantly likable. He didn't speak much English at the beginning, but as he learned, he became quite forthcoming, talking of his home in Valencia and telling stories and jokes around the evening campfire. He laughed easily and inspired laughter in others.

Ramirez, on the other hand, was very quiet, even shy. His clean-cut, boyish face nearly always held a serious expression. Though lacking in physical strength, he proved an excellent worker. He picked the language up faster than Domingo, though he used it less often. Sometimes I would see them off together, practicing their English on each other. That was one thing I picked up on. They were generally together, whether working or resting. I rarely saw one without the other. I asked Black Jack if they were brothers or something, but he merely smiled.

I have to admit that by the time we finished, the *Bonnie Mary* was looking like a new ship. However arduous the work had been, the result was well worthwhile. As we stood before the gleaming ship, Captain Cunningham declared she had the best crew sailing the seas and would fight anyone who said otherwise. She gave out an extra rum ration for everyone and announced that the next day, when the tide came up, we would push off and resume our course to Jamaica.

We had a good supper and settled in, looking forward to being back on the water. One thing I will say of my years at sea is that I have never slept so well as then. Admittedly, this was first because I'd never worked so hard and would finish off the day bone-tired. Over time, I found the caress of the sea to be most soothing. Those few in my life who have been in a position to know have told me I sleep more soundly in rough seas than on dry land. But I fear I'm getting ahead of myself.

I must have been sound asleep for two or three hours when it happened. I remember awakening to find a hand clapped over my mouth. "Not a word, you," said a voice in my ear. "Get dressed." Someone threw my clothes at me. In the dark, I could vaguely see three silhouettes against the darkness. Of their faces I could see nothing, but their swords caught the moonlight. I thought to call for help but was too afraid.

I dressed quickly as I could, tugging on my breeches and shirt, and was then pulled unceremoniously to my feet. A sack dropped over my head. My hands were pulled behind me and bound together, and I felt a knife prod me in the back. "Start walking," said the voice.

I was marched along the shore for a while, my escorts trudging wordlessly alongside me. From time to time, one or another would take my arm and steer me in a different direction. It became apparent we were going inland, as I felt the sand give way to the thick carpet of greenery that covered the forest floor. They marched me forward, pausing on occasion to turn me round and round, as if I could have kept my bearings in these circumstances. Looking back, the walk cannot have been more than a few minutes, but it certainly felt longer. The three who had taken me did not speak, only prodding me forward or steering me along. Around me, the sound of the sea gave way to the rustling of creatures in the underbrush and the calling of the night birds.

I first realized we had arrived wherever we were meant to be going when I felt a space opening out before me. We couldn't be all the way through the woods, a clearing then. My escorts restrained me, and I heard a voice up ahead call out. "Halt! Who comes?"

"We bring the prisoner to the dock!" It was the same voice that had spoken to me before.

"Bring them, then," Someone pulled the sack off my head. It was indeed a clearing, right in the middle of the forest. Hooded figures filled the clearing, some holding torches.

I looked around in desperation, trying to work out what was going on. "What is this?" I cried. "Where are the rest of the crew?"

"Silence!" A hand clapped me on the back of the head. "Approach the dock, ye blatherskate." The hooded mob parted to make a path forward, down which I was unceremoniously shoved. Three more hooded figures sat behind a table covered with a red velvet cloth, motionless, waiting.

I could feel the mob closing ranks behind me, cutting off any hope of escape. The leftmost of the three seated figures turned its head toward me. "The prisoner will state her name." The voice came in a low growl, not at all dissimilar to that of my escort.

"I don't—"

"The prisoner will state her name!" The angry murmurs behind me felt threatening. I was still groggy from being rudely awakened, and in a rather bewildered state. I tried to shake the cobwebs out of my head. Whatever was happening, I needed to keep my head sharp and deal with it.

"Molly Donnelly McCormick."

The figure harrumphed and wrote on a sheet of foolscap on the table before him. I couldn't see what was on it, but it looked like an awful lot of writing.

The figure on the right spoke up. "Now then, Molly Donnelly McCormick, you are charged with the following." They lifted the sheet and commenced to read. "First, that you secured employment on the ship *Cecilia* under false pretenses, viz. disguising yourself as a boy. In doing so, you put yourself and your former captain in harm's way, with no thought to the consequences if you got caught. This reckless disregard for others is shameful, indeed, and bespeaks a woman of low virtue.

"Further, you are charged that, when a group of pyrates attacked the aforesaid ship *Cecilia*, you did conspire with the captain of that band of brigands to take you with them, casting your lot in with the very thieves who stole from your erstwhile employer. You deliberately deceived said employer and caused them great emotional distress, in a manner most despicable.

"Next, not two weeks past, said pyrates were waylaid by a ship of the Royal Spanish Navy. While the soldiers were in the process of pacifying the pyrate crew that they may be brought to justice, you did willfully aid and abet said pyrate crew, offering violence to the representatives of the Spanish crown. First, you ran powder for the pyrate's cannons. Then, when the pyrates boarded the Spanish vessel and attacked her crew, you did willfully assault the captain of said ship, deliberately seeking to impair him in the execution of his lawful duties.

"Finally, when said captain was about to execute the chief of the brigands—a notoriously virtueless woman herself—you did cry out to her, alerting her to the subterfuge and allowing her to escape with her pack of thieves, once again subverting the cause of justice." The hooded figure laid down the charge list and lifted their chin to me. "How do you plead?"

My head swam as the charges were read out. Who were these people, and what was going on? I daresay you, reader, sitting comfortably in your home, have no doubt worked out what was happening. I beg you to recall that I was in a most grievous state of mind and in no position to examine my situation cooly. I could only tremble in fear and stammer that it wasn't like that.

"Not like that!?" The figure on the right pounded their fist on the table. "Then you deny the charges? We have multiple witnesses prepared to swear to every one of these things! Would you have us believe that every one of them is lying? Mm? Is that it?"

"No! I...I..." Words would not come. I sagged. "It's true," I said. "But what I did, I did not do to harm. I went with the pyrates because they on the *Cecelia* were about to discover I was a girl. I feared for my safety. One of the crew was already suspicious. If he had known for sure..." I shuddered, not allowing myself to even complete the thought.

The clearing was quiet, my accusers seeming to consider my defense. The one who had read the charges spoke again, softer now. "And your actions against the Spaniards?"

I hung my head. "I know I ought to have thrown my lot in with them, or at least not interfered, but...well, they attacked without provocation. The pyrates even tried to steer clear of them. When I saw their captain, guarded from any harm and ready to pick off pyrates one by one, well...it wasn't right, that's all. A real captain would have led his men into the fray. Like Captain Cunningham did. I was upset by what I saw and couldn't just stand by and watch it happen."

The figure on the left spoke. "Your sins are great, yet you are not yet beyond redemption. This court graciously offers you the chance to redeem yourself in the eyes of G—d and man. All you need to do is betray the pyrates to us, that we may bring swift and holy justice upon them. Will you do this?"

I didn't answer right away. Some part of me screamed to take the chance offered, to swear myself to goodness and obedience. At that moment, even going home and marrying old Mr. Hennessy seemed appealing. What was I doing halfway across the world? I must be mad.

But even as I opened my mouth to speak, I knew that I could not agree to betray the crew of the *Bonnie Mary*. Though it had only been a few weeks, I had come to know so many of the crew. Many had been kindness itself to me, and while I was not of their number, I felt…home. That's the word. It felt like when I was back home, surrounded by people I cared for and who cared for me. There had never been anything like that aboard the *Cecilia*. As I looked at the shadowy figures, I knew my choice. Pyrates they may be—outlaws, and thieves, and G—d alone knew what else—but they had been decent to me, and I knew that. Even if it was my duty to put them into the hands of the law, I should never forgive myself doing so.

I managed to shake my head. "No," I whispered.

"No?" said the one on the left. "What do you mean, no?"

"I mean, I can't." I looked up at the three figures. "It wouldn't be right, that's all."

"You know what they are, right? And you know what your duty is, yes? Clearly, this is the right thing to do. We will take you home, and you can go back to being a respectable G—d-fearing citizen. Think well, child. This may be your last chance to escape the very fires of hell itself."

"I know that, sir, and I'm sorry. I…I can't explain it. I know it's the right thing, but…" I faltered. Thirteen is a h—l of an age to have to comprehend that there are different kinds of right, I can tell you. I didn't have the knowing of it then, and even today, I am uncertain I could explain it properly. But I have learned to listen to that voice within myself. Just then it was telling me that turning the pyrates over to these people, whoever they might be, would be quite the worst thing I could do.

The three at the table exchanged looks. There was a murmur behind me, as the hooded watchers moved closer. The seated figure in the middle, who up 'til this point had been silent, turned first to their left and then to their right. Each silently inclined their head. At last, the central figure began to speak.

"Molly Donnelly McCormick," the person intoned. This voice was somewhat higher than the others, though every bit as menacing. "You have admitted your guilt in the charges presented before this court. You have offered no remorse, and when offered a chance to redeem yourself, you refused. It is clear to us that you are lost to decent society, an irredeemable reprobate, a lost soul no better than the companions with whom you have so foolishly cast your lot. It is therefore the decision of this court that you shall share their fate." The figure paused. "Bring forth the sword."

Hands came out of nowhere, gripping my arms and forcing me down onto my knees. Another hooded figure stepped forward, carrying a rapier on a velvet cushion. It's odd, looking back. At the time, I was quite sure I was going to die, but I swear to you, reader, I felt no fear. There was only a feeling of calm, of knowing that soon it would all be over. I closed my eyes, murmuring a quiet prayer to G—d, and awaited the blow.

Something rapped me on my left shoulder. Before I could turn to see what it was, it moved to my right, repeating the motion. I looked up just in time to see the central hooded figure hand the sword back to its bearer, who stepped back respectfully. The three figures were standing before me, the one in the middle stretching out their arms in benediction. As they spoke, all the figures around me threw off their hoods.

"Congratulations, me girl," said Captain Cunningham. "You're one of us now!"

Chapter Eight

THE CELEBRATION THAT FOLLOWED was a merry one. My health was toasted several times. A bonfire was lit in the middle of the clearing, and dancing and singing filled the rest of the night. In the middle of everything sat I, head still swimming with the reality of it all.

Captain Cunningham beckoned me over. "Feeling all right, girl?"

I nodded. "Yes, Cap'n. Still a wee bit rattled though."

"Well, it's to be expected. Sorry about all the cloaks and that, but we have to make sure of you, see, before we can allow someone full membership into our company. You really find out who someone is when they fear their life is in danger, see."

"I suppose that's true enough. Still a bit rum though. Er, if you'll pardon my saying so, ma'am."

"Nah, you ain't wrong. And it's Cap'n. One of us now, remember? But you were never going to come to harm, you have my word on that."

"Actually," I said, taking a ginger sip of the rum that had been thrust into my hand a few minutes before, "If you don't mind me asking, Captain, what would have happened if I had agreed to betray you all?"

The captain shrugged. "Well, given your tender years and that, you'd have woken up in an inn in a nearby port town with enough money to buy your passage home. Of course, that's not the only way we handle those who aren't suited to the life. Depends on how you react, really. Here, Kwame!" She turned to Mr. Sanyang, who had converted the table to a bar and was busy playing landlord. "Who was that one fella we had before? The skinny one with the elbow in his neck?"

Sanyang didn't look up. "That was that Harrison fellow, wasn't it?"

"Aye, that was him. Cor, you never saw such a crawler. Positively eager to turn us all over, he was. And after we'd fished him out of the sea and all. Wish I could have seen his face when he woke up on a strange beach with nothing to see for miles...oh, don't look at me like that. There was a fishing village on the other side of the island. I'm sure he found it, eventually."

"But as I was saying. You've got a strong sense of honor, and that'll serve you well if you've the wisdom to listen to it. That Spaniard might well have done for me if you hadn't intervened. I won't forget that in a hurry, my girl. Oh! That reminds me..." She stepped behind the table a moment and reemerged holding a brace of pistols. "Grabbed 'em before we decamped," she explained. "Reckon the señor is better off without 'em. Go on, girl. Take 'em. You earned 'em."

I turned the pistols over in my hands, examining them in the torchlight. The Spaniard's pistols were fine quality and had been well taken care of. I felt a twinge of guilt, not over the way I had gotten them, but a feeling that one such as I shouldn't have such fine things. Growing up, we had never had much in the way of what you would call luxuries. What we had was sturdy and practical, and that was enough. Anything of a refined nature, where effort had been made in beautiful crafting, was not for us, only for our betters. I had never considered this unspoken conviction until I held those two fine pistols in my hands, felt the weight of them, and understood that they were mine. "I have got to learn how to shoot these," I said to myself.

Captain Cunningham laughed and slapped me on the back. "Indeed y'should! Now look, you take care of those. It isn't everyone who gets such fine weapons, you know. I'll have someone show ye how to look after 'em." She cupped her hands around her mouth and shouted at the group. "It's time we wrap this up, you lot. Big day tomorrow and all that. We'll have one more toast, if you'll join me. To Molly!"

"To Molly!" the crew chorused.

Black Jack walked beside me as we made our way back to camp. "Now, understand as you're not a member of the company yet, not officially. That will come when you sign the articles. That'll make you a full member of our band, entitled to vote and have a share of any plunder and that. Long as you remain in good standing, o'course."

"What's the articles?" I asked.

"The code we live by. Every one of us signs on to agree to abide by the code, you see. You'll find out more later. Don't worry. It's nothing onerous. I daresay you had a set of rules to abide by on your other ship?"

"Oh, you can be sure of that."

"Ha! Well, you'll find these to be much the same, at least in terms of the usual business of crewing a ship. Naturally, we have our own special rules, bein' as we are seekers of fortune and that. And of course, bein' one of us now, you can have a say in the articles, as what may need changin' or addin' on. But you needn't worry about all that now. Let's get you off to the camp. If you'll take my advice, you'll put your hammock up by the stream. Believe me, in the morning, you'll be glad for fresh water close at hand."

The advice proved most provident when, come the dawn, I was excused duty on account of experiencing my first hangover. It was the custom of the crew, when initiating one into their ranks, to render them utterly useless for anything on the following day. It is also one reason why the initiations occurred on land. Had we been at sea, I would have found myself in a frightful state.

It was rather after midday when I was sufficiently recovered to join my comrades. The props and braces had been taken down and the camp broken up. We only awaited the tide to come in so we could push off. Maggie had a meal of salted fish and potatoes waiting for me, which foods she swore by as a remedy for hangovers. I must admit I felt all the better for something in my stomach, and when we pushed off, I was on deck with the others, though not really in a position to help out.

The next morning, I was summoned to the captain's cabin. She and the other officers were there when I arrived. Before me, on the captain's desk, was a sheet of paper and a ledger book. "Good morning," Captain Cunningham said, nodding me to a seat. "I trust you're feeling better by now?"

"Yes, Captain. Thank you."

"Good. Now, we'll make port sometime tomorrow. At that time you may leave us, if you wish. If, however, you wish to stay with us, you must become a full member of our company, with all the rights and responsibilities thereof. Black Jack tells me you can read. Is this so?"

"Yes, Captain. Write too."

"Very well." She pushed the paper toward me. "These are our company articles. If you sign on with us, you shall agree to abide by them. If you break any, the punishments are there as well. I would like you to take a moment to read them through. If you have any questions, don't be afraid to ask 'em."

"I will, ma'am—I mean, Captain." I took the paper and began to read. To this day, I recall the code by which I was to spend the rest of my life. Indeed, when, in the fullness of time, I did find myself in charge of my own ship, 'tis the very code I used with my own crew. The articles were simple enough, very much in line with those used by other crews. For me, it was the door into my new world.

Scallywag!

1. Every member of the crew to have a Vote in the Business of the Company, and Title to Goods seized, as long as no scarcity exists. Further, every member to have one Share of all takings. The captain to have two Shares, and officers one Share and a half each. Likewise ship's carpenter, doctor, and cook to have one and a half Shares, their particular skills being vital to the crew's survival.

2. All crew to keep their Weapons clean and Fit for Use. Failure to do so shall result in forfeiture of Share and any other punishment the Company shall see fit.

3. All crew to Obey Orders, and to observe discipline as expected of them. Likewise, all crew will stand their watch in turn. Failure to do so, or to be drunk at thy duties, or when in Engagement, shall result in lashings and other punishments as seen fit.

4. All plunder retrieved to be Shared in Common. Anyone found secreting items for themselves shall be cast off from the company, their nose slit, and themselves put off at the next port. Likewise, if any crew should be found to be stealing from another, this selfsame punishment to be enacted. Should a member of the crew be particularly desirous of a certain item, they may formally request it of the quartermaster, said request to be granted at the pleasure of the Company.

5. No member of the crew shall in any wise interfere with the virtue of another without their leave. Anyone found to have done so to be punished with death.

6. Any Quarrels among the crew to be settled by appeal to the quartermaster, who shall endeavour to Reconcile the Aggrieved parties. If this is not possible, said parties will be Escorted to Shore at the next available opportunity. Combat will be with swords or fists, victory coming with first blood or if the other party yields. Any brawling shall

result in lashings and any other punishment as determined by the Company.

7. All crew to do their share when Engaged in Battle. Acts of cowardice, turncoating, &c, to be punished by immediate expulsion from the Company and marooning, or death if deemed sufficiently serious.

8. Any member of the Company injured while in service of the *Bonnie Mary* and her captain shall receive recompense in proportion (800 for a limb, 400 for an eye, &c). If a member is so wounded that they can no longer perform their duties, they may, at their election, remain a member of the Company in good standing, or receive a Pension and transport to a Port of their Choice.

9. Snapping of guns, smoking, and naked candles in the Hold to be punished with lashings, and lights to be put out at eight o'clock.

10. No drinking or gaming while on duty. Violations to be punished with the lash, &c.

I raised a hand, hesitantly. "Er…"
"Aye?"
"Snapping of guns?"
Mr. Sanyang leaned forward. "That means to pull the trigger of your gun when you're not trying to shoot. You can strike sparks or even shoot someone if you've left your weapon loaded. And of course, if you do it down in the hold with all the powder…" He didn't need to finish the sentence.

"I see." I gulped. The idea certainly gave one pause. "Does that happen often?"

He shrugged. "Not really, only among the most poorly run companies. If we thought you were likely to do that, we wouldn't have given you those pistols."

"Ah, right." I cast my eyes over the list again. Truth be told, I really couldn't quarrel with it. The rules and responsibilities were very like what I had signed under Captain Sykes, but there hadn't been much about compensation and so forth. I found myself wondering what would have happened if one lost a limb under his command. Probably, he would have told them to pray over it.

The officers were watching me quietly. "Do you have any other questions?" asked the captain.

"N-no, I don't believe so, Captain. It's just...well, it's a big step, isn't it? I mean, you've all been very kind to me, and I shall always be grateful, but..."

"But you're not sure you want to mix in with a bunch of bloodthirsty marauders." Captain Cunningham was grinning. "Nah, I understand. Well, you've got 'til we make land to decide. But know you'll always have friends on the *Bonnie Mary*, whatever you do." She nodded toward the paper. "Go along and take it with you. Think the thing over. Just let me know when you've made your decision. Dismissed."

I spent the rest of the day at my duties, though in truth, my mind was quite elsewhere. It was as if my brain, my heart, and my gut were all at war. It was all I could do to keep at my work. Many times, the day went on, it would seem that one side had won the day, but then the other would redouble, and I'd be right back at it, going round and round. The reader will not be surprised that by the time evening came, I was tired out and no closer to a decision.

After supper, I was up on the main deck, leaning on the rail and staring out to sea, still no closer to an answer than I had been. I didn't even notice when Anna joined me. She didn't say anything at first, only looking out to sea with me, waiting. When I did finally notice her, I started, letting out a little gasp. She just laughed and gave me an understanding smile. "Not an easy decision to make, is it?"

"I..." I sagged a little. "No, it isn't. I mean, you lot have been nothing but welcoming to me, and I appreciate it, I truly do. But...well, I just don't know if I'm cut out to be a pyrate, you see? It's like I would love to stay among you, but at the same time, I shouldn't, if you see what I mean? I keep arguing with myself. Driving me spare, it is."

Anna nodded sympathetically. "Oh, I know exactly what you mean. A nice, obedient, G—d-fearing young lady raised to do what's right, then suddenly here you are. It's a real trial and no mistake. But I'll tell you one thing. There is not a day when I have regretted throwing in my lot with these people. Even the bad days. Especially the bad days, now I think of it. That's when you need people by your side. And there are no finer people to have, let me tell you, than the ones on this very ship."

I smiled a little, despite myself. "That's good to know," I said, "though I am rather curious about you. I mean, you…you don't really seem like a pyrate, if you'll pardon my saying."

She just laughed. "Well, you're not wrong. I daresay I'm about as far from most people's idea of a pyrate as you can get." She leaned forward on the railing, gazing out at the sea and the moon draping silver across the waves. "It has been…quite the journey," she said quietly. "Quite the journey indeed."

"I expect it has."

"Would you like to hear it? How I joined up, I mean. I think you might find my story useful. At the very least, I daresay you could find some similarities between your tale and mine. It might help make your decision easier. That is, if you were at all interested."

"I think I would like that, yes."

"All right. Let's find somewhere we can sit down, and I'll tell you all about it."

We moved to the forecastle, where we settled ourselves on a couple of boxes. Anna sat back quietly for a moment, seeming reflective as she prepared to tell her story. As evening turned to night, I listened with silence to her tale.

Chapter Nine

(BEING THE NARRATIVE OF Anna C., I'll step back and let you hear from herself.)

"I suppose it will not surprise you to hear that I never set out to be a pyrate. In fact, I came out here to the West Indies in the role of a teacher. The mission society to which I belonged was building several schools with an eye toward bringing civilization to the people of the new lands. There were, oh, about a half dozen of us, all freshly scrubbed and straight out of school, along with a group of missionaries, some clergy, and a few chaperones. Everything one would need, excepting of course, anyone knowledgeable about the new lands and how to survive. The Lord will provide, was our motto. And He did. For a start, he provided a storm that pummeled the boat before we got halfway across and swept two of the crew overboard. After that, He provided rats in the provisions, and an outbreak of scurvy, and rough seas all the way to the island of Antigua, where we made land.

"I tell you now, I was never so glad to set foot on dry land as when we lit on that shore. We'd lost a few people to illness, besides the two crewmembers. By that point, we were all of an ill humor. I, myself, was laid up at an inn for the better part of a week before I was ready to continue my journey.

"The plan was to establish schools in different colonies. Each place would get a schoolteacher and a clergyman, plus one or more missionaries to go out and, er, 'gather the flock,' as it were. Once everyone had quite recovered from the crossing, we began to go our separate ways. My party was heading south, to Barbados, where we hoped to establish ourselves in Bridgetown. We were able to secure a ship to take us there in short order. So, armed with righteousness of purpose and not quite all of the naivety we started with, we set off.

"I remember thinking, as we cast off, that at least this voyage would be mercifully swift and uneventful. Now I'm not saying I was a slow learner in those days, but...let us just say my faith had thus far been untempered by experience. What was supposed to be only a few days' voyage became two months before I ever set foot on that particular island. By that point...well...you may guess for yourself.

"I had thought the storms we experienced on the first voyage were awful, but they were nothing compared to what hit us halfway to Barbados. It truly felt like the sea was doing everything in its power to be rid of us. The crew did their best to keep us afloat, but the situation was grim, to say the least. We passengers were below decks, praying and pleading for deliverance. In the end, it was all for naught. I tell you, girl, until my dying day, I shall remember the sound the ship made as it broke apart. Splintering timbers, ripping sails, the shouts of the crew. It was h—l.

"To this day, I truly do not know if the others survived. Perhaps I was the only one who did, or perhaps they were all rescued together and I was the only one unaccounted for. I remember grabbing onto some rope bound around a few crates and hanging on. Somehow, when it was all over, I was still there. A Dutch trader found me. They were coming into port at Martinique, which we were, happily, quite near. The captain had to head back north once he was finished but allowed that I should be able to find a ship heading to Barbados easily enough. And so it was, shaken from yet another calamity and quite alone in the world, that I set foot in the Wheel and Bell.

"I suppose you might have had sailors' inns back where you come from. But take it from me, girl, you never saw such a place as this. I thought I might find a captain there willing to let me take passage with them. Though no self-respecting captain would set foot in a place like that. The instant I walked in, I realized I had made a horrible mistake. The place was full of drunken sailors and tavern wenches, all in a state of debauchery I had yet to see the likes of. I remember standing in the doorway, just paralysed. It was as if so much was happening before my eyes that I couldn't take it all in. All the while I stood gaping like a fool.

"Of course, it took no time at all for some of them to notice me. There were some hoots, and whistles, and shouts of the kind I shall not bother you with. If I am any judge, you can probably work them out for yourself. I think those last were what shook me enough out of my stupor to try and make my exit. But it was already too late. This scrawny, unshaven man with about three teeth in his head leered as he blocked my way, pushing me back. 'Now, now, missy,' he said, 'no need to leave. Ye only just got here. Come an' have a drink with ol' Tumble-Down Tom.'

"I tried to back away and blurted out something about how I was flattered by the invitation, but I thought I might be in the wrong place. He just grabbed me by the wrist. Quite hard. 'You're not thinkin' of spurning ol' Tom's hospitality, are you?' I could feel his nails digging into my skin as he pulled me toward the bar. I caught a whiff of him as he pulled me near. Lord, you never knew such a smell! The stale booze wasn't even close to being the worst of it. Between that and the situation I found myself in, I don't mind telling you my stomach began to turn. So many horrible possibilities went through in my mind, and they all ended badly. I felt quite helpless. I couldn't run with his grip on me. What *could* I do? Well, it was all pretty dire, I can tell you.

"Out of nowhere, I heard this voice. 'Leave it, Tom. She's well out of your league.' There, leaning against the bar, a rather handsome (and fairly less scruffy) sailor held a mug of ale in his hand and a rather captivating grin on his face. He took a swig of his drink. 'Let 'er go, mate. She clearly don't belong here. You're scarin' the lady.'

'Mind your own business,' Tom said. 'I reckon she wants to stay. In fact, I reckon there's nowhere in the world she'd rather be.' He turned his grip, twisting my arm a little. 'Ain't that right, missy?'

"I was terrified. I was certainly not going to agree with him, but what would happen to me if I said no? Well, it didn't bear thinking about. I don't think I managed to stammer out anything even remotely coherent before the other sailor intervened. He downed the last of his beer, put the mug on the bar with a sigh, and came striding up to us. 'I said, let her go, Tom.' By then, a fair number of people in the tavern had stopped what they were doing to watch. Being in the middle of everyone's attention did absolutely nothing for my mood, I can tell you. The sailor turned to me and nodded. 'It's all right, miss. Nothin's gonna happen to you. I'll see to that.'

'You ain't seein' to nothing, Dutch,' said Tom. 'I reckon I'm gonna show this girl a good time, me.'

"Then Dutch—yes, that Dutch—looked him dead in the eye, and she said, 'Tom, boy, you ain't shown a woman a good time since you stopped nursing.' Well, *that* got a laugh. Even I giggled a little. Though Tom certainly didn't like it. I don't think he much enjoyed being the center of attention either. I suppose it must have occurred to him that there were now an awful lot of witnesses to whatever he'd had in mind. I felt his grip loosen, but not quite enough to pull away.

"'Listen 'ere,' he said. 'You're one to talk. We all know about you, don't we?' And he spat on the floor in front of Dutch.

"She did not rise to his taunt, just shook her head and said, 'Tom, there ain't a bawd from here to Hispaniola what hasn't had you fall asleep on top of her. This lady clearly ain't in the trade, so you'll be wastin' your time. Now I ain't gonna tell you again. Leave her be.'

"Tom growled at her like some sort of animal and tightened his grip around my wrist again. 'P—s off.' I noticed him sneaking his other hand to his belt. Well, I was certain he had a dagger or something, and in any second there would be bloodshed and G—d alone knew what else.

"I don't know what made me do it. Maybe it was just desperation, or anger at how he was about to attack this nice person who was trying to defend me. I've always had a very strong sense of righteousness, you know. Well anyway, I pulled back my knee and gave it to him right in the culyons.

"Ha! That got his attention, enough for him to let go of my wrist anyway. I scurried out of the way, quick as I could, the instant I realized what I'd done. No lie, I was terrified he might just go straight to cutting me up then and there. I realized I'd best get out while he was still doubled over and wheezing. I guess Dutch realized the same thing because she dashed over and grabbed my hand.

"'Come on!' she shouted. 'Let's get you out of here.' Out we went, up the docks, round one corner, then another, working our way inland. Finally, we came to a pleasant little open area with a few benches and so on. 'All right,' she said. 'We can rest here. Tom talks a good game, but there's not much to 'em really. You all right, miss?'

"Now, the pub had been rather dark, as they do tend to be. Out in the daylight, I finally got a proper look at my rescuer. It was only then I realized that something was off. I had noticed they were rather on the short side, and there was a timbre to the voice I would have expected from a younger man. But in the Caribbean sun, there was no denying it. I remember staring at her, not quite sure of what I saw. I did eventually remember my manners and gave her a nod. 'I think I will be all right, yes. Thank you, er...uhm...'

"'Just call me Dutch, miss. Everyone does.' Now I should tell you that it's not at all uncommon for people to be a bit confused about Dutch. I mean, as to whether she's a boy or a girl. To tell the truth, I think she rather enjoys it. I have seen her make a game of watching people try to figure it out without asking her outright. All the while she keeps her answers as ambiguous as possible. Sometimes she can keep a person on the hook for days. Fortunately for my sanity, she took pity on me, and said, 'And yes, I am a girl.'

"'Well,' I said to her, 'I suppose that makes what you did back there all the more remarkable. I don't quite know what I would have done had you not intervened.'

"'Eh, it wouldn't have come to that. The boys at the Wheel like their fun, but they wouldn't have let you come to any real harm. You get a few like Tom, of course, but most of 'em are just talk. By the way, what were you doing in there?'"

"I started to tell her about the school in Barbados, but then I had to explain about the wreck. Of course, that led back to me falling ill in Antigua, and all the things that had happened on the voyage over. Well, before I knew it, I was crying hysterically. I guess it had all been building up and the incident at the pub pushed me over the brink. I'd been so full of hope, you see, when we first set out, thinking of all the good, fine things we would do. I'd expected everything to be wonderful, and everything had gone so wrong, just one disaster after another. I felt like it had all been a big mistake, that things were going to keep going from worse to worse. I tell you, I never felt so alone and scared in my life as I did sitting there, pouring my heart out to her.

"Bless her heart, though, she didn't say a word. She just leaned me to her side and put an arm around me, letting me cry. When it was all over, she lent me her kerchief and said I ought to talk to her captain. She reckoned they would swing by Barbados eventually and could give me a lift along if I didn't mind working my passage. At that point, I didn't have much to lose.

"Captain Cunningham was very sympathetic and said I could sail with them to Barbados if I helped out in the galley. Mark you, I was more than a little bit leery about sailing with a bunch of pyrates. But they were a nice enough bunch, and honestly, I wanted to stay close to Dutch. In all my time in the West Indies, she was the only person I truly felt safe around.

"Well. I won't bore you with the details of the voyage, but as I say, we wound up having a lot of adventures on the way. By the time we actually did make it to Barbados, I was a full-fledged member of the crew and no longer inclined to a teacher's life."

When Anna finished her tale, I studied her face and saw my own journey reflected there. I also realized my struggles were not as horrific as they'd seemed.

"Now, I know you have a lot on your mind, weighing up this and that, but let me tell you something," Anna said. "The years I have spent with this crew have been the best of my life. Sometimes it's rough. We get lean times, same as everyone. It's dangerous too. I've seen more than one mate fall. But these people...they're like family, in a way. Better, really, because we chose each other. I don't know what your plans are, but I can tell you that you'll find no finer crew in the Caribbean than that of the *Bonnie Mary*. Yes, we are bandits when all is said and done. That's something you would have to square with your conscience. But I can honestly say, with my hand to G—d, that I have never regretted my decision."

After she left, I stayed leaning on the rail, staring out to the sea. Truth be told, I was glad Anna had told me her story. It made me feel I had a better chance of fitting in with them than I had reckoned on. Since those days, I've come to understand that I had wanted to stay on from the start. Anna's story gave me what I needed to square things with myself. The very next morning, I went to the captain and signed on.

I was a full-fledged pyrate.

Chapter Ten

ABOUT TWO YEARS AFTER I signed on, I had my first brush with the extraordinary. We were busy chasing the Spaniards around and harrying them whenever possible. The Royal Navy had upped the bounty on attacking French and Spanish ships, and we were all too happy to oblige. During these skirmishes, Domingo and Ramirez proved invaluable, adding their knowledge of the Spaniards' capabilities and tactics to our own. They were also, not surprisingly, rather good at bringing others to join our cause. It wasn't long before we had a half dozen of their fellow countrymen, including Dr. Acosta, a ship's surgeon who insisted on attending to one of his wounded countrymen after a battle and never got around to leaving. The reader may rightly guess we were quite busy in those days. The rewards were plenty, and I look upon those days with fond memories.

    By that time, I was very much coming into my own as a buccaneer. I had seen my share of battles. I had "killed my man" and then some. The pistols I had been awarded from the incident with the Spanish captain became my constant companions in any battle, and truth be told, I got to where I was able to wield them with considerable skill. I daresay, most who take up the gun can shoot a bottle off a rail from a distance of twenty paces. To do so on a ship, when the waves are rolling you from side to side and the wind can't make up its mind as to what it's about, takes a real refinement of skill.

    We were about three days out from Port Royal, ready to hunt up some more Spaniards, when we found ourselves in an unfamiliar area. The Spaniards had been sailing somewhat farther to the east of the islands in an attempt to stay out of the main seaways, and we had become accustomed to going out farther afield after our quarry. A fog moved in overnight, quite unlike what one typically sees in these climes. The sun was little more than a pale glow in the gray. We were sailing blind, and we knew it.

    There was something else. I've never been able to say quite what, only that we sensed something down in the bones…This was a bad place. We were on the alert. By noon, the whole crew was on edge. There had been talk of turning the ship around, but it was decided that would only make things worse. And so, with empty grayness all around us, we pushed forward.

It must have been around midafternoon when we came upon the small island. We couldn't see anything in the way of settlements, not so much as a lone fishing shack. It was not the most inviting of places, but under the circumstances, we were glad enough to see any land at all. After a quick discussion, we brought the ship in close and let her lay at anchor until the fog should lift. A small group of us, with Mr. Sanyang in charge, were dispatched to the island to see if there were any provisions to be had.

We came ashore, struck by the lifelessness of the place. There were no trees, no animals, just patches of grass and scrub covering hills of naked, rock-strewn earth. The land was utterly desolate. The reader may have their doubts when I declare that it was even worse than the cell I now inhabit, but no one expects to find life in a dungeon. On the island, it felt like life had been there, then fled or was chased away. Hand on my heart, I do declare it was all the worse for that desolation. Indeed, so forlorn was the place that I didn't notice the dead body on the beach until I was nearly upon it.

The body had been there a good while, I should think at least a year. Simple clerical robes surrounded what remained of the man, who lay in repose with his head on one of the larger stones that littered the shore. His hands were folded over his chest. He held in them a crucifix and rosary beads. We stood a while, taking in the gruesome sight. Mr. Sanyang was first to speak.

"Died in his sleep, poor soul." He looked around. "Likely nothing to eat or drink around here. On the other hand, nothing to attack him either. Doesn't surprise me. I doubt there's anything here bigger than a sand flea." He paced around the dead man, shaking his head. He stopped suddenly. "What is that?"

I looked in the shadow next to the body and saw the shape. I picked up the weather-worn journal and found a few feather quills had been carefully secreted between the pages, where the writing was still readable: *The journal of Brother Amos McPherson and his missionary journeys among the West Indies.* I leafed through Brother Amos's travels from island to island, preaching the gospel, and so on. One page near the back was bookmarked with a bit of red ribbon.

> *To whosoever finds this: I beg you, this moment, to quit this island at once. I came seeking to spread the Word of G—d, but there is nothing and no one here. You will find only death and unholy things. I have resign'd myself to my fate, but let me warn you from sharing it. Please take this journal to Father Oswald at the priory in Hispaniola, that he may know I died in service to the Lord. May G—d shine His blessings upon you.*

Mr. Sanyang let out a low whistle. "Death and unholy things, he says?" He looked around at the desolate landscape. "I can almost believe it."

"So what do we do?" asked Dutch. "I don't think there's anything here worth finding, myself."

Mr. Sanyang shrugged. "We explore the island, like we were told. Though I agree we're not likely to find much, at least we will be able to say we did it." He looked back down at the body. "Our weapons…" he hesitated. "We probably won't need them. But be ready. Just in case."

We began the trek inland, following a path which was even more bereft of vegetation than the rest of the island. We climbed a hill from which we gained a view of the island as a whole. A rise encircled the roughly ovoid island with a sort of valley at its middle. The landscape was as bleak here as elsewhere, with the only signs of life being some rubble down in the very center of the island.

"Crater," said Black Jack.

I turned to him. "How's that?"

"Crater. Sometimes a volcano erupts under the sea and works its way up to the surface. We're standing on the rim of a crater, by my reckoning. That's why it goes all down in the middle there. Only…" he frowned, glaring at the vista before us.

"Only what?"

"Well, I seem to recall hearin' as how volcano ash makes for excellent soil. That's why things grow so well round the islands. But this place"—he waved an arm vaguely—"only thing you could grow is old, as me mam used to say."

Mr. Sanyang nodded. "That is odd. Don't know much about it myself. Maybe something bad in the soil. Anyway, let's get down there. Looks like the remains of a village."

So it was. There had been a few dozen huts, mostly of stone, and a larger structure in the middle. As we investigated, it became clear that the state of the place was down to more than mere time and nature. Someone had gone to a lot of trouble to destroy each building as thoroughly as possible. I don't believe there was one hut that hadn't been razed almost to the ground.

That was far from the most disturbing thing.

I have mentioned the larger structure in the middle. It alone was untouched by whoever had done the rest, and indeed it looked to be entirely intact. A single, narrow doorway led into darkness of the rough, oddly angled structure. At the four corners of the building, someone had carved crude statues of creatures in odd-fitting robes. Each figure's face had been chipped off.

"Don't like the looks of that," said Mr. Sanyang. "This doesn't look like normal tribal warfare. Somebody wanted to be *sure*. I wonder if—"

"Here!" Paulo, one of the other crew members who had come with us on the boat, had wandered around the back of the massive structure and was now beckoning us to join him. "Come and look at this!"

We hurried round to where he stood by a giant mound of ashes, nearly half as tall as he. Old bones and such protruded from the cone of gray powder. It was a sight to turn the stomach, and the years have done nothing to dull the horror I felt when I first laid eyes on it. Black Jack poked at the ashes with his sword, dislodging some and exposing more bones. "Human, all right," he said. "Must've been the entire village."

"What?" I asked. "Everyone?"

Wordlessly, he nudged the remains of a ribcage near the bottom of the heap. You didn't have to be an expert to see it didn't come from any adult.

Mr. Sanyang frowned. He squatted down, looking at the charred remains. "This is wrong."

"Well, I should say so," said Dutch.

"No, I mean...well, raiders are nothing new in these waters, but as a general rule, they tend to take slaves. This was no ordinary attack. Somebody wanted to make sure there was nothing left. Also, you notice this?" He kicked at a charred old chunk of wood, which promptly disintegrated.

We looked at each other and shrugged. "Looks like perfectly ordinary firewood to me," said Black Jack.

"Right. And where do you think that came from? No trees round here, right? They must have brought it special. Whoever did this, they knew exactly what they were about." He stood and turned toward the large building. "I think I want to see what is in there."

"Not sure I'm with you there, sir," said Paulo, eyeing the structure.

"Well, you can stand guard outside if you like. Rest of you, I know someone has a flint and tinder. These here scrubs ought to make fine torches. No dallying. I'd like to be quit of this place before nightfall."

Inside, the building was just one big, open space. The walls had been covered with carvings and what might have been paintings long ago. Here and there were small fragments which had survived, a leg here, a bit of a man in robes there. Nothing one could actually identify, you understand, but somehow it all added up to something very nasty.

The main feature of the chamber was a nearly circular hole about a fathom wide and right in the middle of the space. Dutch held her torch over the pit and let it go. We all watched it tumble down and down until it disappeared altogether.

"Criminy," murmured Black Jack, "don't that thing even have a bottom?"

Mr. Sanyang said nothing. He worked his way around the pit, the rest of us following after him. On the other side was a black stone, possibly an altar by the look of it. Behind that was a throne of sorts, a carved stone thing, curious to see in such a place as this. On it sat the remains of a red-robed figure. Six spears pierced it, two at the feet, two at the hands, one straight through the skull, and the last dead center of the heart. Black Jack let out a low whistle.

"D—n, they wanted to make sure, didn't they?"

Mr. Sanyang leaned forward, studying the corpse. It alone of all the others had not been burnt. It sat on its throne, entirely intact. Its skin was dry and grayish brown, like a mummy. The eyes were long gone, but there was something in what was left of the face, a coldness that spoke of evil and...something else. I stepped forward, trying to get a closer look...

"Easy, girl!" Dutch grabbed at me as I staggered backward, tugging me away from the hole.

I stumbled to the side and hit the ground with a thump. I lay for a moment, trying to collect myself. Dutch knelt beside me. "You all right, girl? You look dead pale."

I pulled myself together. "Sorry," I said. "I thought I saw a bug. Something, anyway." I shook my head, trying to right myself. As I did, I saw a gleam on the floor right next to the throne. I crawled closer, curious…

The thing turned out to be a medallion of sorts, a disc of green soapstone attached to a leather thong. On both sides of the stone, someone had carved a symbol. Strange symbols filled the spaces between the seven points of the star. The symbols were simple in structure, but quite unlike anything I had seen before. I turned the medallion over in my hands, trying to make sense of it.

Dutch helped me up and eyed the thing curiously. "What's that, then?"

"Looks like some kind of talisman," said Black Jack. "Belonged to this feller, most like?"

Mr. Sanyang shook his head. "More likely one of the raiders," he said. "Nowhere they'd get stone like that around here. Looks like a protection amulet. Sometimes the tribes around here will wear 'em when they go off on dangerous business." He smiled. "You go ahead and keep it. It will bring you luck."

I nodded and carefully slipped the thong around my neck and tucked the medallion under my shirt. It was odd, but when I wore it, I felt…different, somehow. Safer. I almost forgot what had made me jump back in the first place.

Mr. Sanyang glanced out the open doorway. It did seem that the sky was getting darker. "Well, I believe there's nothing else to be seen here. I reckon we can get back to the boat before sunset if we go now. That is," he smiled, "unless anyone wants to search around some more?"

The reader will easily guess that we had no desire to remain there one minute more than necessary. We hurried back to our dinghy and rowed back to the ship. A full report was made to Captain Cunningham, and my new acquisition duly shown off.

The next morning, the fog had lessened considerably. Captain Cunningham sent a detail to the island to collect the friar's remains, that they may be given a proper burial when we returned him and the journal to Hispaniola. It not being good to carry a dead body round any longer than you have to, we dispatched the errand with all speed.

Scallywag!

    The medallion I kept on my person and have, indeed, worn it to this very day. In all this time, I have never yet told a soul what it was I saw that made me jump back so. Probably they would not believe me if I had. I scarcely believe it myself. But the truth is, as I gazed at the long-dead face of that dreadful corpse, I could swear that just for a moment it turned, ever so slightly, so as to meet my gaze.

Chapter Eleven

THE READER WILL INDULGE me if I skip about somewhat. Life onboard ship was, more often than not, rather dull. Long stretches of sailing about were followed by brief bursts of activity, as we made raids on those ships we were targeting at any given time. Captain Cunningham was something of an expert at playing the crowned heads of Europe against each other. Sometimes we hunted the English on behalf of the Spanish, sometimes the other way round. It all depended on what was advantageous to us at the time. As long as we kept our letters of marque in order and didn't do enough to gain the permanent enmity of our current quarry, we could go on quite well for a very long time.

So things went for another year or thereabouts, nothing much out of the usual until the great typhoon hit during an unusually brutal autumn, that being the time most inclined to storms at sea. More than a few captains put their ships to shore to ride out the worst of it. Indeed, we were on the way to our home port when the storm came at us out of nowhere. Bad enough that the steady, light rain falling from the cloudy sky chilled the bone and wearied the soul. Without any warning, a gust of wind threatened to tear the mainsheet. The waves soon swelled up the side of the ship. Before we knew it, we were in the middle of a howling gale.

The reader may well imagine how it is to have sails up with a typhoon blowing. We scrambled like mad, battening down to ride it out. Trimming the sails was our first priority. I and several others ran to the halyard lines to bring down the sheets. These, I should explain, are lines used to raise and lower the yard, to which the sails are bound. Each sail had a crew assigned to it, whose job it was to bring the sheets in as quickly as possible. (In calmer times, the captain would declare a contest as to which team could get their sail down and secured the fastest, with an extra ration of rum for the winners. I later used this stratagem to train my own crew and commend it wholeheartedly to the reader.) I was part of the crew assigned to the top sheet of the mainmast. We set to as the storm raged around us. I swear, 'til my dying day I shall remember the roar of the wind and the lurching of the ship as she pitched from wave to wave.

Scallywag!

We loosed the halyard and began to bring the sail down as fast as we safely could. All around us, the other crews were bringing theirs in as well. It was still rough going, but it did mean we were not being buffeted quite so violently as before. I began to feel a bit of hope that we would be able to ride this out, more or less, intact. Sadly, this was not what the fates had in store for us.

The sheet was not quite halfway down when the rope slackened. The yard refused to go any farther. It quickly became apparent that the rope had gone askew on the pulley. This happened from time to time and was generally a nuisance. At the moment, it was a dire emergency. Storm winds in the sail could capsize the ship. There was nothing for it but that someone would have to go up and get it unstuck. As the nimblest member of my group, it was clear who it must be.

I ran for the ratlines, staggering across the deck as the wind and rain lashed at me. The boat was rocking precariously, making for a risky proposition indeed. I gripped the line with one hand and placed a boot on the rail. The next time the boat rocked upward, I made use of the additional momentum to swing myself up and onto the lines. There then followed an ordeal where I climbed up as quickly as I could while the movement of the boat was with me, then hung on as best I could when the waves swung the boat back. It was a nightmare of a climb. (No idle words here. To this day, I sometimes dream of that hellish storm.) Even going as fast as I dared, the climb took twice as long as it normally would have. I crawled to where the yard met the mast and inspected the problem. The wind had moved the sail enough to get the line off-center. I waved down to my crew and signaled them to pull upward.

As they did, I braced myself against the mast and pressed at the rope with my boot, putting all my strength into the effort. It didn't work right away. The crew had to tug repeatedly at the line. At last it gave, and I felt the rope shunt into its accustomed place.

We had the sheet down in a trice after that, and from my vantage point, I could see that the other groups had gotten theirs down as well. Thus satisfied, I made my way back to the ratlines and swung myself onto them, just as the ship took a particularly rough wave.

I felt the whole craft lurch under me, the lines wrenched from my grip. I tried to grab hold again, but there was no chance. I tumbled down toward the raging sea. All was the roar of the wind, the gallows-creaking of the ship, and the shouts of the crew as I tumbled down the rope line, bounced off the rail, and plunged into the unforgiving waves.

K. L. Mitchell

The reader would be forgiven for believing that my narrative must needs end there. Indeed, as I hit the waves, I was certain I was done for. I remember the impact as I crashed into the waters and began to sink. Below the surface of the raging sea, the water was warm and calm as it enfolded me.

I have since spoken with others who have experienced this brush with fate. It seems this sense of halcyon is not an uncommon thing. It's odd. One would expect their last moments to be full of panicking and thrashing about, but instead there is this feeling of letting go. You just...wait for it to happen. So it was, as I watched the hull of the ship disappear above me. I recall feeling like I was dreaming. So odd to feel the world fading away like that, like you're drifting off into a lovely dream. I put up no resistance at all and let the world fade away. Or at least, I began to.

But everything changed. I began to feel a sort of burning itch inside me, growing outward. There was a sensation that made me think of lightning, and a sudden warmth upon my chest. I moved my hand to the spot and felt the medallion I had found on the abandoned island. It had grown very warm and somehow married itself to my skin. Meanwhile, the strange sensations continued to flood through my body. I felt constrained, unable to move my legs as if they were bound by some inexplicable force. Somehow, this was considerably more concerning than the fact that I was drowning. I began to panic, thrashing against whatever was happening. I felt the seawater flow into my lungs, and then...out? And as I tumbled in slow motion beneath the waves, I threw my head back and screamed.

That was the moment. Somehow, the surprise of hearing my own scream, underwater, snapped me out of my moment of terror. As I drifted in place, awareness slowly stole over me that I was breathing—or something very like breathing—and all the pain had melted away. I was alive. Somehow, in defiance of all logic and sense, I was all right. Perhaps my mind was playing a trick, placating me with one last moment of peace before the sea claimed me for good. But it felt too real. I could hear the muted roar of the sea echoing all around me and could even see just as clearly as I could in the open sky. A school of butterflyfish swam by me, utterly unconcerned by my presence. I reached out to them and tried to pet one before thinking better of it.

A glimmer of silver below me caught my eye. I tried to arrange myself to see what it was, but had the most enormous difficulty in maneuvering, to the point that I resorted to relying on my arms to steer myself. The glint of silver stayed on the edge of my vision no matter which way I turned. I kicked at the water in frustration, and a gleaming fish tail intruded itself upon my vision.

It took a moment for my mind to adapt. I looked myself over, and there was no denying what I saw. I had somehow been turned into a mermaid. Presumably, the amulet had some power to protect me against drowning. Even as I write this, it seems quite fantastic and unbelievable, but as I drifted in the blue Caribbean waters, the truth was surprisingly easy to accept. I essayed a flick of my tail and went corkscrewing off in entirely the wrong direction. I laughed and tried again, this time managing to move forward though my tail nearly met my hands.

So. I wasn't drowning, but now what? I looked back up at the boat, still directly above me. It seemed that the storm was beginning to abate. They are sometimes wont to go as quickly as they arrive. I thought of swimming back up to the surface but was unsure if I could even get their attention. Perhaps if I just waited the storm out, then tried? It would be a challenge to explain how I had survived, but perhaps I would manage something…

Some movement caught the corner of my eye, where the blue of the water deepened into darkness. Emerging from the depths was…well, it was another mermaid. I suppose I should not have been surprised, really. After all, where there is one, may there not be another? She was young, about my age as far as I could tell. Her long, white hair billowed out behind her. Her skin likewise was startlingly pale. She was adorned in gleaming silver ornaments, with blue gemstones that mirrored the ocean itself. She kept at a distance, eyeing me with a mix of curiosity and fear. I daresay I must have looked rather the same from her perspective, though in my case, it was less fear than heart-thumping panic.

She was, without a doubt, the loveliest creature I had ever seen. Though most girls my age would be long since married, I had never felt any particular stirrings in that direction. It was as if tilting in the "lists of love" was something that happened to other people. I was not overmuch bothered by this and, indeed, gave it little thought, there being other things to set my mind to. But I swear to you, reader, that as I gazed down at her, I knew exactly how her lips would feel against mine. Such stirrings I felt as I gazed upon her beauty I had never felt before. The reader may well laugh, but truthfully, I wasn't sure what was happening. For a moment, I thought it a by-product of my transformation. I reached a hand out to her, utterly mesmerized.

There was a splash from up above, and something came plunging down into the sea, obscured in a cloud of bubbles. I turned back to where the mergirl had been, but only the distant sight of her tail flicking as she retreated into the depths remained.

I turned back to the source of the interruption in time to see the bubbles part and reveal Black Jack, holding his breath and with a rope around his waist. He squinted in my direction, unsure of what he was seeing. I realized he must not be able to see me properly down here, but even so…I tucked my tail behind me as best I could and swam toward him, waving an arm.

His eyes widened as I approached. Had he seen something he shouldn't? Hard to say. In any case, if he had been daft enough to go plunging into storm-tossed waves after me, I was certainly not going to let him go back empty-handed. Besides which, I was scared. Not just because of the storm and the transformation. It occurred to me that I was entirely alone. The other mermaid had gone off to heaven knows where. If the *Bonnie Mary* gave me up, I would be all by myself in the middle of the sea with no one and nothing. The thought fairly squeezed my heart with terror, and I darted to Jack and clung to him with a ferocity that must have taken him by considerable surprise.

Startled though he was, he nevertheless had the presence of mind to tug repeatedly on the rope that snaked up to the surface. A moment later, I felt the line go taut. Quicker than it takes to tell, we broke through the waves. Immediately, the world swam out of focus, and I felt a wrenching pain all through my body. It felt like I had swallowed half the sea and was trying to sick it up all at once. By the time they dragged the two of us up on deck, I was something of a mess. I lay there curled up, coughing up water, and sobbing, and shivering, and generally going straight to pieces.

I have oft noticed that in a dire situation, there are some, myself included, who do not panic, but they sort of…store their fear away. For later, as it were. Only when the thing is well and truly taken care of does all the bile and terror come flooding back with nothing to stop them. As I lay on the deck, the horror of everything that had happened hit me all at once. I remember how utterly incoherent I was, unable to stop sobbing.

Someone was holding my hand in theirs. I squeezed hard, afraid if I let go I'd go right back into the sea. Beside me, I heard the voice of Dr. Acosta, the ship's surgeon. "She'll be all right," he said. "Help me get her to the infirmary. A little rest and she'll be right as rain."

"Good to hear." It was Captain Cunningham. I collected myself enough to look up at her. She was standing over me, looking very concerned. "Someone want to tell me what happened?"

A crew member pointed. "She went up to free the halyard on the mainsail when it got stuck. Got it all right, but then a wave hit and she went over. Black Jack here made us fetch a rope and went in after her."

"Did he really?" The captain turned to Jack, who, as it turned out, was the one holding my hand. "Jack, that was a very reckless and irresponsible thing to do."

He smiled up at her. "Well, Cap'n, after all, I *do* have a reputation to maintain."

She laughed. "Right enough. Get her to the infirmary then. And Mr. Sanyang? Extra rum ration that man." She slapped Black Jack on the shoulder with a smile. "Well done." She turned to the others. "Has anyone got a blanket?"

I just managed to speak up. "Thank you, Mis—er, Captain, but I'm not cold."

"Tain't for cold, missy," she replied, nudging the toe of her boot against my legs, which had somehow returned. "Only you seem to've lost your drawers."

Chapter Twelve

"A MERMAID, YA SAY?" Captain Cunningham stroked her chin. "Interesting."

I spent the rest of the day in the infirmary on Dr. Acosta's insistence. He said that I should try to get some rest, but I spent most of the time turning the events of the storm over in my head. Foremost on my mind was the question of what to tell the others. On the one hand, I felt like I really ought to be as honest as possible with them, they being my fellow crewmates and all. But on the other hand...If someone came up to you and told you they'd been turned into a mermaid, and seen another one while they were down there, what would you think? Quite.

In the end, I figured if I couldn't trust my crewmates, I couldn't trust anyone. When the captain came by to check on me that night, I told her everything. She listened patiently without interrupting, then went and got a few of the officers. I was then bid to tell the story again, which I did.

To my astonishment, none of them seemed all that surprised. "Mermaids people these waters 'tis said of old," said James, the bosun. "Never seen one myself o'course."

"I daresay they keep out of the way of land dwellers," added Mr. Sanyang. "Not that I can blame them."

"True," said Heinz, our quartermaster. "But I have heard stories from the natives round here. Some islands used to trade with 'em back before our lot showed up, so they say. Reckon they had to stop then."

The captain snorted. "Most likely, yes." She rubbed her temples, thinking. "And you say it's down to that amulet of yours, there, girl?"

I nodded. "Yes, Cap'n. I believe 'tis so. It went all warm while I was in the water, and I think it attached itself to my skin." I craned my neck down to look at my chest. If I squinted, I could just fancy I saw the red mark where it had fastened itself.

Mr. Sanyang grinned. "See, now? I told you that thing would bring you luck!" He reached toward it, then hesitated. "Do you mind if I...?"

I nodded. "Go ahead."

He gingerly took the amulet, lifting it toward the light. He turned it round in his hand, examining it with the others. "Looks a bit like jade," said Heinz.

Scallywag!

"Not quite heavy enough for jade, I think. Besides, the way the light catches it...bit like an abalone shell." Mr. Sanyang moved it back and forth, watching the light dance across its surface. "Could be a similar thing, perhaps?" He shrugged and laid it gently back on my shirt.

"Curious," muttered the captain. "Most curious." She turned to the others. "I think it's probably best if we get a wee bit of outside help on this one."

"Have you got someone in mind, Captain?"

She nodded, then turned to me with a smile. "All right, you. Go ahead and rest the night here. I'll be wanting you up and about in the morning. Can ya do that?"

"Yes, Captain!"

"Good." She stood and rubbed her hands together. "Because I think it's time we went to visit the admiral."

Shortly thereafter, we changed course, heading away from the main shipping routes and into the middle of the Caribbean. It was quite the isolated spot. For the majority of the trip, we never saw so much as a sign of another ship. From time to time, Jansen, the navigator, would go up to the forecastle by himself, then we would change course slightly. One evening, while on watch, I saw him standing there, cupping some sort of metal object in his hand and studying it carefully. I thought of walking over and asking him what it was but thought better of it. There were few enough secrets amongst the crew, but something about the way he stood gave off a feeling that whatever he was doing was a private thing and not to be interrupted. I held in my curiosity and bided my time.

The mystery extended to the admiral himself, as I quickly discovered when I tried to ask about him. Crew members who had been around longer said they had indeed met him, but none were willing to talk about it. Even Black Jack, who generally took delight with explaining things to me seemed unusually shy on that account. "I dunno as I should tell ya," he explained one day when we were working on deck. "I mean, if we're going because of your necklace there, it stands to reason they'll have you along as well. But I don't know that for sure, y'see." He shrugged. "It's a bit of a secret, is the old admiral. If the captain an' them reckon you should know, then rest assured, they'll tell ye."

And so it was that, three days later, we came upon the oldest ship I have ever seen. The wood was black with age, the sails dark and stained. From a distance, it looked like a derelict ship, one which, by rights, ought to have been claimed by the sea ages ago. As we came closer, it became clear that the ship, in defiance of all expectation, was in rather good shape. Someone was looking after it. Several someones, in fact. As we hove to, I could see it was manned by a handful of old men, with grizzled beards and faces of old leather that bespoke a lifetime at sea.

We came up on the ship slowly at first, the captain sending up a green flag with an insignia I had not seen before. We held ourselves at bay for a few tense minutes until another flag of the same design was run up on the other vessel. Whereupon we dropped anchor, and a skiff was prepared to go over to the other ship. As I helped with the sails, Mr. Sanyang came up and put a hand on my shoulder. "Come on," he said. "The captain says you're to come with us. You have your amulet with you?"

I lay my hand on the spot where, under my shirt, I could feel the disc against my chest. "Right here, yes."

"Good." He led me across to the skiff, where the captain and a couple of other crewmen were waiting.

"All right," said Captain Cunningham, "in you go, lass. We're going to pay a little visit."

"Now then," said the captain once we were underway. "It's time you learned about the admiral. There's not many as even knows he exists, so you can consider yourself one o' the privileged few. The fact is, he ain't an admiral so much as...well, the oldest captain on these here seas by a long chalk. He don't give orders over the rest of us, but any captain with a lick of sense to 'em knows that he's got more knowledge and experience in these here waters than any three people you'd care to name. And if you need some advice or got a question, the admiral's your man." She looked up at Mr. Sanyang. "Ain't that right?"

He nodded. "That's true enough." He took a long draw on his pipe and fixed the captain with a look. "You gonna tell her the rest?"

She just grinned. "How about I let you do the honors?"

He shrugged. "All right." He turned to me and looked me straight in the eye. "The thing about him, y'see, the thing that makes him the admiral, is that...y'see, it's this way...he's dead. But also, he ain't. That is to say, his body is dead, but his spirit ain't departed."

Captain Cunningham nodded. "Now, no doubt you think you're being fed a line. The ol' captain an' Mr. Sanyang having you on, but it's G—d's truth. He was one of the first white men to sail these here waters, back before there were any real colonies to speak of. When he got old, to where he couldn't sail no more, he cut a deal with a houngan, that's a vodou priest to you. Dunno what he gave for it, but they made a magic for him so's he could keep sailin' as long as he liked. Long as he stayed on his ship, it would remain true, and no storm could take it. And what is more, he would never die, less'n he set foot on land again. That suited the ol' man just fine, as he had no desire to go ashore again anyway."

"Aye, but it wasn't what you'd call a perfect arrangement," said Mr. Sanyang. "Like I said, he may still be around, but his body...well, there ain't much left of it these days, and that's the truth. It ain't a pretty sight, girl. And I'm telling you now so you won't be surprised. He looks and sounds like death itself, and I ain't even gonna mention the smell. But like Cap'n says, no one knows these waters better'n him."

I had little enough time to digest this revelation before we came up alongside the ship. It was old, older than anything that should still be afloat. Up at the bow, someone had carefully painted *The Admiral*. The fine gilt paint seemed as old as the rest of the ship, yet still gleamed like it was new.

We headed up the rope ladder that had been cast down for us and proceeded to the main deck. There wasn't much of a crew, mostly old salts who eyed us with a slightly diffident air. Captain Cunningham took off her hat and bowed low to a leathery old coot with a layer of gray stubble on his chin and no less than six gold hoops in his ears. "Permission to come aboard," she said. "Captain Cunningham of the *Bonnie Mary* and party. We crave an audience with the admiral."

The old man snorted, idly scratching the side of his nose. "Aye? Well, 'at's as may be. Himself is havin' a kip, but I'll see if he's awake yet." He nodded toward a wooden bench in the shade of the main cabin. "Ye can wait there if'n ya like."

Captain Cunningham bowed again. "That will be most agreeable, thank'ee." We filed over and took our seats. The old man disappeared into the cabin, and the rest of the crew dispersed back to whatever it was they had been doing.

I found myself next to Mr. Sanyang. Normally, he viewed the world through an impassive mask of a face, but I could see he was somewhat unnerved. I leaned a little closer. "Sir? May I ask a question?"

He nodded. "Better out here than in there, I suppose. What is it, McCormick?"

"These men—the crew, I mean. They all seem a little..."

He nodded. "Oh, that. Aye. It's not uncommon for a man who has spent his life on the sea to want to finish off his days here. He knows he'll find a welcome berth, and a like-minded crew. They don't go in for privateering and all that. Most of 'em have had all the excitement a lifetime can handle. But if you can't quite step away from the sea, then this is about as peaceful a place as any to while away the time, waitin' for the end." He leaned in with a conspiratorial whisper. "And I'll tell you another thing. You see these old gray beards here? A fair number of 'em are former captains themselves."

I looked at him with suspicion. "What, really?"

"G—d's truth. Let's see...ah!" he nodded his head toward a balding man, rather heavyset and jowly, who was calmly mending a ratline. "See him yonder?"

"Aye?"

"Ever hear of Captain Oswalt? Of the *Nightshade*?"

"Him? Yeah, he was a terrible pyrate! The sailors back home used to tell stories about him, and he..." I looked back at the old man, then up at Mr. Sanyang. "You're not serious."

"Dead serious, m'girl. In the flesh and all. Met him before, last time we were here. Nice old fellow. Got an accent you could cut cheese with. But he ain't the only one, not by a long way."

Just then, the door to the cabin opened, and the old man we had spoken to put his head round.

"All right, you lot. The admiral will see you now."

Chapter Thirteen

IT TOOK A MOMENT for my eyes to adjust to the dark as we were escorted into the admiral's cabin. A couple of old hurricane lamps supplemented the meager sunlight coming through the closed slats of the windows. As my eyes became accustomed, a picture slowly formed before me of the unusual surroundings in which I found myself. It has been said that if someone lives somewhere long enough, the place becomes an extension of themselves, a second face, as it were. The admiral had been residing in this cabin a long time, and one could read it as easily as a book. Most of the room was decorated with faded glory: plush cushions, ornately carved woods, wall-to-wall finery, and not a thing less than a hundred years old. In the back of the cabin, I could just see a massive four-poster bed. Gold ropes held back curtains of red velvet. The bed must have been quite the fine thing once. In its present state, I wouldn't have gone near it for all the mites and things that must have taken up residence over the years.

As to the admiral himself, he was exactly as the captain & Mr. Sanyang had described him, though that hardly prevented me from letting out a gasp. I had never seen a zombi before and have seen precious few since. I cannot call myself an expert, but for a fact, I do know that most people tend to get them wrong. The thing about a zombi, you see, is they must have a reason to come back. It's no easy task. Staving off the reaper takes an act of considerable will. I remember the moment I clapped eyes on the admiral. I genuinely believed I was looking at a corpse, some sun-dried mummy that had long since given up his ghost, but then I saw his eyes. Bright green the irises were, almost like they had a light of their own. As I stared, I felt the power of the old admiral's will wash over me. Here was a man who had been through things unimaginable, someone with limitless reserves of cunning and determination. By my troth, he had more life in him than many people walking around breathing.

He wore old finery, a lavish, red coat over a blouse yellowed with age. A tricorn hat sat atop a rather long periwig, the ringlets hanging well down past his shoulder. He was seated in an old chair which had been fixed with wheels, his body being evidently too frail to move itself around.

Bony fingers gripped the arms of his chair as if he might fall out any second.

Captain Cunningham bowed low. "Thank you for seeing us, Admiral. Captain Cunningham of the *Bonnie Mary*, with my mate Mr. Sanyang and Molly McCormick, of my company. We come to seek your knowledge concerning a relic Miss McCormick came across just recently." She turned to me. "Go on. Show him the amulet."

I slipped the leather cord from around my neck and held the amulet out to the old man, who grasped my wrist with a speed I would never have credited him for. Truth is, I nearly cried out. He pulled my hand close, peering intently at the medallion. "Light," he croaked, his voice like dry stone.

One of his attendants hurried over with one of the hurricane lamps. He lifted the disc delicately in his bony fingers, turning it this way and that. At last, he looked up at me with a quizzical expression, then harrumphed and released my wrist. I stepped back as quickly as politeness would allow and secured the amulet once more around my neck.

"A most unusual find," he murmured. He turned to Captain Cunningham. "You, girl. You ever hear tell of the An'ui?"

The captain furrowed her brow. "Not that I recall, sir, no."

He nodded. "Before yer time, I expect. It's their workmanship, arright. I ken it well, even as long as it's been." He took a deep breath. "The An'ui, they were…well, children of the sea. It was what their name meant, y'see. A rare and secretive race they were. Time was they would come up on land to trade and such, but their real home was the sea. I even met 'em a few times meself. This was in the old days, mind, before every Tom and Jack came runnin' to plant their flags. There was magic, y'see. The old peoples hadn't been chased into hiding, like they had back home. There were such fantastic sights…" He sighed, his eyes growing wistful. "And I have lived to see them fade away, one by one. Like as not, one day they will all be gone, and take the old admiral with 'em."

One of his attendants coughed. "The amulet, Admiral, beggin' your pardon."

"Hm? Oh. Yes. Right. Well, they used it to move back and forth between the land and sea, y'ken. Mostly for doin' trade and sech with tribes they trusted. Not heard of them bein' out and about, mind. Where d'ye say you got this one?"

Mr. Sanyang spoke up. "We were investigating an island. Looks like some kind of massacre had been there. She found it off in a corner of this...well, I suppose it was meant to be a temple."

The admiral nodded. He let out a horrible laugh, little more than a hoarse whisper. "Ah, yes, from time to time, they'd get up to that too. Not as raiders, mind. Just...they weren't the only ones in communion wit' the old mysteries. Some of the tribes, out in the more isolated islands, they got up to things even the Conquistadores couldn't match for cruelty." He nodded to himself. "Probably that belonged to one of their people, one as didn't make it back."

"It looked like they burned all the bodies," I said. "There were women and children as well."

"A nasty business indeed. But I tell you true, they wouldn't do it if it weren't needful. Sometimes you got to rip the thing out root and branch." He balled his hand into a fist and swept it upward with a sardonic gleam in his eye. "Root and branch!"

There was something terrible about the way his eyes gleamed. Up 'til that declaration, he had been...well, scary enough, certainly, but not actually threatening. In the flickering lamplight, his face looked more skull-like than ever, and for a moment, his eyes gleamed with malice. I found myself taking a step back in spite of myself.

He must have noticed, as he quickly composed himself. "Sorry there, missy, didn't mean to startle ye. Things was...a bit rougher in those days. Closer to the bone, as ye might say. Safer now, o'course. That's the other side of it. One day it'll be all safe, all the old ways gone. They reckon they're bringing light to the world, but when there's nothing but light, what's a keen man to do?" He shook his head, looking downcast. "Well, I suppose that's the way of things and no mistake. But look, you"—he jabbed a bony old finger at me—"you keep holt of that amulet, d'ye hear? This be a relic of a time what was, and what shan't be again. I don't reckon as there's another of its like to be found on dry land. It'll bring you luck, like as not."

Mr. Sanyang smiled down at me. "You see? I told you myself, didn't I?"

Captain Cunningham nudged me. "Tell him about the mermaid."

I told the admiral of the incident in the storm and my going overboard. When I finished, he nodded sagely. "Well, now. That does put a rare complexion on it. It's good to hear the An'ui are still in these waters. Seems to me there's hope for this ol' world yet." He leaned forward again. "But mark ye, If ye're wise, you'll not tell anyone else about this. It's already treasure enough, but if word got out..." He shook his head. "I've seen men kill and die for far, far less."

I gulped but managed to nod. "Yes, sir. I understand."

"Good lass. Always good to have an extra card up your sleeve, eh?" His chuckle was echoed by others of his crew. He settled back, sagging a little into his clothes. "And now I must beg your indulgence. These old bones, they tire easily, damn 'em. The gentlemen will see you out." He looked up at Captain Cunningham. "Always good to see you, my girl. Quite the fine captain you have become and no mistake." To Mr. Sanyang, he nodded his head respectfully. "You look after this lot, hear? I know ye shall." He turned to me. "And as for you, young lady, I shall follow your career with interest, yes indeed. Return any time you like, girl. You've got the freedom of the old admiral's ship for the asking."

Captain Cunningham bowed again, sweeping her hat off in the process. Mr. Sanyang bowed, and I followed his example. "Thank you kindly for the audience, Admiral," said the captain. "Fair winds to ye 'til we meet again."

"Same to you, girl. Same to you." The old admiral leaned back in his chair, eyes half-lidding as he fell silent. Beside us, one of the attendants touched a finger to his lips and led us back outside.

"Right," said the captain as we made our way back to the ship. "If anyone should ask, all you need tell 'em is how you found it on an island and fancied it. That's all anyone needs to know, yes?"

"Understood, Cap'n," I replied. "May I ask a question?"

"Well, y'can ask."

"How did we get here? To the admiral, I mean. I saw Jansen messing with...well, something or other. I figured it was to do with the admiral, but I didn't like to ask."

"Oh, that. It's a compass, y'see. A special one. I dunno the doin's of it, but apparently ya take a regular old compass, and there's some work with the blood of the person you're trying to find, and a houngan's gotta say words over it or such like. Anyhow, it always points to the person you're looking for. This is a fine rare magic, and rarer still are the ones as lead a body to the admiral." She leaned forward and smiled. "Tell ya this, girl. People think we privateers are always hankerin' after gold, an' jewels, an' that. But some of the grandest treasures are wee things ya wouldn't look at twice." She winked. "There's a lesson there, so there is."

Back on board the vessel, Captain Cunningham hailed Jansen. "All right, mate. We've had our business with the admiral, and I do think 'tis time to head to port. Where's the nearest land?"

Jansen indicated a map he had rolled out on a table. "Well Cap'n, we had to turn around a bit to catch up with 'em, but near as I can figure it, we're right around the seventeenth parallel, probably south of Cuba. We might be closer to Jamaica, mind, or even Hispaniola, but I reckon we're farther west than that. Either way, if we point 'er north, we're bound to hit something right soon."

"Good enough. Mr. Sanyang, get us underway. I'll be in my quarters for the next little bit." The mate saluted, and the captain departed. Halfway to her door, she turned around. "Oh! Nearly forgot."

Mr. Sanyang just smiled. "I'll have the hot water sent up directly, ma'am."

She smiled back. "Good man. You've got the helm." With that, she went to her cabin and closed the door.

I looked up at the first mate, puzzled. "Hot water?" I asked.

He didn't answer right away, glancing first from side to side to make sure we were unheard. Then he leaned down to me and grinned. "The admiral is a fine old fellow," he said, "and it's a wise captain indeed that takes his counsel. But the cap'n, she's a bit fastidious, y'know. Whenever we get back from visiting him, she needs a hot bath and a change of clothes before she's quite herself again. Now, you run down to the galley and tell them the captain wants a bath, though if I know Maggie, she's probably already got some hot water ready to go. Off you go, now."

So we changed course and headed north. The sea was nicely calm as we headed landward, and there was a feeling of pleasant anticipation onboard. Of course, once a crew found its way to a port town, most of 'em engaged in the time-honored practices of unloadin' their worldly goods for the benefit of the various taverns and brothels.

Now, I won't say I never frequented the occasional inn, but pyrate or not, being a young woman of slight build made them not the most ideal spots to spend my leisure time. And as for the other...the reader may well imagine naught was there for me that I could figure. Generally, some of the women of the crew would set out together to explore the town, safety being in numbers, and I would often tag along. Anna and Dutch would find an inn away from the noise and bustle of the docklands, to which they would repair until it was time to leave. It took some time for me to understand why. In any case, the prospect of shore leave lightened the spirit, and the next two days passed quickly and pleasantly.

On the evening of the third night, when the sun was just dipping below the horizon, the lookout spotted land. All of us on deck hurried to take a look. Sure enough, just ahead and a wee bit to starboard, we could see a strip of land. It wasn't a large island, but as night fell and the stars came out, we began to discern lights ahead.

Captain Cunningham summoned Jansen to her side. "Looks a likely enough place," she said. "Any idea where we are?"

Jansen shook his head. "No, Cap'n. I don't see anything on my charts. We're not near enough to Cuba. If it were Jamaica, we'd have hit land by now. Too small for them anyway." He shrugged. "Must be a relatively new settlement. They're popping up all over these days, Lord knows. Shall we set course for them?"

The captain thought it over, then nodded. "Where there's lights, there's civilization. If nothing else, we can stop and refresh ourselves. Bring us in toward the lights. If they have a pier, we'll dock there. If not, we can send a dinghy in the morning."

He saluted. "Right you are, ma'am."

And thus it was that we, with the last slivers of light slipping over the edge of the horizon, came upon the town. A cheerier, better-appointed port you would be lucky to find. The lights shone on clean cobbled streets. Men, women, and children bustled along cheerfully, and the sounds of laughter and music found their way to our ears. As we came closer, a pier came into view, and a man ran out with a lanthorn to guide us in as we approached. Soon, several others were eagerly helping us to tie down and get situated. Black Jack nudged me as we cinched the guylines together. "Well, they do seem to be glad to see us, don't they?"

I nodded. "Must not get many visitors, away out here and all."

There was a commotion on the docks. As the captain and her senior officers strode down the gangplank, a hefty, red-faced man in muttonchops bustled forward to greet them. He stood still a moment, wheezing a little and trying to collect himself. Captain Cunningham nodded to Mr. Sanyang, who stepped forward.

Scallywag!

"Captain Cunningham of the *Bonnie Mary* extends her greetings and requests permission for her crew to come ashore."

"Oh, of course! Of course!" The mayor—for such he was—took off his hat and bowed toward her. "Yes, by all means. I'm afraid we don't have a lot of visitors here, so you are most welcome! Yes," he raised his voice, turning his head upward so all the crew could hear, "you are all welcome to Donovan's Cape!"

Chapter Fourteen

THE READER MAY NOT be surprised to learn that not every port town is thrilled to have a crew of pyrates come ashore. We're a raucous lot. Months of lookin' at nothing but each other and the sea does, as I mentioned before, make a body a bit reckless. Thus it was that we ladies and gentlemen of fortune were always on the lookout for places that welcomed our presence—or at least our coin. Generally, we could expect to be tolerated, provided we didn't wear out our welcome. But these people seemed genuinely delighted to have us there. It wasn't long before we were all strolling about on the main street, admiring the fountains and window boxes filled with colorful tropical blooms. It really was quite an idyll. Something in the warmth and cheeriness of the place spread to ourselves, and even the roughest soul among us was soon scrubbed up and ambling along the road, tipping their hat to the ladies as they went by.

It wasn't long before we found ourselves in The King's Head. The town's main inn was a fine place, clean and bright, and nearly full to the rafters. It turned out to be the de facto social spot for the town, so alongside workingmen and women, there were entire families, chatting amicably, playing noddy or piquet, or just listening to the small band of musicians in the corner. They were quite good, actually, and when they played a set of old Irish tunes, it stirred up a degree of homesickness I hadn't felt in a long while.

While I was off in this misty-eyed recollection, one of the young ladies of the village came up to me. She was about my age, perhaps a year or two older. She had honey blond hair, sparkling emerald eyes, and a face that positively shone in the golden light of the tavern. She smiled at me, waiting until I came back to myself enough to notice her. "Hello," she said. "Something on your mind?"

I blushed, shaking the cobwebs from my brain. "Sorry," I said. "Just a little homesick is all." I nodded my head toward the musicians, who were in the middle of "The Girl I Left Behind Me." "Haven't heard this tune in a long time. Me da used to sing it, you see."

She brightened. "Ha! I knew you for an Irish lass the moment I saw you!" She put forth her hand. "Aimee Fitzpatrick."

Scallywag!

"Molly McCormick." I reached for her hand but hesitated, unsure of whether to shake it or what. She spied my difficulty and, with a short laugh, squeezed my hand briefly before sitting down next to me.

"So, Miss McCormick," she said, making herself comfortable. "How long have ya been away from old Éire?"

"Let's see..." I took a moment to cipher. "Three years and a bit. Goodness."

She laughed. "Time flies, eh?" She leaned back, looking wistful. "We came here when I was only a little girl. I don't have many memories of the old country, but to hear Mum and Dad, it was another Eden. What did you think?"

"I daresay Eden wouldn't be quite so cold and wet." I laughed. "Mind you, I've seen lots of islands round these parts that could pass for paradise."

She smiled at that and leaned closer. I caught a whiff of her intoxicating scent that put me in mind of morning dew gleaming on the petals of a rose. "Indeed?" she said. "And what would you say of our little island, then?"

I grinned sheepishly. "Well, I haven't seen much of it, but I like what I've seen so far."

She just laughed. "I should hope so!" She sat with me, watching the revelers. "Your crew is a lively bunch."

"Aye, that's true enough. Though I think we're just glad to get a little leave. Been a long time at sea, you know."

She nodded. "I always think it sounds so romantic. Sailing the seas, braving storms, crossing swords with deadly enemies and that."

"There is a *bit* of that, though to tell the truth, it's mostly just a job. Still, I can't complain. I've had worse, heaven knows."

She leaned close again. "Perhaps you might tell me some of your adventures, eh?"

I shrugged. "Might do, might do. Though in truth you'd hardly credit some of 'em."

"Well, I tell you what," she said and laughed. "I see you've an empty cup. Why not I fill it for you, and you can try one of your stories on me?"

"Fair enough."

Just then, there was a bit of commotion at the door. A scraggly old fellow in old, soiled clothes and a patchy beard strode in. "Evenin' to ye!" he crowed, strutting about like a gamecock. "Elwin, me love, start us off with a grog, eh?" He stopped halfway to the bar, taking in the room.

"Aye? And do we have visitors t'night? Well, that's a fine thing indeed! Seems a celebration's in order!"

The atmosphere in the room...changed. Not too much, mind. The smiles were still there, with just a wee bit of strain about the corners, if you take my meaning. If you've ever had company along, and some daft older relative wandered in and decided this was the time to be sociable, you will know what I mean. The new arrival strode up to the bar, where the barmaid dutifully slipped him a mug of grog. He turned and saluted the company. "A good even' t'ye! Amos Bickle, they call me! Washed up on these shores thirty year' ago. Bloody paradise, this. Of course, it do take some adjusting, yeah?" He threw back his head and laughed at his own private joke.

A distinguished older man hurried over to him. "All right, Amos. No need to talk our guests' ears off, eh? Have your grog."

"Ah, right." The old man stared into his mug. "Ferget what I was saying, don't I?" He looked up at us. "Still, it is awful good to see such as ye. Ol' Amos, he don't see many new faces around, sure he don't." He took a long pull of his grog and looked thoughtful. "Of course, circumstances bein' what they are, well..."

"Tell you what, Amos," said the other man. "I've got a nice bottle of Old Dastardly in my office. Would you do me the honor of sharing it with me?"

Amos looked up at him, then back at us. His eyes twinkled. "Ohhhh! They dinnae know, do they? Dearie me! Well, ev'ry man knows his price, an' a bottle is well enough fer me. Lead the way, gov'ner." The older man hooked his arm in Amos's and began to steer him toward the door. Just as they were leaving, Amos turned back and called over his shoulder. "Look me up in the morning! I'll be at the usual place!" And he was gone.

"Zounds," I muttered to myself. I turned back to Aimee. "Who was that, then?"

She colored a little. "Oh, him? Just old Amos. He landed here some years ago, and...well, we sort of look after him, you see."

I nodded. "I guess he probably does need looking after."

"Oh aye, but he's harmless, really. Just...has his ways."

"Ah."

"But never mind him. Grog, was it? And you were going to tell me one of your adventures." She giggled and bustled away, disappearing toward the bar.

"Well," said a voice behind me, "you're doing pretty well for yourself, ain'tcha girl?"

At the next table, Dutch and Anna were smiling at me. Dutch raised her mug in a mock salute. I looked back and forth between the two of them, trying to work out what they meant. Anna, seeing my confusion, leaned forward. "The girl," she said. "Dutch means you're doing rather well for yourself there."

"That's right," Dutch grinned. "Well in, y'are."

"I..." The reader may hardly credit it, but G—d is my witness, I had no inkling what those two were talking about.

Anna turned to Dutch and sighed theatrically. "Oh, dear. She really has no idea, does she?"

Dutch rolled her eyes. "Lord save us from useless bl—dy sapphics," she declared.

"Useless bl—dy whats?"

"What we *mean*," said Anna kindly, "is that the girl likes you. Fancies you, I mean."

"Wants your body."

"Yes, thank you, Dutch. I think I can handle this."

"What," I said, "her? But...but she's a girl."

"And...?"

"Well, I mean! If she's a girl and I'm a girl, then how can that possibly..."

And then I understood. Anna and Dutch. Always inseparable. Hardly ever one without the other. Like sisters, I had always thought. But no, that wasn't right, was it? More like...

...like a couple.

The two of them watched with amusement as I realized the truth. Dutch nudged Anna with her elbow. "Comes the dawn." She grinned.

"Wait...you two?"

"Yes."

"Really?"

"Oh, yes."

"...how?"

Anna laughed. "Oh, I hardly think that's a topic for polite conversation!"

Dutch joined in. "We could loan her some books. Maybe the one with the watercolors?"

"Don't you dare!" Anna punched playfully at Dutch's arm. "Poor girl's confused enough as it is." She turned back to me. "The fact is, there's honestly not much to it. There are girls who fancy girls, and boys who fancy boys. Hell, there're some as likes 'em both. Though I think you're not quite ready for that."

"Aye," said Dutch. "We'll save that for the advanced course."

"The point is," said Anna, "this rather nice young lady seems to fancy you. And if I'm any judge, you were rather enjoying her company yourself, hmm?"

I colored a little. "Well, I mean, she is rather nice..."

"And...?"

"And she smells good," I murmured.

"Does she, now? Dear me. And does she make you feel all tingly, then?"

"I...well, a bit..."

Anna chuckled. "Young fella me lass, we can see it from here." She reached over and patted my hand. "Now look, you. I daresay these are uncharted waters for you, yes? Ah, thought so. Well, best I can tell you is let your heart be your compass. And when love reaches out, don't be afraid to take its hand."

Dutch grinned at Anna. "Well put."

The other woman smiled. "Well, it worked for me, didn't it?" Anna turned back to me and was about to say something when her expression changed. "Ah! Looks like she's coming back. Remember what we said, girl." She nudged at Dutch, and the two women turned their attention away from me.

Aimee returned, two mugs of grog in her hands. "There we are." She sat back down and took a light pull of her drink. "Now then," she said, "give us a story. Tell me...yes, tell me how you came to sea."

So I told her of my old village, and old man Hennessy, and how I disguised myself as a boy to get away. She found this bit particularly amusing and remarked that I probably made a very handsome lad. I wasn't quite sure what to make of that, truth be told, but she did seem to mean it as a compliment. I took it as such. I told her about the voyage across the sea, then the attack by the pyrate crew, and how I became one of their number. When I finished, she leaned back and took me in. "Well, my goodness. That's quite the adventure you had. And you've been with them ever since?"

I nodded. "Same crew and all. If you had told me four years ago that I would be halfway across the world, and a pyrate no less, I'd have thought you mad."

She giggled again. "Well, I think it suits you. I rather like a swashbuckler, myself." Off in the corner, the musicians started a high-spirited jig from my days back home. Aimee's face lit up as she heard the opening notes. "Oh! I love this one!" She turned back to me. "Tell me, Mallory—I mean Molly—do you dance?"

I fidgeted nervously. "I—well, not really. I mean, a bit, but..." There was a hand at my back, and of a sudden I felt myself shoved forward and onto my feet. I spun around to glare at whoever had done it, but Anna and Dutch were both looking the other way. Not like I'd ever get them to own up. At any rate, it was too late. Aimee took my hand and bustled me onto the dance floor.

Several couples had already gathered for the dance, and Aimee weaved us expertly past them until we found a free spot. She put her hands on her hips, took a step back, and began. I tried to match her movements but only managed a clumsy approximation, generally a step or two behind hers. At length, she took my hand and motioned me to stop. "You're overthinking. Look, just follow the rhythm, right? You just move your feet in time. You can start with doing one at a time if you like, then work your way up to both. But don't worry about doing the same thing as me. All right? Then let's try again."

This time, I will admit, I did rather better. Relieved of trying to duplicate her moves, I found myself following the music much more smoothly, not to mention the less I had to worry about getting it right, the more I could concentrate on the lovely girl before me. In truth, it was genuinely fun, and by the time the landlord called last orders, I was quite exhausted.

The next thing I knew, we were strolling together in the flower-scented night, arm in arm. I remember some part of me thinking that I really ought to head for the ship, but the momentum of the evening, as you might say, easily overwhelmed any such thoughts. We sat side by side on a bench, Aimee's body nestled against mine, as we stared up at the crescent moon and the night sky blanketed with stars. I showed her how to find Polaris and told her some of the old stories that various people on the crew had told me about the other stars, legends that went back a thousand years or more.

I think we must have sat there together for quite a while before the clouds began to fill my head. I yawned, then turned a worried smile to Aimee. "Sorry. Fair takes it out of you, this dancing."

She just smiled and ruffled my hair. "Let's get you to bed."

I didn't argue. We wound through the cobblestone streets, now quiet as the city came to rest. There was a door, then some stairs, and finally the sensation of a mattress and linen sheets. Aimee stood before me, her body silhouetted against the moonlight.

"What—"

She stopped me with a finger to my lips. "Please," she whispered. "Don't say anything. Maybe it will be all right. Just...let me have this."

She lay down by my side. Outside, the night was quiet except for the distant calls of birds. What little light there was brushed the world in silver edges. I felt her move closer to me and smelled the sweet scent return just before her lips met mine. Those lips...If I close my eyes, I swear I can taste them, even now...her body draped over mine, and for a long time, we held each other in a quiet embrace. After a while, she stood up again and stretched like a cat, silhouetted in the frame of the open window. Without a word, she began to remove her clothing.

I shall draw a veil of modesty over the rest of the night's activities. Suffice it to say, it was an experience without compare in all my life up to that point. It seemed to me that everything that had happened in my life had conspired to bring me here to this place and this night.

In my opinion, it was well worth the trip.

Chapter Fifteen

I WOKE A LITTLE past dawn. I remember becoming gradually aware of my unusual surroundings (Aimee's bed being rather nicer than my own modest bunk back on the ship). The momentary confusion gave way to memories of the previous night. That woke me up right enough, and I reached out for Aimee.

She wasn't there.

Sitting up, I took a look around the room. There was no sign of her. In fact, there was no sign that anyone had been there in ages. The place had that musty, forgotten feel you get from a place long abandoned. Odd, when we arrived the night before, just a handful of hours ago, it had been a perfectly lovely home. I distinctly remembered feeling self-conscious in such a well-appointed place. But now, as I looked around, it was all faded and timeworn.

I rolled out of bed and found my clothes on the floor where they had been discarded. Aimee's should have been right by them. I tried to tell myself she just had to run off to work, or to get breakfast or somesuch, but the fact was, I knew something was deeply wrong. I dressed quickly and hurried through the house, calling her name. No reply came, and every room was in the same state as the bedchamber.

It was then that I noticed the silence. Recall that I was born and raised in a port town. I knew full well the business of such a town would be well underway. I should have heard people running errands, merchants crying their wares, children running about, and so on. But d—d if I could hear anything outside.

Going out into the streets, I saw not a soul. The whole town stretched out before me, somehow grayer and older than it had seemed before. Not a soul was to be seen. I began to panic a bit. Where was everybody? Was I the only one left? Worse, maybe I was the one who was missing, slipped unawares into some faerie kingdom like my gran used to tell us stories about. I ran down the hill toward the docks, praying the ship would still be there when I arrived, but secretly fearing it wouldn't. You cannot imagine how my heart leapt as I heard familiar voices up ahead. I turned a corner to the docks to see several of our crew in serious conversation.

Black Jack saw me hurrying toward them and beckoned me over. "All right, Mol. Still among the living, I see?"

I nodded, somewhat out of breath. "What's going on? Where is everyone?"

"Well, that's the question of the hour, innit?" Black Jack rubbed his bald head. "Looks like all our people are accounted for, barring a couple. We got runners hunting them up. But as for the townsfolk, well, ain't seen one of 'em all morning. And that ain't all. Have a look." He gestured toward the tavern where we had been the night before.

I had an idea of what I was going to see but went to have a look anyway. Sure enough, the place was not just empty but abandoned. A layer of dust coated the counters, a film of grime on the few bottles and mugs that were still around. I found the table where Aimee and I had been, still there but looking so much older and worn. I tried to reconcile it with my memories of the previous night, but it was just impossible. I couldn't get it to make sense.

Black Jack caught my expression as I came back out again. "Bit of a puzzler, innit? We were trying to work it out. I thought I'd dreamed it myself, but it seems we mustv'e all had the same dream."

"Faeries," James whispered. "Me mam used to tell me about 'em. They'd invite you off to their home, and there'd be singin' and dancin' and that. Then you wake up and you're all alone an' thirty years gone. Time's different for 'em, she says."

Jansen the navigator squinted at the morning sun. "Well, it's coming up right where I'd expect it this time o'year. Besides, lots of the crew bunked up on the ship, and it's only been one night for them as well."

Out in front of the dock, the captain was deep in discussion with the other officers. There was a shout, and a small group of men emerged from a side street. "Found 'em," called the one in front. "Drunk in a bloody alley, weren't they?" The shamefaced stragglers saluted the captain and hurried back to the ship as quickly as they could.

"Well, I think that's everyone," said Jansen. "We might as well head toward the ship as well. Faeries or not, I don't much fancy sticking around here, and I daresay the captain will feel the same."

You may well imagine there was no objection. We had just started toward the dock, when Black Jack stopped. He held up his hand for silence. "Hol' up," he said. "Anyone else hear...singing?"

We stopped and listened, ears straining. The sound was faint at first but grew as the singer came closer. It was not a good singing voice: rather

Scallywag!

scratchy and hoarse, really. But right then and there, it could have been a chorus of angels for how glad we were to be hearing it. It was coming from the main street, and several of us hurried back to see who it was.

The old man, Amos, was strolling unsteadily down the street. He held an empty bottle in one hand and was using it to conduct himself as he sang.

Johnny's gone to sea, m'dear,
Poor Johnny's gone to sea.
These em'rald shores he'll ne'ermore see
Since Johnny's gone to sea.

The old man froze in midstep, catching sight of us. "Well, blow me!" He cackled. "Still around, are ye? Was beginnin' to think as I'd dreamt ye. Suppose ya haven't got a wee hair of the dog? I'm dead parched, me."

The better part of the crew watched as he wolfed down his third hard tack. "Been years since I had a decent ship's biscuit," he mumbled, crumbs tumbling onto his beard. "They've got good grub, mind," he said, nodding in the direction of the shore, "but somehow they just can't make it right on land. I think 'tis the sea air." He took a long swig of rum and smacked his lips.

Captain Cunningham leaned into view. She had been watching him impassively since we first brought him aboard. She hadn't said much, though she'd hardly taken her eyes off the old man. "Well now," she said, "I dare say that should fix a man right for breakfast, and now I'm hoping you'll tell us just what is going on."

He looked up at her, his boiled-egg eyes looking somewhat uncertain before realization dawned. "Oh! Ye mean the town!"

"Yes. I mean the town. Now would you, please?"

"All right, all right." He took another draw at the rum and assumed a thoughtful expression. "Well, I don't know the why of it—I think I may've asked once, but it's all gone now—but I can tell you the what. It was in...G—d strike me, '50? Or '51? Well, I was a sailor then, signed to the *Pheasant* out of Edinburgh. We had just come to haul some timber to St. Edward when—"

"The town. Please."

"Oh aye, aye. The town. Well, there was a wreck, is the short of it, and I was washed up on the shore. I found the town just as ya seen it today. Figured it musta been a colony that got abandoned. You know how it is. Well, I fair turned the place upside-down looking for any sort of grub or something to drink, but there weren't a crumb left in the place. Did find the remains of an orchard over on the landward side, so I reckoned if I died it wouldn't be of scurvy, anyway.

"I was feelin' pretty well disheartened, as ye may reckon. I sloped off to one of the old houses and found a bed that looked comfortable enough and lay down for a rest. Weren't more'n a couple hours later, I'm woke up by this lady screamin' her head off at me. She was wantin' to know who I was, and how I got in her room, an' all that. And of course, here's me wondering what happened to the empty town I had been in. She were screaming and I were screaming, a real scene it was. Fortunately, some people came runnin' and before ya know it, I was before the mayor, telling him all about the shipwreck an' that.

"Well, the point of it is they're under a curse, or a blessing, or somethin' of that kidney. Never quite got it straight in me head. But durin' the day the town is all dead an' empty an' that, but at night everyone comes back and the whole place's like new again."

"Are you serious?"

"'Upon my word. Even the food an' drink an' that. Ye can eat a crust of bread one night, and the next night it's right back where it was. Tis the same with everything round here. It's like the same night over 'n' over. Exceptin' of course you remember all the nights what come before."

"Good G—d," whispered the captain. She moved over and put a hand on his shoulder. "Well look here, we can get you off to a proper port if you like."

The old man smiled up at her. "D—d decent of you, Cap'n, but in fact I rather like it here. Always plenty of food an' drink, no tabs to pay, a nice wee cottage they put me up in for nothing. I've a cosy little berth, all told, especially at my age. An' besides," he confided, "I'm dead important round here, me."

Captain Cunningham raised an eyebrow. "Indeed? Are you, then?"

"Mm-hm." He took another long pull of his drink. "See, anything they does in the town, anything they change, it goes back to how it was before. So nothin' changes 'cept the memory, you see? But if I do something...well, it's like I'm exempt, somehow. If I paint a shed, it stays painted. If someone asks me to write somethin' down for 'em, it'll be

Scallywag!

there the next night, sure as anything. So basically I does for the town and in exchange I'm livin' the good life. Ye're not the first to offer, an' I do appreciate it, but as I say, I'm rather disinclined to leave."

Afterward, the officers went up to the captain's cabin for a discussion. When they came out, they announced that, as there was some maintenance and things that needed attending to, we would be staying on at least one more night. By this point, the ship's gossip chain had done its work, and everyone was quite aware of what the old man had said. Consequently, there wasn't much in the way of grumbling. Of course, that was the cue for Bosun James to start handin' out work for everyone. In fairness, things needed doing, and with another night on the town to look forward to, you couldn't complain too much. I myself couldn't stop thinking of Aimee and all the questions I wanted to ask her.

Dusk came soon enough. Just as the sky was darkening, the city lit up again. I happened to be on deck, and I can vividly remember how the empty, forlorn buildings began to change. A shadow passed over them, in a manner of speaking, or more like one falling away. Windows that had been dark gradually filled with light. The age and neglect of the place melted away. Voices drifted in the wind as if coming from a long way away. In less than a minute, the thing was done.

A few minutes later, the captain and other officers headed down the gangplank. As they headed toward the town, I could hear her talking to Mr. Sanyang. I didn't catch it all, but when I heard "that bloody mayor" and "get some answers," it was clear enough she wasn't going for a social call.

I took a little more than usual care getting ready to go ashore. I didn't have much in the way of fancy clothes, of course, but I gave myself a good, proper scrubbing and washed and brushed my hair. Anna even volunteered a few drops of juice from a vanilla pod she had, applying them to either side of my neck. I cleaned off my tricorn hat, polished my boots, and strapped a sword to my belt. It was all a bit makeshift, but as I looked in the one old mirror hanging in the crew quarters, I had to admit that it was not overall a bad effect.

Anna and Dutch bustled around, helping me get ready and peppering me with advice. They seemed almost as excited as I was. As I descended the gangplank to the pier, I could just hear Anna behind me saying something about "how soon they come of age." I chose to ignore the remark and steered my feet toward the tavern.

Aimee was already there, sitting by herself near the door. She spotted me the moment I came in, her face brightening. "There you are!" She indicated the seat next to hers. "I was afraid you wouldn't come. I am so sorry I didn't explain. It's just...I didn't want to scare you away, that's all. You've no idea how lonely it gets, and only the same faces every day, and it was so lovely, at least I thought it was, and then tonight everyone came down and you didn't, and I thought you were mad at me, but here you are and oh, say you aren't mad, do!"

Truth be told, I had been going back and forth with myself on whether I was mad or not. The whole thing had been a most 'markable night, and the business of the morning had put me in more of a state than I had originally realized. When I walked into the tavern that night, 'tis a fact that I had no idea how I was going to react. Fortunately, her panicked outburst softened those ill feelings I had over the whole thing, washed away by my laughter as I squeezed her hand. "It's all right. It is, honestly. I mean, you really ought to have said something, left a note, or like that. Waking up this morning was a bit of a fright, I can tell you."

She blushed and nodded. "You're right, of course. And I am truly sorry. It's just... sometimes we tell people and they leave right away. I couldn't bear thinking of it. Especially since..." she trailed off and shrugged helplessly. "Well, it's been a long time."

I nodded and gave her hand another squeeze. "Look, it's a bit noisy in here, and I think I'd rather be somewhere we can talk. Let's see if we can't get ourselves some privacy, eh?"

She smiled and nodded. "I think that would be a very fine idea, Miss McCormick." I rose to my feet alongside her, just in time for my stomach to let off a long, loud rumble.

I colored a bit as she giggled, then gave her a weak smile. "Actually, might we get some dinner first? It's been rather a long day."

She laughed. "Indeed. Dinner it is."

After dinner, we walked along the quiet streets, talking of this and that, sharing each other's life stories. I told her about my life back home, and some of the things I had done and seen at sea. She told me about her childhood growing up in the town. Before long, this led to the town itself and the strange curse it appeared to be under.

"Honestly, we've no idea what it is." She shrugged. "I remember the last day. There had been clouds all week, but that day they were so thick it was practically night. You know how it is when there's a storm coming and the air feels sort of different? It was like that, but…it was thick, the air, I mean. Felt like you were wading in the sea. As the day got later, it got worse. By evening, everyone had more or less given up on the day and turned in early.

"Next thing I know, I wake up and it's still dark. I rolled over, went back to sleep a couple of times, waiting for the sun, but it never showed up. Eventually, I heard voices outside. People were getting upset. Well, it took us a few days to realize what was going on, and it was quite a shock as you, no doubt, can imagine. We tried sending some lads off in a skiff to get help, but the next night, there they were, right back in their homes. We've been stuck here ever since."

I winced. "I'm sorry to hear it. And you never worked out the cause?"

"Never have. If you have any ideas, we'd love to hear 'em."

"And you just stay the same age forever?"

"Not quite. It seems that we are still aging, only much more slowly. I reckon I'm a couple of years older than when it started, but can't be sure. My friend Sarah's gran actually died of old age. Madness overtook a man. He tried to take his own life, but came back just the same. So I guess we have to bide our time and wait."

Aimee and I had wandered down to the docks. The sky was rich with stars, the sound of the waves soft and enchanting. We found a spot at the end of a pier and sat in silence, looking up at the sky.

"Molly?"

"Yes?"

"I suppose your lot is leaving in the morning?"

"Dunno. Probably."

"Stay with me. Just for tonight, I mean. Until the sun comes up. Please, I don't want to be alone."

I nodded and slipped an arm around her to draw her close. She lay her head on my shoulder and slipped her hand in mine. We stayed that way, gazing out at the world until a sliver of light appeared on the horizon. As we watched the sky change, she clung to me, squeezing my hand with hers. I held on to her, not saying a word. What could a person say?

Presently, the sun pushed its way above the horizon. I felt her body change, growing softer and less substantial. We looked into each other's eyes, as she faded. I could see the sun taking her place, then I was alone.

That morning, we sailed off toward Port Royal. We never returned, though I always meant to. Even as my life has grown busier and my responsibilities greater, I have never forgotten the words she whispered as she faded from my sight. "Remember me."

I always will, Aimee. I always will.

Chapter Sixteen

BY THIS POINT, I had begun to work my way up a little. James, still our bos'n, had taken me under his wing, so to say, and was teaching me how to organize and lead. I will admit that I was quite nervous at first—most of the crew were older than I, after all. But, in fact, I got very little resistance. Turns out privateers are not particularly ambitious when it comes to power. Occasionally you do get one, mind, who covets authority (or at least the trappings thereof). These are the ones who will spend years patiently organizing a *coup d'état*, only to realize once they have seized power that they have no idea what to do with it. Happily, Captain Cunningham taught me a technique to deal with such as them, which has stood me in good stead for many years. One appears to acquiesce to their desire for power and puts them in charge of some tedious thing that no one else wants to worry about, with the implication that they are being given their first step upon the ladder. Occasionally, it must be admitted, they will rise to the occasion and prove themselves worthy. More often than not, they will decide it's not for them after all.

In any case, the majority of the crew were there to do their work, get some treasure, and look forward to the next shore leave. I can well understand this attitude. Being made responsible for the persons one has worked with for so long is a jarring change. It turns out there is a lot of work-behind-the-work, if I may phrase it so, that goes into making sure the crew can do their job. Take the bos'n. A certain amount of work needs doing, and a group of people set to do it, and you've got to make sure everyone does their fair share. No one gets too much or too little, and somehow everything gets done. What's more, one must always be cognizant of who works well together and who doesn't, who's feeling poorly, and so on, and so on. It's less tiring than spending all day clambering around the ratlines, but decidedly less enjoyable.

After a year of helping James, I had more or less learned the ins and outs of the job. I assumed I was being given additional duties because James needed help. Being one of the few who could read and write, I had been the natural choice. In fact, Captain Cunningham had other things in mind.

We were busy that year. The Dutch had put out an especial bounty on Portuguese ships, and we had been thus employed, bringing in as many as we could. We'd had a pretty good run of it, as I recall, so on this particular day, when we saw the familiar flag on a distant schooner, we didn't hesitate to turn to and head to intercept.

The relatively small ship was about a hundred ton by the looks, a bit small pickings for a ship of our size. Nevertheless, the bounty was worthy. We didn't expect them to open fire on us before we'd even raised the black flag.

"D—nation!" Black Jack cried, as the first volley of cannon blasted forth. "To the guns! Now!" What followed was a short but furious battle. We sent off three full volleys all told, two of them striking home. They returned fire until our third volley hit the lower parts of the ship, whereupon they changed their tune. They withdrew their cannons and tried to turn away and outrun us. You saw that from time to time. A crew would fire to scare you off. If you called their bluff, they would back down right enough. In any case, it wasn't long before we caught them up and boarded the ship.

It wasn't a large crew, though a bit more than one would expect for the size of the ship. Captain Cunningham led the boarding party, as always, sauntering up to a stern-looking man with a blue chin and a permanent scowl. "Right!" she declared. "This ship is hereby seized by the authority of His Majesty King Charles the—*sh—te!*" The captain ducked as a musket ball flew by her head.

The reaction was immediate. Every man-jack of us brandished our weapons and pointed them at the crew. I had brought along my pistols, of course, and kept them trained on the other captain. Captain Cunningham stepped forward, all swagger washed away in a tide of anger. "Right," she said with a growl. "All your weapons. Throw 'em down onto the deck. Now. And by G—d, if so much as one of you tries to keep one hidden about your person, we will slaughter the lot of you."

This had the desired effect. There was a prolonged cacophony of swords, knives, and so on being surrendered. Captain Cunningham waited until it was over, then turned to us. "As soon as they're done, I want each one of 'em searched. Right down to the bone." I distinctly heard the noise of a couple more knives hitting the deck.

"Better. Now then, as I was saying..." she trailed off as a little black child scurried out of the cargo hatch. He can't have been more than three or four, if I were any judge. He stared at us with large, silent eyes and scurried down into the darkness again.

Scallywag!

The whole ship went quiet for a moment. Without taking her eyes off the crew, Captain Cunningham beckoned. "James? Heinz? One of you lot go down there and see what kind of cargo these people have."

"Wait," said Mr. Sanyang. "I'll go."

The captain turned to him. "You sure, mate? I mean, you know what could be down there."

"I know, yes. I know. Probably best I'm the one who checks."

"Well, all right. But bring some others with you? They might have more crew down there."

"Yes, Captain." His eyes flickered around the assembled group. "You…you…and, actually, is Molly here?"

I raised one of my pistols. "Right here."

"Yes, you come too." Puzzled, I fell in with Mr. Sanyang and the others as we headed to the cargo hold.

Reader, this I tell you, in all my years at sea, I have seen many things that boggled the mind, both wondrous and horrible. I have explored lost cities, spoken with the dead, encountered curses and magic, and even stared right into the maw of the Leviathan itself. In all that time, I have never seen anything that so repelled me as what we found below.

The cargo decks had been modified so that they had twice as many levels as they normally would by the simple expedient of putting another deck in the middle of each. Of course, this meant that each resulting level was low enough that one had to duck to be able to move about. It struck me as a very odd arrangement. For a moment, I couldn't see the sense of it. Before I could give the matter much consideration, the smell of the place hit me like a brick.

It was as vile a combination of smells as ever I've encountered, like a privy mixed with an infirmary and mingled with sweat, decay, and the memory of death. Worst of all was the all-pervading scent of despair. Don't ever let anyone tell you despair doesn't have a smell. I've smelt it and never wish to do so again. I felt dizzy and nauseated from it all and had to lean against a pillar until I was able to settle. The other crew seemed likewise affected, but Mr. Sanyang just stood there, perfectly still, his fists clenched so hard they were shaking.

My eyes began to adjust, and I saw the shapes as they resolved in the darkness. They were men, black like Mr. Sanyang himself, lying side by side down the length of the hold on both sides. A long chain stretched at their feet, which were manacled to the chain at the ankles. Some were groaning or muttering to themselves. A few were even singing in a forlorn sort of way, seeking comfort in the dark. For the most part, they lay perfectly still, waiting to see what fate had in store for them next.

Slaves.

"Well, blow me," said one of our crew. "It's a sodding Guineaman." I had heard about them, of course. They take their name from the Gulf of Guinea in Africa.

I stared at this hell on Earth, made all the worse by the fact that it was done not by devils, but people.

When Mr. Sanyang finally spoke, his voice was low, menacing, the sound of a man doing everything he could to keep his temper. "Molly," he said, "check below. There'll be women and children there, I suspect."

I nodded and hurried off down the steps, as much to get clear of him as anything. As a friend of mine says, one does not need to believe in a volcano god to see the smoke coming out of the crater. Down below, the hold was at least normal height. One could stand upright if one chose to. As my eyes adjusted to the deeper darkness, it seemed to me very few had bothered to do so. The hold was indeed full of women, dressed in the colorful cloth of their native land. Many of them were accompanied by little children. I saw some about the age of my brothers when I first set off, and even babes in arms. The sight of it made me feel so helpless. What could one do in the face of this?

They noticed my silhouette against the doorway. I suppose they must have recognized it as an unfamiliar one. Without a word, it seemed like every pair of eyes turned toward me, shining white in the murky darkness. None of them said anything. In fact, it occurred to me that not one of them had said anything at all. All my life, when I've been around a room full of women and children, there was a sort of constant cacophony, the women talking, the children laughing or singing (or screaming and crying). But down here, there was nothing but silence.

All eyes on me, I felt the pressure to say something. I coughed, fumbled for something to say. "Er," I said, realizing there was no way they'd understand what I was saying but carrying on anyway. "I don't know what's going to happen next, but…I think things are going to be different soon. Er, I…" I trailed off lamely and gestured up to where Mr. Sanyang was. "I'd better go back up. Erm, 'scuse me."

When I returned, Mr. Sanyang was shouting something I couldn't understand. He paused, listening, and tried again. This time, an answer came—faintly—from one of the men manacled nearby. Mr. Sanyang ducked down and moved as quickly as he could to the other man's side.

Scallywag!

A rapid conversation followed in hushed tones. Those of us who had come down belowdecks with him looked at each other, but no one knew what was happening.

In only a minute, he came back out again, shaking his head. "G—d but it reeks down here. Let's head back up."

When we stepped back out into the fresh air, it became clear that our crewmates had not been idle. The slavers were bound and manacled and were now slumped against the captain's cabin. The small pile of weapons had been cleared away, no doubt already *en route* to our hold. Mr. Sanyang strode up to Captain Cunningham, the rest of us trailing along in his wake. She must have read his expression as we approached, for she didn't even ask what we had found. "That bad, old friend?"

"They're Akan, same as me," he said. "Raiders came. Killed off all the old ones, took everyone else. Half the people, they don't know what happened to them. Another boat, I'm thinking."

Captain Cunningham made a face. "I see. And the women?"

Mr. Sanyang turned to me. "In the bottom hold," I said. "Quite a few of them. Children too. Even saw some babies."

"Dear, oh dear." The captain tutted as she turned to face the slaver crew. "I mean, far be it from me to point fingers an' that. Man's got to make a living and all, but babbies?" She glared at the cowering group for a moment. "What shall we do with 'em, Mr. Sanyang?"

He coughed. "Well, Captain, you know we've been discussing me taking a command of my own. I think I would like to do that now."

She didn't look surprised. "Had a feelin' you might. Well, if you reckon you're ready. You'll need a few hands to help run the thing. Got some people in mind?"

He nodded. "I've got some mates I've talked to, said they'd join up if I asked them."

"All right, then. Round 'em up. We'll make sure you got plenty of supplies and that. It's your ship now, Mr. Sanyang."

In no time, the ship was a hive of activity. Supplies and medicine were hauled over, their human cargo freed and allowed up onto the deck. I remember them now, blinking in the first sunlight most of them had seen in days. Our ship surgeon, Dr. Acosta, bustled from one ailing soul to another, providing what aid he could. Mr. Sanyang stood in the middle of it all, barking orders and conversing with his fellow countrymen. In no time at all, the ship was made ready with a small crew which opted to join him on the new ship. There was a short ceremony up on deck, and we all drank to the new captain's health.

Afterward, I went up to Mr. Sanyang. "Is this really it? You're leaving us forever?"

He nodded. "Well, I won't say forever. We'll meet from time to time, I wager. And of course, we're sailing under the same flag, so we'll still be with you. Just in a different way, you might call it."

"Well, I'll surely miss you, Mis—I mean, *Captain* Sanyang. Wish I'd known you were planning to leave."

"Oh, it's not so much a surprise. Ol' Cunningham, you might say, she's got an eye for talent. She finds someone likely, she likes to start training 'em up. There's a few damn good captains out there right now that got their start with her. As some day you may discover," he said cryptically.

"If you say so. But tell me...the other crew," I nodded toward the hatch where the slavers had been dragged belowdecks, "what's going to happen to them?"

"Oh, we'll keep 'em around a while. After all," he grinned, "someone has got to clean that hold down there."

"Well, I just hope they do a thorough job. It's like one giant privy."

"They will, don't you worry. Oh yes indeed, they will." His smile flashed white in the Caribbean sun.

The Africans, once they realized what was happening, quickly stepped up and began making the ship their own. They'd begun to make dinner and lay blankets out on deck. We set sail a little while later, leaving Sanyang and his new ship behind. As we departed, I could hear them singing. It was simple enough music. One person would sing out a line, then everyone else would sing it back. And yet, as the sun set and the music drifted out over the sea, I found it entrancing. Something about it reminded me of going to church on Sundays and the hymns we would sing. There was that same feeling. Couldn't understand the words, of course, but you really didn't have to. To have such a day as that end in music is one of the mysteries of the world I will never fully understand.

Chapter Seventeen

THERE WAS A BIT of a to-do after all that. With the first mate gone, there was a gap in the ranks. The captain suggested that James be moved up to take Mr. Sanyang's place, and this was duly passed. When he recommended I be promoted to bosun's mate…Well, I was going to say it surprised me. But if I'm honest, it didn't really, not much. It had been clear for a while that he was grooming me for the job. I just hadn't thought it would happen so soon. Still, I couldn't complain. I'd gotten used to the work, and the rest of the crew had gotten used to me doing it. Mostly, I took care of the scheduling of the day's activities and made sure everything on deck was right. James was still the bosun, of course, and he would handle the larger responsibilities of that office, but over time, he trained me in those as well. There was a lot of brainwork, but it beat being a rope monkey. I was technically an officer, which meant an extra quarter share of the taking. My new private room was a tiny thing, smaller than the bed I'd had at home, but it had a door I could close and a board that folded down from the wall, which I could use for a desk. I thought myself quite fortunate.

By this time I had been on the ship for about five years and was as at home on the *Bonnie Mary* as if I'd been born there. We'd had crew come and go, but there was always a core group of stalwarts who found the situation to their liking. I was grateful for Anna, and Dutch, and Black Jack, of course. Maggie stayed on for a few more years before handing in her apron for good. I understand she lives in Bermuda now. I myself never entertained the idea of joining another crew. To this day, I think of her as my ship. Even if I never shall see her again.

About two years ago, we got word of an English merchant vessel beached on a remote island where it was getting some needed repair work. We knew the place well. Not much more than a large, isolated cove and a nice long beach fronting a forest full of excellent timber. A good place, if you needed to hole up for a bit. Unless, of course, someone knew you were there.

We set sail at once.

It was about two days from where we were, so there was a worry they'd have finished their business and gone by the time we arrived. However, as the little island came into view, the ship was plainly visible through the glass. We headed for the narrow gap, which provided the only way in or out. No need to hurry. They weren't going anywhere. Even if they did see us coming, there was nothing they could do. We'd be in and out right quick.

That was the plan anyway.

As we entered the cove, I heard the distant boom of a cannon. Several of us ran to the fore to see if our intended victims were trying to drive us away, but as far as we could tell, there was no activity at all. Surely, the ship should be swarming with working crew, shouldn't it? I felt the hairs rising up on the back of my neck. Suddenly, it all felt very wrong.

Captain Cunningham was standing at the prow, looking through the spyglass and frowning. I pulled myself together. "Captain? Captain?"

She turned and looked at me. "What's on your mind, girl?"

"I think we should hard about, Captain. Right now."

She glanced back at the other ship, her lips set in a thin line. "I think you're right," she muttered. "Hard about!" she bellowed, turning to the crew. "Get us out of here! Lively, now!"

We all scrambled to our stations, shifting sails and hanging on as the helmsman spun the wheel about. The cove was big enough that we could easily turn around once we got past the opening, but speed was the real problem. If something was about to happen, it would likely be soon. If we were still there...well.

We were too late. All along the shoreline, teams of gunners pushed cannons out of their hiding places. Before we could react, those nearest the exit fired, neatly dropping their shots right where we would have to go if we were to flee.

"Captain!" shouted Jansen. "Shall we man the guns?"

She hesitated, then shook her head. "No. I think they want us to stay put." She turned back and raised her voice again. "Get us the rest of the way about, but don't move until I say."

I hurried to the prow and peered toward the open sea. It didn't take me long to find what I was looking for. First one, then another bowsprit appeared, coming round the bay. I felt my stomach drop, as the ships came into view, men-of-war. We watched them enter the bay, flanking the inlet. Handling one would have been tricky. Two was out of the question.

"Well, bugger me." Black Jack stood next to me, gazing at the ships. "Got us good and proper, didn't they?" He squinted at the ships, shielding his eyes from the sun. "I thought we were all right with the Royal Navy. Odd, that."

"It's not them," said another. "Look." We all turned our attention to the standards waving above each ship. As they flapped in the breeze, a familiar image met our eyes.

"Well, blow me," Black Jack spat. "The bleedin' Company."

The reader will doubtless be aware of the British East India Company, and how it has, over the course of the last eighty years, become the dominant force in trading with the East Indies (despite the best attempts of the Dutch to displace them). What may be less well-known is that there is also a West India Company trying to establish itself in these selfsame waters. I suspect they will not succeed, as they lack the early advantage their elder brother enjoyed. Still, one cannot deny their ambition. In the few years since they began, they have been doing everything they can to claw a monopoly out of the New World. Just how desperate they were, we had not begun to understand.

A ship sailed between the two large ones, smaller, but better appointed. This was no cargo ship, and no man-of-war. Ornate, light, and nimble, a passenger ship then. And one for very important passengers indeed.

Behind me, I heard someone say, "Orders, Captain?"

"Hold to," she said. "If they wanted to slaughter us, they'd have done so by now. Not sure what they're about."

"Unless they're trying to take us all alive."

"Well, if that's the case, you have my permission to do what you can. Until then, no one is to raise a weapon without my say. Is that understood?"

There was a chorus of assent. I checked my pistols, feeling their reassuring weight in my hands.

The smaller boat came alongside. It too was a Company ship, lightly armed as far as cannon, but with a line of troops on deck, their guns pointed at all of us. A gangplank was lowered, and the troops marched onto the ship, corralling us in the afterdeck. Only Captain Cunningham stood out in the open, waiting. If she was affrighted, she certainly didn't show any sign.

A small entourage came up from belowdecks, a trio of well-dressed men who moved like they expected the rest of the world to get out of their way. They strode across to our ship, barely giving the rest of us so much as a glance before turning to Captain Cunningham.

The man in the middle, by all appearances the leader, stepped forward. He was tall and lean, with a stylish periwig and bow spectacles adorning his nose. "This is your ship?"

The captain bowed. "I have that honor. And who might I be addressing?"

"I am Lord Armstrong, acting on behalf of the directors of the British West Indies Company. We are seizing this ship and its contents, as well as yourself and your crew. Any resistance on your part will be quite fatal, I assure you."

Captain Cunningham glared at him. "Oh, aye? And what makes you think you can do that?"

"We are operating under the authority of the Crown. Also, we have you outgunned by a considerable margin." He smiled in a humorless little way. "I expect if the former does not exact your cooperation, the second most likely shall."

"We do have letters of marque, you know. And to my certain knowledge, we've not interfered with any of your company ships."

"That's as may be. But the fact remains that you are pyrates. And that means that we may take any action at our discretion. Now let me tell you what is going to happen. My men are going to remove anything from this ship found to be ill-gotten gains. Then you, your senior officers, and the majority of your crew will be detained, along with your ship. You will be held until we are done with you. Now, you will order your crew to stand down and surrender their weapons."

She glared at him for a moment, then gave us a nod. With extreme reluctance and much grumbling, we passed our weapons forward where they were placed together on the deck. Several of the guards came forward with chests and collected our weapons, while the rest held us at bay with their muskets. I couldn't help but think of how we'd done the same to those slavers not so long before, and felt the bile turn in my stomach.

While this was happening, the two larger ships came into the bay. Armstrong nodded approvingly as he saw them approach. "Now then, when the other ships arrive, my men will escort yours down to our brig. Don't worry, we've space enough for you all. If you are wise and cooperate, this will be over before you know it."

Captain Cunningham snorted. "Be easier just to kill us outright," she said.

Armstrong just smiled. "A helpful suggestion. But we have other plans. Here comes the first ship. Step lively now and remember what I said."

As I look around the cell in which I write these memoirs, I cannot help but reflect on how different it is from that ship. The room is small and the accommodations similar, but at the very least, I have the space to myself. The brig we found ourselves in consisted of ten separate cells, into each of which five to seven of us were placed. We were belowdecks, below the portholes. The only light came from lanthorns that hung from the timbers above. The mood was glum, to put it mildly. It was as if the fight had been taken out of us. That we could be lured so easily into a trap and disarmed with no more difficulty than taking a toy from a child...well, it hurt. No doubt about it.

There were four of us in my cell, viz. myself, Anna and Dutch, and Maggie. We comprised the female portion of the crew (not counting the captain herself, of course). I suppose they thought they were being gallant by putting us in a separate cell, as if we hadn't been living side by side with the rest of the crew for years. In any event, it did mean we got a bit more room, even if Dutch seemed particularly rankled by the arrangement. Mind, she would have been even more upset if they had separated her and Anna. For myself, I was too sick with worry to care much about the accommodations.

"What do you think they are going to do with us?" I asked, not for the first time.

Maggie lit her pipe. "Difficult to say, m'dear," she said. "I've been sailing these here waters a goodly long time, and I've seen a lot. But this is...well, it's bloody odd, is what."

"Don't see what's so odd about it," said Dutch. "They set a trap for us. They caught us. Now we're all going to get hanged." She sneered. "What's there to understand?"

Maggie puffed reflectively. "Aye, well. That's the question, though, innit? Did they lay a trap for us? From what I hear tell, when they came aboard, they didn't know who we are. Or at least they didn't know Captain Cunningham. I'm thinkin' that we weren't the quarry so much as any pyrates they could get their hands on."

"True," said Anna, "but I rather doubt that improves our situation. Probably they're starting a campaign to clear us all out of these waters, and we're just the first to be lured into their trap."

"Assuming we are the first," I said.

Anna turned to me. "How's that?"

"Well, I mean, I've only been at this a few years. But even to me it seems like there're fewer of us about. I've heard the older crew members talk about how it used to be. Let's face it. We're useful as long as we are safely employed to go after rivals. Maybe they've decided we're not worth it anymore. Probably, they don't want anyone going around what they don't have control over. You know the English. Sharing is not exactly in their nature."

"Ahem."

"Sorry, Anna."

Maggie mused on this. "A fair point," she said. "And yet if they wish to get rid of us, they're going about it in an odd way. Keeping us cooped up like this. And we're still in the bay. I'd have thought they would have set sail by now. Feels like they're saving us. Be blowed if I know for what though."

"Probably want a nice show trial. Make an example of us," murmured Dutch.

There was a commotion up front. An order was shouted and the brig unlocked. The two guards watching over us stood to attention. After a hurried conversation with someone I couldn't see, they proceeded to the cages. The first one took a deep breath and shouted, "Attention! When you hear your name, you will call out and approach your cell door. If you refuse or resist in any way, you will be shot." He looked down at the small slip of paper he had been given. "Black Jack Conway!"

"Aye!" He was in a cage across from us. He waited as they opened the cell door and manacled his wrists. In a trice, he was spirited out of the brig and out of sight.

"Dutch Aarden!"

"Right here," Dutch said. The guard looked at her in mild surprise but didn't say anything. In a moment, she was gone as well.

"Paulo Rodriguez!"

He was two cells down from us. He said nothing as they led him away, though if looks could kill, he'd have seen to 'em all.

Scallywag!

The guard paused. He called another guard over and tapped at the paper. I couldn't hear what they were saying, but somehow a bad feeling came welling up from my gut.

"Molly McCormick!"

Chapter Eighteen

THE FOUR OF US were led up through the ship, flanked on all sides by guards. We had no time for examining our surroundings, as the reader may well imagine, but we didn't need to see much to get an idea of the scale of the operation. They could have dismantled our ship and taken it home with them, if they so desired. There were two rows of guns with enough ammo to hold out against a fleet. Whatever the Company was up to, they weren't about to be caught out for want of preparation.

The quarters we were led to were sumptuously appointed and larger than our captain's by a considerable measure. Actually, as I sit here and think of it, I feel fairly certain it wasn't the captain's at all, but almost certainly that of Lord Armstrong. No doubt, he was the real authority on the ship, a fact I cannot imagine engendered good feelings in the actual captain and officers. Nevertheless, we were marched in and made to stand in line while Armstrong and a couple of his men looked us over.

"Curious," he declared. "Not one but two women. Not who I would have chosen. Are you quite sure about your selection?"

He moved aside. Behind him, with a guard on either side of her, sat Captain Cunningham. She seemed unharmed from where I was standing, though it was sure enough that her pride had taken a beating. "I'm sure," she managed.

Armstrong merely shrugged. "It is as you say. Now then, you lot. We're going to be extra generous and give you an opportunity to save your captain, your ship, and even your own miserable hides. Simply put, you are going to do a little job for us. If you are successful, you might not wind up on a gibbet. With me so far?"

Black Jack put a hand up. "Beggin' your pardon, but if you're wanting us to go after someone, why, we'd do it anyway, no need for all of this."

Lord Armstrong shook his head. "Not someone, something. A treasure of sorts. I understand you lot love nothing more than going after hidden treasure? Yes?" He reached down to a silver tray and plucked a chunk of fresh pineapple. He took a moment to savor the morsel, then turned his attention back to us. "Tell me, have you ever heard tell of the *Pearly Jack*?"

Well! The four of us looked at each other in surprise, trying to work out if the man was joking. It is perhaps the case that the reader does not know the story, but when we sailed these seas, the legend was quite well-known. The *Pearly Jack* had been a cargo ship, delivering raw materials and bringing back spices and other tropical items. It was, by all accounts, a wholly unremarkable ship, one of many plying their trade across the ocean. One day when it was due to dock in Barbados, the ship arrived right on schedule. As the *Pearly Jack* approached, it became clear no crew was aboard to guide her in. A quick-thinking dock master sent out a group to board her and bring her in safely. Once she was secured, a thorough search showed no sign of any crew. The lifeboats were still in position, and there were no signs of violence to ship or crew. The ship had somehow carried on, pilotless, crewless, until it reached its destination.

The cargo seemed to be all present and accounted for. The ship was secured to the docks, the cargo unloaded, and a watchman stationed to keep an eye on things until it could be properly searched. When morning broke, the ship was gone. The watchman himself was found curled up on the pier, incoherent with fright. They say it took him weeks to recover, but he could never go near a ship in the dark ever again.

The *Pearly Jack*, meanwhile, set off on its own course, making a sort of circuit of the area south of Puerto Rico. It was an empty stretch of water, a deep-down area far from any land. Occasionally, ships crisscrossing the sea on their way to the mainland would spot her in the distance and give her a wide berth. A couple of attempts had been made to board and salvage her, and neither was successful. The *Pearly Jack* was exactly the sort of legend that tended to get passed from crew to crew until it was part of our common lore. Had we heard of the *Pearly Jack*? Had we indeed!

He must have read the answer in our faces, for he smiled humorlessly and rubbed his hands together. "Good. Well, we have reason to believe a certain trinket is aboard the ship, a shell, in fact. One of those I believe they call a conch. You will rendezvous with the *Pearly Jack*, board her, retrieve the shell, and return to us. In the meantime, your captain and crewmates will wait here for your return. Do as you're bid, and you may live to tell the tale. Come back without the shell, and you all die. Try to make a runner, and we will put the biggest price on your heads the Caribbean has ever seen. I understand the area the *Pearly Jack* sails is well-known, so you should have no difficulty finding her and coming back. I think a fortnight is more than enough time, don't you?"

"A fortnight?" asked Black Jack. "That seems a bit short, is all."

"Nonsense. You shouldn't have any trouble at all. In and out, what could be simpler?"

"Then send your own people to do it!" Dutch snapped.

Lord Armstrong looked at her disdainfully. "And why would I do that when I have you? The fact is, the ship is still an unknown quantity. It is considered dangerous, and I understand those who board it seldom return. Naturally, I would not desire to expend my men when I can just as easily use you lot. Besides, you're pyrates, are you not? You should be used to burglary and subterfuge and so on. And if you should fail..." he shrugged. "Well, we have so many more of you. We can take our time."

"Bastard," muttered Dutch.

Armstrong looked at her for a long moment. "Mister Bridges," he said, "does the injunction against hitting a lady extend to pyrates?"

A junior officer behind him stepped forward. "Hard to see how it would, sir."

"Ah, good." He nodded to one of the guards, who struck Dutch across the mouth. She made ready to leap at him, but Jack and I hastily grabbed at her arms and held her back. "Not now, not now," I heard Jack whisper. "Save it for later. It'll be soon enough."

"Now, then. You will be taken hence to one of my ships where you will be transported to the area the *Jack* is known to frequent. From there it will be your task to search the area until it is found. You will then be sent across on a dinghy, board the ship, and retrieve the artifact by whatever means necessary. Understand that is your number one priority. You will do what you have to, make whatever sacrifice you must, but you *will* retrieve the shell. The survival of the rest of your people depends upon it. Do I make myself clear?"

"Abundantly." Black Jack made no attempt to keep the bitterness out of his voice.

"Splendid. Swift studies all." Lord Armstrong then turned to Captain Cunningham, who had remained silent throughout. "Have you anything to say to your, er, 'men' before we send them off?"

She didn't speak at first, taking a moment to look us over. "Right," she said. "I know you four. You're rock solid, and you know your business. If anyone can do this, it's you lot. But hear me. I want you to be careful, right? Take every precaution. Do what you must, but keep each other safe. You know the old stories as well as I do, but we don't know what's on that ship. Whatever you do, come back. All four of ya. Don't worry about us. We'll be here waiting."

Scallywag!

"Touching." Armstrong nodded to a guard, and we were escorted away. As we departed, I turned to take one last look at the captain. In my years of sailing with her, I had seen her in every mood, but never had I seen her so utterly forlorn.

Of the voyage that followed, I will not say much. We were bundled onto a company ship, not one of the men-of-war but a smaller cargo trader. The officers and crew were all Company men, and as such held no great love for our kind. I had expected we would spend the voyage sitting in the brig until the ship was sighted. The captain had other ideas. Every morning, we were allowed up on deck for "exercise," by which they meant putting us to every tedious, demeaning chore they could find. I swear to you, reader, that in the space of the time we spent on that ship, I personally must have scrubbed every damn inch of it. It was like my first days at sea, only worse. The regular crew took great delight in making our lives hell. I remember thinking back to old Cheese, bastard though he was, and how there had only been one of him, not a whole boatload. Some of them even tried their hand at Dutch and myself, figuring they could take advantage of the situation. Happily, we were able to disabuse them of that idea with great speed and were left alone after that.

It was three days down to the waters the old ship was known to frequent. From there, we began to patrol. We found our duties changed to seeking out any sign of the *Pearly Jack*. With no small trepidation, I kept watch with the others. Clearly, finding the ship and retrieving this shell they were so hot about was of utmost importance. But boarding a ghost ship...it didn't bode well. Even the crew laid off hazing us, their nerves too strained.

A day went by, then two. We were every one of us on watch, sighting in every direction. Even the crew who were off duty would join us in scanning the sea night and day. There was a feeling of...well, I won't say camaraderie. Perhaps truce is the word I'm looking for. We may have been on opposing sides, but the truth was that when it comes down to blood and bone, it's man versus sea. A capricious mistress she is, yet those of us who have dedicated our lives to her cannot help but stay under her spell. In any case, everyone had rather too much on their mind to bother with enmity.

I remember a particular incident that occurred on the third night. I had drawn middle watch, that being the one from midnight to four. The moon was a crescent sliver above the water, and the murmur of waves against the ship's hull was quite relaxing. From time to time, when I felt drowsy, I would pace around the deck a time or two to reinvigorate the blood. The ship itself was deathly quiet, the only movement coming from those who, like I, were keeping vigil.

I heard unfamiliar bootsteps come up behind me, and a thump. I turned around to see a member of the crew, an officer by the look of him. He scowled at me. "You there," he said. "Pick that up."

I looked where he indicated. Glory be if there wasn't an orange on the deck. Now me, I hadn't had a proper orange in quite a while. We tended to be out for extended periods of time, and our rations tended toward things that would keep while at sea. Fruit was plentiful among the islands, so we were always sure to take on supplies. But it did tend to be potluck what we got and when. Oranges were found more toward the mainland and were comparatively rare out this way. Needless to say, I wasted no time in retrieving it.

"Right," he said. "Get rid of it. I'd better not see that thing next time I come by. Understood?"

I, thank goodness, had just enough sense in my head to salute and reply, "Yes sir. I'll dispose of it right away."

"See that you do." Without another word, he was gone. I saw him heading to where Paulo was standing watch, no doubt with another orange in hand. In any case, you may believe that I wasted no time disposing of the one he had given me. My parents would have jumped to see how quickly I obeyed that order.

So our vigil went. As the days ticked by with no sign of the *Pearly Jack,* the crew began to grow restive, as did we ourselves. The deadline was weighing on our minds to the point where our fear was subsumed by a desire to get it over with and get back. I understand there was even some question as to whether we were in the right waters, but it was determined that we were where we were meant to be. For a ship that seemed so ready to appear before unwary eyes, the *Pearly Jack* was unaccountably shy of we who were actively searching for her.

Scallywag!

It was on the morning of the fifth day of our vigil when we heard the cry from the lookout. Everyone dropped what they were doing and hurried to the rail, craning our necks to see. The captain was sent for and surveyed the distant vessel with his glass. "That's it," he declared. "Move to intercept." It was rather far off at first, but fortunately the wind was in our favor. The phantom vessel did not appear to be in any particular hurry. As we closed with her, preparations were made for our boarding.

The ship itself was still under sail, and while it was proceeding slowly, it was nevertheless moving along with no visible means of stopping it. As such, it was decided we would overtake the ship somewhat before deploying the longboat. Instead of tiring ourselves out by trying to catch up with her, we could let her come to us. Once we boarded, we were to drop anchor, if possible, then commence our search. A small dispatch of crew were to row us across and wait, having secured the boat to the ship, yet ready to go as soon as we had finished.

"I don't like it," Paulo muttered as we made our preparations. "We can row over just as well as they. Why are they sending their men along? Do they think we're going to row off into the sunset or something?"

"I don't think that's it," I replied. "I expect that they're afraid we'll all get killed and they'll have to send someone to fetch back the boat." I checked the standard Company cutlass I had been issued, made to be cheap and replaceable. The blade felt off-balance and heavier than it should. Clearly, it was designed for those who use swords as blunt objects. I waved it through the air a few times and thought longingly of my pistols.

"Aye, that's one possibility," said Black Jack. "But you know what I think? I think that if we don't find that bloody shell, we're not getting a ride back. In fact, I wouldn't put it past this lot to have us hand it over, then bug off and leave us behind."

Dutch made a face. "Ugh. You think so?"

"Wouldn't put it past 'em."

"All right then." Dutch ran her hand through her close-cropped hair, her face grim. "No handing the thing over until we're safely back on their ship, agreed?"

"Agreed."

"Right."

"Aye."

"Good." Black Jack looked up. We could hear the increasing activity on deck. It was almost time. "Everyone ready? Right then." He turned to face the rest of us. "Let's get this over and done with. The captain and all our mates are depending on us." He sheathed his sword and turned to the steps leading up. "Let's show 'em what the lads and lasses of the *Bonnie Mary* can do."

Chapter Nineteen

AS WE APPROACHED THE *Pearly Jack*, we could feel its influence stretching out beyond the ship itself. The blazing hot Caribbean sun had faded into a damp chill as the cloudless sky was replaced with a gray mist. Even the Company men whose job it was to row us across were understandably quite disturbed by this turn of events, for (as one pointed out) the *Jack* had been plainly seen from their vessel, but as we came up alongside her, the other ship was nearly invisible despite being well within shouting distance.

They tied off alongside the ship and we climbed aboard, one by one. First order of business was to drop the anchor, which happily proved to be intact and the chain sound, if rather timeworn. This having been done, we turned our attention to the matter at hand.

"Well," said Black Jack, "if'n I had to guess, I reckon the first place to check would be the captain's cabin. Unless someone has a better idea?"

I shrugged. "As good a starting point as any, I reckon."

Dutch nodded. "Works for me."

Paulo unsheathed his sword. "Let's go, then."

The old boards creaked under our boots as we headed aft. The wood was old, older even than the admiral's boat, though clearly not as well looked after. Still, it seemed solid enough. Presumably, whatever kept it voyaging around was also keeping it proof against wood rot and the various other pestilences that can scuttle a neglected ship.

The door to the great cabin was nothing particularly fancy, just a stout oak plank door with iron hinges and a large keyhole. What was not present, however, was a key. Black Jack swore under his breath and tried the door. Locked. Of course it was.

I shall spare the reader the details of the several minutes that followed. Suffice to say, we tried picking it, prying it, carving our way through the wood, and even battering the thing down. The end result of which was merely a few loose splinters and four sore shoulders. Dutch was all for going back and getting some more effective tools. (Though why precisely she expected a merchant ship to have a morningstar on board is something of a mystery to me.) We concluded we were better off searching the rest of the ship for the key. If by chance we happened to discover the shell in the process, why, that was all to the better.

The first place we investigated was the group of smaller cabins that made up the officers' quarters. A couple of them were locked as well, but we were able to gain entrance to what proved to be the navigator's room. It was a mess of charts, spread out or tacked to every flat surface, with a cluster of compasses, old pencil stubs, and all the other esoteric tools of that discipline. As I think back, it looked quite like Jansen's cabin back on the *Mary*. Over the years, I have come to believe that there is nothing a navigator so despises as to not see a map in front of him wheresoever he may turn.

In the middle of the desk clutter was a journal, which Black Jack prodded, then opened to a random page. Pages of numbers and scrawled notes greeted us. He flipped through pages in a desultory way, then stepped back. "Navigator's log. Might be something worthwhile there. Molly, you're the best reader of our lot. You have a go at it."

I nodded and seated myself before the desk. Most of it was latitude readings, bearings, all the minutiae of the navigator's art. All very important, of course, but not what one would call riveting reading. I scanned a few pages before feeling my eyes start to glaze over. I realized I was going about it all wrong and promptly flipped to the back.

A few pages from the last entry, I found what I was looking for. For the benefit of the others, I read aloud.

> 14 May. Fog continues. Believe we should still be bearing due west from St. Kitt's, but with no visibility, I cannot verify. If only the fog would lift! Even for a few moments could get bearings w/stars, for now having to dead-reckon. Crew on edge, fog not natural. Beginning to agree with them.

> 15 May. Great rumbling and disturbance last night. An almost perfect ring of land came up around our boat, about half a furlong, side to side, by my estimate. Most curious the land is, too, not like the sea-washed stone one would expect. More like a wall of four-sided towers, all deep gray. Put me in mind of the stone I saw in Santo Domingo. It was round like a large egg, but someone had split it in half, and the insides were surrounded by crystals all around it like shining teeth. They are like that, though I do not care for their gray aspect.

The only thing here is a small bit of land, dead center of the circle. There's another one of those gray structures, but broader and squatter, Captain reckons he can see a doorway. Expect he'll send a party over to investigate. Not like we can go anywhere.
Addendum—
Mate Peters, &c, back from exploring. Showed us the prize they found. Very nice indeed, but I still wonder at what it all means. Peters made it sound like we were meant to take it, but how can he be sure? I seem to think I hear rumblings similar to what we heard before. Does it mean this wall of stone is about to recede? I dearly hope so.

16 May. The wall of stone and the little island are gone, nothing but calm seas before us. Still bl—y fog though. Worse, boat is moving despite no wind. Seems to be maintaining course, but no way to tell?
I will be glad when we make shore.

I skimmed through the few entries that followed. They were little more than vague guesses as to location and heading, mixed with consternation at the ship having taken control of its own and the never-lifting fog. The very last entry, alone on its own page, undated, read simply, *Land.*

"And that's it?" Dutch craned her neck over my shoulder to see.

"That's it." I shrugged, flipping the pages a little. "Beats me what happened to them. Maybe there's more in one of the other cabins?"

Black Jack nodded. "I think I want to find the cabin for this Mate Peters. I reckon he might have a thing or two to say."

As we filed out, I reached for the log to take with us but hesitated. It wasn't that I was squeamish about taking something not mine—a fine pyrate I would be if I were—but it did feel...different. It was like the thing belonged there, and if I took it, it would be out of place. I know full well how silly this sounds, but I left it behind, nonetheless, and hurried after the others.

We found the cabin of the quartermaster next. It too was locked, but happily, the doors down here were not quite so sturdily built as the captain's. Paulo was able to knock it open with a few kicks. Inside was nothing of interest except the ledgers in which the ship's cargo and supplies were tracked, and a rather exotic array of drawings of the female form, executed with rather more desire than technical skill. I shall not intrude upon the reader's time by giving examples. Suffice to say the quartermaster, whoever he may have been, had some rather exotic interests.

Truth be told, it did break the tension a bit. Whatever mystery had occurred here, the ones who experienced it were men just like any others. It was almost comforting, if you can say that about a picture of a...ah, but I promised I wouldn't tell, didn't I?

The next room we explored was different. The walls were...well, we saw a *few* images of the type the quartermaster enjoyed so much, but they had been overrun by bizarre scrawls, symbols, and grotesque curves that seemed to me to come from some infernal alphabet. We stood in the small cabin, taking it all in.

"I don't suppose anyone recognizes any of these?" Black Jack rubbed his head, frowning. "Mol, you recognize this?"

"Not at all," I said. "Never seen anything like it."

"Looks a bit...alchemical," Dutch hazarded. "I seen pictures once, when I was a girl."

"I was thinking witchcraft," offered Paulo. "If the devil-bought have a tongue, this is it."

Black Jack harrumphed. "And how much do you want to bet this here is our boy, Peters?" He poked at the effects on the small desk and nodded. "Ah, yes. Here we are." Under a few papers covered in more of the eldritch scrawls, he found another book, which he passed wordlessly to me.

I flipped through to the back and read.

> *May 15th: Capn sent me and some others to go check out the little island. Took Wilson Maddox and the boy Stephan. The island was basically a flat gray stone with nothing on it save the building. Looks to be made of the same stuff as the island, and in fact could not see the join between them, nor any sign of stones being cut & shaped for its construction. Wilson said as how it looked like it*

Scallywag!

had been carved out of the rock & not built but I never see something so well carved as that. The sides I swear are dead flat even tho the corners be all askew. No windows but an open doorway so we go in.

I went in first and the floor moved beneath my boot, causing me to cry out, &c. Maddox held his lanthorn to the floor and we see it is of pumice. It were floating on the water hence moving, but fortunately held our weight no problem only bobbing a little when we moved around. Nothing in the room but a plinth a couple hands wide and up to my waist. The top had been hollowed out into a bowl, and inside there was a conch shell. As I drew it out the light hit it and we seen it is all colors and shining inside and out. Wilson says how he has never seen one like that before, and the others have not either, nor me. It is warm somehow, and for a moment I think I hear whispers but it goes away. Suddenly I am feeling it is v. important and we must get it to the capn. I tell others to look around to see if anything else, but room is small so nothing to see. Stephan points up to ceiling though, hole in middle like chimney. Maddox's lanthorn shows it only goes up a little ways before closing off again. Stephan reckons when this place is under the sea, the floor floats up and the plinth goes into the ceiling. Then I see it is the right size and place for that exactly, and must allow he is prob right. So it can only be got at when it comes to the surface. Dead strange in my opinion. Nothing else there so we go back.

Showed the shell to the capn and he says it is Remarkable. He gives me an extra shilling for the find and puts it in his cabinet. I feel like I should be mad but only am relieved the thing is Safe. Everyone on board anxious about stone wall but I feel calm & not worried. I think it was Providence that brought us here and that we were meant to find it. We have done what we were meant & I am confident we will be on our way in the morning.

> *May 16th: stone wall and island all gone as I thought would be. Did have most strange dreams at night, dreamed I was at the building where we found the shell. But it was under the water, and the door was blocked with the pumice-stone. It seemed I was there many ages, standing guard over it. I had memories, not my own but of the dream. There was something important about it, and great danger should it be taken. It seemed I understood all this in my dream, but when I woke up it was gone. Did not speak of dream to others, though noticed all seemed troubled which I thought was down to fog.*
>
> *May 17th: still fog, ship going with swiftness but we know not where. Heard others discussing dreams and discovered they are having same dream as me. Even capn says so & is much worried. Cannot see anything for mist, must keep constant lookout for fear of other ships. Feel anxious but not scared, like there is nothing to be afraid of.*

It went off into a ramble after that part, so I skipped ahead until I found the last entry—that is, the last in English.

> *We understand now. It has been kept safe for so long and must be for yet a time more. We are chosen and so it shall ever be until we may lay our burden down. Rebecca, if you read this, know that I love you & always shall, but we have been elected for a great duty. Do not mourn me, but know you are in my heart always.*

"And?" Black Jack prodded when I had finished.

"And that's it," I said. "After that, it turns into this gibberish like on the walls. Look."

Black Jack leaned back against the wall, stroking his beard. "I don't like it," he declared. "For two pins I'd turn around and bog off this ship this minute, if it weren't for the captain an' them. Well, what do we do now?"

Scallywag!

"The navigator's diary said the shell was in the captain's care," Dutch pointed out. "I guess we're back to finding our way into that again."

Black Jack groaned, rubbing his still-sore shoulder. "Oh, aye. I was afraid that would be it. All right, come on, you lot. Back up on deck." He turned to go, then froze in his tracks. "What was that?"

"What was what?"

"Just now, d'ja hear that?"

We looked at each other in confusion. "I don't hear anyth—." I felt the hairs stand up on the back of my neck. Whispers, a chorus of them, came just on the edge of hearing. A quick glance at the others showed they heard it too. The words...they weren't words, not really. They were more shaped sounds, holding no meaning within them, like how apple means an apple, but the sounds were the meaning themselves. Do not ask how I understood this. At the same time, I felt my eyes drawn to the walls of the cabin, which the unfortunate Mate Peters had covered in his strange writings. And while I could no more read them than before, somehow I understood their meaning.

It was that all those who had come upon this ship seeking its treasure were instead fated to serve as its guardians until such time as the burden may be lifted. That in the meantime, they would float the seas eternal, unknown to the eyes of mortal man, protecting the most worthy treasure. And that now, we too, would be joining them.

Chapter Twenty

I FELT A CHILL run down my spine, as the full import of the situation came upon me. All the others who had come aboard, never to return...they too had been pressed into guarding this infernal thing. Were we truly damned? Beside me, Paulo moaned. He staggered back, thumping against the wall in his haste.

"Bugger," muttered Black Jack. "I don't suppose you lot are feelin' that?"

"We are," said Dutch. "We all are." She set her mouth grimly and turned to the open hallway. "I'm not havin' it. Anna will be expectin' me back, and I ain't disappointed her yet." She began to stalk toward the steps that led up to the deck. "Come on."

The rest of us looked at each other, but what else could we do? We fell in behind her and were soon back up on the deck.

Somehow, while we'd been down below, things had changed up there. The fog was still thick as anything, of course, but now it felt...warm, comforting. There was something soothing about it. It felt like we had been away for so long, and had at last come home, and we would never have a reason to leave. Around us, the mist resolved to just-visible patches of light and shade in the shapes of men.

"Ah," said Black Jack. "The rest of the honor guard, come to welcome us." The irony in his voice fell flat, as if the fog itself was eating it away. True indeed, the shapes that surrounded us were not menacing, but somehow welcoming. We were not trapped, no. We were *selected*. It was an honor to be here, to gaze upon the Horn of Azatot and bask in its radiant presence. Fortunate were we. I felt the world outside slipping away. One of the shapes near me reached out their hand. My mind in a daze, I reached out to accept the welcome of my new brother...

There was a blur of motion in the corner of my vision, and Dutch slapped my hand away. She put herself in front of me, fiercely looking me in the eyes. "Molly! Focus, girl! This is not our fate! You hear me? Think of Captain Cunningham and the rest of the crew! Think of my Anna! Would you leave them to their fate, eh? Never to know what's become of us?"

I couldn't answer. I felt frozen in place. The temptation...Reader, you cannot know how strong the pull to accept this early ticket to paradise.

Scallywag!

We could leave behind all the strife of the world and spend our endless days roaming the seas and adoring the divine treasure.

Deep down, I knew she was right. We could not tarry here. People were depending on us. With a sigh, I shook my head to clear it of the fog.

The four of us were surrounded. There were maybe a dozen shapes, little more than spectres in the mist. We felt no menace, but at the same time, it was clear that we were not to leave without their permission. Black Jack rested his hand on his sword hilt but made no move to draw. "All right, you lot," he said quietly, "if any of you've got ideas, I'm open to hearing 'em."

Dutch cracked her neck. "I say we fight 'em. They're ghosts, what the hell are they going to do?"

Paulo shook his head. "Don't reckon that will work. Never heard of someone fighting a ghost before. Might as well stab the fog."

"We'll see about that." Dutch lunged forward, swinging wild. Her sword passed easily through the nearest shape, which shook as if laughing. There was no other effect at all.

"Worth a shot anyhow." She put her sword back, eyeing the shapes warily.

"Right through em," Paulo muttered to himself. I saw his eyes flicker in the direction of the railing. "Wait!" I cried, but he was already running.

He barreled through the ghostly figures around us and leapt. As his hand touched the rail, everything started to slow down. First one foot, then another, left the ground as he vaulted in slow motion. He got just about halfway over before stopping completely, his face frozen in an expression of grim determination.

Black Jack shook his head. "Bugger." He strode toward Paulo, stopping short as the shapes closed in on him. "Hold yer horses," he grumbled. "I'm only fetching him back. That's allowed, innit? I mean, you lot have made yer point." Dutch and I joined him, and together we wordlessly pulled our friend back. It was sluggish work, like pulling a fellow through tar, but we managed. Once his feet hit the deck again, he staggered forward and fell to his knees, gasping. I knelt next to him, putting a hand on his shoulder. "You all right, mate?"

He shook his head. "Be all right in a minute...shoulda known better. Had to try though." He clutched his head in his hands, moaning.

Black Jack glared at the ghostly shapes. Several of them appeared to be holding their hands out, awaiting our joining them.

It occurred to me they were very patient with us. I suppose they figured they had all the time in the world to wait.

"Don't suppose anyone has any other ideas? How 'bout you, Molly-girl? I reckon you're the clever one amongst us."

"I'm sorry. Haven't a clue." I shrugged helplessly. "I don't reckon there is a way out of it. If there were, somebody'd have found it by now. I reckon we're stuck here until..."

Until.

There was an expectant hush as the others waited for me to complete my thought. Finally, Black Jack coughed. "Er, you were saying, Mol?"

"Huh? Oh! Yes. Well, I was just thinking. These people here—" I waved at the shadowy figures that still surrounded us. "Well, they're here to guard this thing, aren't they? And I guess so are we now. Right?"

"Right."

"Okay. But who from? And for how long? It sounds like the whole point was to keep this magic shell or whatever it is safe. But they can't have it locked away forever, can they? Seems to me they're waiting for something or someone." I turned to the shapes around us. "Am I right?"

One of the figures appeared to nod. I continued.

"All right. So how do you know who you are guarding it for? Sooner or later, someone has to come for it. There must be a way you can know, right? Some sort of trial or something?"

As one, the shapes turned to face the door to the captain's cabin. A faint click echoed in the silence.

The four of us approached the door cautiously. Black Jack, taking point as was his wont, laid a hand on the door. He moved his other hand to his sword, then thought better of it. He glanced back at us, then tugged at the handle.

The door swung open on silent hinges, offering no resistance, and we made our way in.

A typical captain's cabin, though a bit less gaudy than some, was decorated with but a few woodcuts. A lone shelf held weather-beaten logbooks, and various maps were laid out with bric-a-brac on the corners to keep them in place. In the back of the cabin, a bed and night table could just be seen. It was, in short, home and workplace in one. Lanthorns flared to life as we stepped in, throwing dancing shadows on the walls and illuminating a bizarre sight.

Scallywag!

On the captain's desk, a crystalline latticework of stone shone all colors of the rainbow. The stone was more or less spherical, with strands forming a cage about the width of a man's torso. Inside was as perfect a specimen of conch as any I have seen in all my days. So perfect was it that one might be persuaded it had not been grown in the way of natural shells, but was, indeed, a made thing. The fact that it shone with the same pearlescent sheen inside and out gave credence to the idea.

For a moment, we did nothing, standing in awe of the thing. Beside me, Paulo took a deep breath. "Now that is the loveliest thing I have ever seen. No wonder those Company sods want it."

"So what do we do?" asked Dutch. "Break through the cage-thing?" She reached for her sword.

"Hold it." Black Jack held up a hand. "That's not the way this goes." He stepped closer, peering curiously.

And then we felt it. Again, there were no words, just the idea fed directly into our minds. The thing had to be kept safe until it was needed. It would be released to one who could show a rightful claim. There would be, could be, no coercion. Either one had a claim, or one did not.

"Well," said Black Jack. "Anyone fancy a go? I don't reckon it'll let me."

That was when I felt the strange, warm glow emanating from my amulet. The Company guards, it not being a weapon or of any particular apparent value, had allowed me to keep it on my person when we were rounded up. I took a cautious step forward. Sure enough, I felt the warmth increase. Only a little, mind, but now I was watching for it I could feel the change, right enough.

I don't think the others said anything as I stepped forward. At least, I do not recall them saying anything. I found my attention fixated entirely upon the shell and its crystalline prison. The closer I got, the more pronounced the warmth of the amulet. I reached out, and...

Looking back, it is hard to describe quite what happened. Even given all that I have seen and done, it is a strange and unworldly memory, one that defies precise recollection.

I recall white emptiness all around me, except for the spot where I stood. This was to all appearances the same crystalline cage as held the shell, grown to the size of a room. And it contained only me.

What followed did not take place in a way that can be adequately described (or at least, not by yours truly). Think of an oral examination, or perhaps a trial, but not quite either. It took place without words. There were only thoughts, ideas traveling from mind to mind without the clumsy vehicle of language. Nevertheless, I shall do my best to put what happened into words for the benefit of the reader.

The presence wished to know if I was a daughter of...well, I didn't get the name, but there was an impression of a woman all in blue and gold, sitting on a stately throne while the world billowed around her. I understood she was some sort of sea goddess. It must have sensed my ignorance, as I could feel its suspicion. This thing (I shall call it the judge) bid me explain how I came by the amulet.

My mind flashed back to the island and the temple with the impaled corpse. I felt ire building up around me and realized the judge was thinking I might have been one of those who had participated in whatever horrible deeds had taken place. I quickly recalled the scenes leading up to the discovery, the bodies, the old priest on the beach. This seemed to mollify the judge, and the enquiry continued.

The judge sent thoughts to me of merpeople, the An'ui. In the flash of a moment, I saw a glorious kingdom under the sea, whose inhabitants were freely trading with those who roamed the land. There was prosperity, harmony, and even some interbreeding, much to my surprise. Other things called the sea their home, noisome things with terrible ways, whose god bade them commit atrocities to slake its thirst. I saw some of the land dwellers make compacts with these beasts, and the deeds done in their name. Then the uprising, as the An'ui struck at the fiendish creatures and their human followers. I saw battles, armies that would dwarf even the Empire. And at the climax of it all, the conch taken up. I felt the desperation of those who wielded it, the fear of what may come.

What happened next, I could not say. The truth of it was hidden from me, leaving only the impression of great and terrible power. All that was shown to me was the aftermath, a scene of devastation. Victory at what must have been an unthinkable cost. The conch taken away, stored in a place where no land or sea dweller could take it until the time came for it to be found again.

Scallywag!

I understood then that the task of keeping the conch safe had been passed to the men of this ship so that it may eventually fall into the hands of another. I must take the thing, I must keep it safe and see that it goes where it must, for a task was awaiting, and the conch must be in the right place at the right time.

The next thought from my mind came unbidden. I found myself thinking of the West India Company, of the measures they had taken to entrap myself and my crewmates into fetching the thing for them. As much as I feared for their safety, I could not withhold the truth that I would be handing the conch over to some very foul people indeed.

I fully expected the judge to reject me outright, to cast us away, one and all, rather than let the conch fall into such hands. Strangely, it seemed unsurprised, and I felt this was right somehow, that the shell must pass into such hands, however briefly, before things were made right. In that moment, in that congress without words, I swear to you I felt a hand on my shoulder and words—actual words—appeared in my mind.

"Things will be made right. But first, you must play your part."

Around me, the crystalline cage began to dissolve. The long, multicolored strands whirled away, leaving only trails of glittering color that faded like dying embers. One after the other vanished into the white expanse, until the very last one disappeared, and I was alone.

I opened my eyes. (When had I closed them?) The conch rested on the captain's desk, the cage gone.

"Strike me!" Behind me, I heard Black Jack and the others. He stepped closer, peering over my shoulder at the extraordinary shell. "How'd you do that, Molly-girl?"

I shook the last vestiges of the white place from my mind. "It is…best if I explain later." I reached out to the shell, hesitated a moment, then took it in both hands. It was heavier than it looked, and cold. Without speaking, I turned around and carried it out of the cabin.

Outside, the shapes in the fog were still waiting. I held the conch up for them to see. "It is done," I said. "Your part in this is over. You may rest." I do not know where those words came from—certainly not from me—but somehow I knew they were the right words to say. One by one, the shapes faded into the fog until only one was left. This last, whom I judged to be the erstwhile captain of this vessel, bowed his head to me before joining his brethren.

Around us, the fog itself began to dissipate, and we heard a low groaning that was coming closer. We looked around in alarm, trying to make sense of it. "What's going on?" cried Dutch, reaching for her sword. It was the sound of old wood warping and flexing, as age and ill-use took their toll.

"It's the ship, innit?" said Paulo. "Whatever's been holdin' it together is gone now. All those years are comin' back on it, if I'm any judge."

Black Jack gave the ship a calculating look. "Aye. I think you're right and all. Time we got off this tub. Lively, now!"

We scrambled for the rope that still hung over the railing. All four of us climbed down to the waiting boat below, myself with some difficulty on account of having to keep the conch in the crook of my arm as I descended. As soon as the last of us was aboard, the men began to row away as fast as they could. No one needed telling to get away.

Almost as they hit the oars, we heard the sound of the mainmast collapsing into the sea. The rowers redoubled their pace, and we held on tight as they got us clear of the ship as fast as they could. By now the fog was a mere shadow of itself, so that the Company ship was plainly visible again. But no eyes were on it. We watched the *Pearly Jack* fall apart, seemingly aging a century in seconds. The hull became rotten with holes, the timber gray and brittle. The last vestiges of fog boiled away under the Caribbean sun just as the ship slipped below the waves, leaving nothing but driftwood and a few lonely pieces of flotsam.

Chapter Twenty-One

To say we caused a stir when climbing aboard the ship, conch in hand, is a vast understatement. It was clear they expected our lot to return empty-handed (or possibly not at all). There was genuine admiration in the captain's voice, though he did his best to hide it. The conch being duly locked in his safe, we were escorted back to the brig and the return trip was underway.

The return was, without a doubt, a good deal pleasanter than the trip out. They still set us to chores and such during the day, but it felt more out of obligation than any particular malice. Indeed, it seemed that the sailors were keeping us at a wary distance. This I found baffling, only to realize that they were intimidated by us—or rather by what we had accomplished. Our little group found this amusing but agreed 'twere best not to push the advantage. The most important thing was getting back with our ship and crew, safe and sound, and nobody wanted to be the one who wrecked that.

It was the third night, our ship due to rendezvous with the others in the morning. I was taking one final watch. One of the other sailors, a plump Company man who had not said two words to any of us since we came on board, sidled up to where I was looking out over the sea.

He coughed. "Er, look. That was pretty impressive, you lot getting the treasure and that."

I shrugged. "Well, getting hard-to-get-at treasures is more or less what we do."

"Huh-huh. I bet. But really, solid work ya did. Dead impressive."

"Oh. Well, ta."

"That, and if you'd failed, they woulda started sending our lot over."

"Ah."

"Yeh." He paused, looking at his nails. He seemed to have something on his mind. "Er, look. You done us a good turn, gettin' that thing. So...guess we sort of owe you."

"Yes?"

"Yeh. See, the thing is, His Lordship...we've done things for him before, you see. An' he likes usin' criminals to do dangerous work for'm. Reckons they're disposable, like. If they die, who's to say? But if they succeed...well, he's not one to worry himself over promises made to the lower elements, if you take my meaning."

"Well, I wish I could say myself surprised. Let me guess, gallows at dawn?"

He shook his head. "Not His Lordship. He's...you've seen a cat when it's got holt of a mouse? He's like that and all. Loves to bat 'em about, then let 'em scurry away. Just when they think they're free, whap." He brought his hand down hard on the rail. "It's like a game to him. And some of us...it ain't Christian, that's all. You may be rogues an' that, but that don't give him permission." He looked around the empty deck. "Just wanted to let you know. Put a word in your ear, sort of thing. Anyway, uhm, right. Bye." And he was off.

As soon as my watch was over, I wasted no time and informed the others.

"Well, bugger." Black Jack sneered as he leaned back in the cell he shared with Paulo. "Can't trust the bastards. You really can't and all."

"Yeah, well. Hands up, everyone who's surprised." Dutch looked from one glum face to the next, not a hand to be seen. "Thought as much. So what do we do about it?"

"Well, we could..." Paulo trailed off with a sigh. "Never mind."

"No, go on, what is it?" I prompted.

He waved a hand dismissively. "Oh, I was just going to say we could hang on to the shell 'til everyone was safe, then float it over to 'em. Of course, that only works if we hadn't handed the bloody thing over to the captain first thing, asses that we are."

"Ah. Well, if it's any help, I don't think they would have let us hang on to it in any case."

"Suppose you're right."

"Don't suppose we could take one of their lot hostage?"

"Shouldn't think so, Dutch. Besides, this fellow doesn't seem like the type to lose sleep over a few ordinary seamen."

"True." We lapsed into silence, each shrouded in our own glum thoughts.

I don't know how long we sat in the darkness, contemplating the bleak prospect ahead. Eventually, we dropped off to sleep, no closer to a solution than when we had begun. It seemed our worst fears had been

Scallywag!

confirmed, but buggered if we knew what we could do about it. At least we were going in with our eyes open, as it were. All we could do was play it as it came. The words of the sailor kept coming back to me. *Just when they think they're free.* Well, I made up my mind that I wouldn't think us truly escaped until we were out of sight of His Lordship and all his bloody cannons.

The next day dawned gray and blustery, the clouds above us rolling hurriedly across the sky like a storm that was overdue to break somewhere. By midmorning, we sighted the island, and it was coming up noon when we sailed into the bay. We sat at anchor for what seemed a hell of a long time, while all around us was nonstop activity from the crew. I don't recall any of us having anything to say. We were all too much on the alert for any sign of betrayal. Other than the wait, nothing seemed to be out of the ordinary. Mind you, that was more than enough.

After what seemed a lifetime, we were let out and herded at gunpoint to a dinghy. We were rowed ashore, where we found the rest of the crew, minus Captain Cunningham, milling around. "They went ahead an' took her over to the ship," explained James. He pointed to where the *Bonnie Mary* sat at anchor in the middle of the bay. "Said as soon as they're gone, we can head back quick as we like. Of course, they only left us the one boat." He turned his head to indicate the single rowboat sitting on the beach. "Mind you, it'll take a while getting people ferried over. I can't tell from here if they left us her other boats, but I figure the first group over can see, then row back across in 'em. Oughta speed things up, anyway."

The four of us looked at each other, unsure of what to say. Black Jack stepped forward. "Well, that might work out right enough, but the thing is, we've got word that they might have some sort of trickery in mind for us." He turned to me. "Go on, Mol. Tell 'em."

I quickly explained about the sailor's warning and how we had spent the time since wondering precisely what we may do about it. James frowned. "Well, it's always bleedin' something, isn't it? All right. Well, forewarned is forearmed, as they do say." He turned to the rest of the crew and cupped his hands. "All right, you lot. I want volunteers for the first boat over—"

Most hands went up.

"—to check for traps an' things. Sabotage, anything like that. We've reason to believe they've got something nasty waiting for us, so I need keen eyes to check her top to bottom. Now, who will go?"

Despite the seriousness of the situation, it was genuinely amusing to watch the forest of hands slink back down again, as if endeavouring to pretend they had never actually been raised in the first place. I think I heard Black Jack chuckle behind me. I daresay he heard me as well.

Jansen put up a tentative hand. "I can go. Got to check they didn't take my charts and that."

"Jansen, you're our only navigator. Can't risk it. Come on, now. Who else?"

"I'll go." No one was more surprised to hear me say it than myself. The words came out of my mouth without bothering to consult with my brain. Still, once said, it couldn't be unsaid. James nodded in my direction. "Good on ya, Mol. Who else?"

We scanned the ranks of the crew. There was a slow showing of hands again. At least some of them must have volunteered out of shame that a mere girl had stepped up before them. In the end, myself, Black Jack, old man Tucker, Rijn, Walleyed Red, and Domingo made a party of six. As soon as the last Company ship was out of sight, we rowed out to the *Bonnie Mary* and climbed aboard.

An eerie silence surrounded us as we stood on deck. I had spent over five years of my life on the ship. Up until then, there had always been something doing. Crew running about, seeing to the ship, gossiping, and singing, and yes, even fighting sometimes, but they were living. Standing there then, the ship felt abandoned and forlorn. I told myself this was only temporary and she'd be her old self again in no time. Some part of me didn't quite believe the lie.

"All right." Black Jack rubbed his hands together. "Rijn, see to the sheets and lines. Tucker, you check the guns. Mol, fetch the captain, then join the rest of us in the cargo hold. We're going to give this place a right going-through, see?"

We agreed, and all went our separate ways. I went first to the captain's cabin, assuming she would be there. I tried knocking, but I heard no response. I began to call out again, only to realize I *could* hear something faint. The muffled sound was accompanied by a sort of irregular thumping. I froze in place, listening hard, then called out again: "Captain! Is that you?"

Scallywag!

There was the sound again. Too faint, not coherent enough for words, almost as if...Of course! They would hardly have left her free. Well, I would see about that, right enough. I grabbed the door handle and tugged it open.

There are times in your life when the world sort of slows down, lets you take notice of things. I seen it but a few times, and always in a moment of crisis.

The door was moving wrong. I had been in and out of the captain's cabin G—d knew how many times and knew the feel of it. Just now, that feel was off. I felt more resistance to it, like it was pulling something.

I pulled my hand away from the door as if it were a snake. The door was only opened a few inches, but continued to swing open of its own volition. I will remember that sight to my dying breath.

The captain was in the middle of the room, bound hand and foot to a chair. There was a lopsided gag over her mouth. Likely she had been trying to work it off before we arrived. An open lanthorn was burning right next to her head. From its handle, a black thread led to the door. The lanthorn was poised at the very edge of one of several powder kegs stacked around the captain. The lid of that keg had been pried off, and as I watched in horror, the lamp slid the last little way to the edge of the powder keg and began to tip.

The captain's eyes met mine in a moment of shared horror. She flicked her eyes toward the lanthorn, then back to me. She twisted and braced her head against it, holding it in place the only way she could. The flames danced around her hair, then slowly began their work. She caught my eye one last time, and with all the strength she could muster, cried out, "*RUN!*"

Her voice may have been muffled from the gag, but you may be assured I understood her right away. For only the briefest moment, I did hesitate. I wanted to run over and free her, drag her away from the powder and the flames. But there was no time, no time. Her hair was already ablaze. Soon the rest of her would be too. Of course, there was naught to put the fire out in the cabin. No surprise they had thought of that. No, the only option was escape.

"Abandon Ship!" I shouted it at the top of my lungs as I ran toward the deck. "Abandon ship! Trap! Jump for it!" Black Jack and the rest had already descended to the hold. "Abandon ship!" I cried down the hatch. "She's gonna blow!"

"What's that?"

"What'd she say?"

"I said the ship's going to blow! It's a trap! Get out now!" Rijn, who had gone up the ratlines to check the mast, took a running jump and dived into the blue waters. Beneath me, I heard the thump of boots as the others scrambled to get out.

My crewmates warned, I betook myself with all speed to the rail, vaulting it without slowing down. As I tumbled downward, I saw Tucker and Domingo diving out of the gunports. Behind them, I thought I could hear Black Jack shouting something. But then I hit the waters, plunging beneath the waves in a cloud of bubbles, just as the world above exploded in a carnation of flame.

Chapter Twenty-Two

THAT NIGHT, AS WE made camp by the shore, the mood was one of utter hopelessness. We'd had tight spots before, to be sure, but we'd always had our ship and our captain guiding us forward. To lose them both at once did not seem possible. It was too big a thought to have. We ate listlessly, making no attempts at conversation, only staring into the fire. There was no talk of the future that I recall. There didn't seem to be one.

Black Jack sat himself down beside me and rested a hand on my shoulder. "I just want you to know," he said quietly, "that there's no one here blames you for what happened. We all knew His Lordship was a rotter. All this is on him an' him alone."

I shrugged. "But we knew that. We were supposed to be looking for traps. I had to rush in without thinking, didn't I? And now we've lost everything."

"Nah, it's not just you. Listen, when we went down to check the powder, there were tripwires hidden between the barrels. I reckon Red must've hit one when we were trying to escape. No doubt there was others we didn't even get a chance to find. One way or another, he wasn't gonna let us get away. Probably got a ship or two sitting just out of sight in case we did manage to get 'er going again. The bastard."

"Expect you're right." We watched the campfire for a while. "So...Red?"

He shook his head. "Couple hours ago. James has got a digging party lined up for the morning. We'll see him all right, him and the captain both."

"Good."

"Yeah."

"Only..."

Black Jack patted my shoulder. "S'alright, girl. Speak your mind."

"What happens next? I mean, we've got no captain, no ship, just one bloody rowboat and what we could salvage from the wreck. Jansen reckons he's lost twenty years of charts and all. I just don't know if there's anything left for us, you know?"

He nodded. "Aye, I'm feeling that myself. Upon my oath, I don't know what will happen next, and I daresay not a man among us does."

"Then what do we do?"

Black Jack sat back. The weariness in his face still held the horror of the day's events, but there was a change, somehow, even if it was a little one. "The first thing we do, we set things to rights here. We mourn our dead, tend to our wounded. Then...we'll have to see. But all that will wait 'til the morning. What we do right now is the only thing we can do."

"And what's that?"

"Just get through the bloody night." And he was off.

The next day was somber indeed. We laid Walleyed Red to rest in a nice grove of trees not far off from the shore. As to the captain, there was really not a lot that we could do. We had no body to lay to rest, no cannon or even pistol shot to see her off. All we could do was remember her as best we could.

"Captain Sarah Cunningham was a da—was a very fine captain, and the *Bonnie Mary* the best-run ship it has been my pleasure to crew." James stood before us, head bowed. "I've been at sea most of my life, in one capacity or another, and a better captain I never set eyes upon. She was the kind of captain one would sail with off the edge of the world if she but bid it. And though she was from us untimely rip'd, I am nonetheless grateful to Providence that I had the very great privilege to serve under her as long as I did. It is a shame we cannot honor her as she deserves, but I do believe we shall every one of us keep her dear in our hearts for as long as we shall live."

A chorus of "amens" from the crew filled the air. James let a somber moment pass, then resumed. "I would now call upon those who have a special memory of the captain that they would like to share."

Black Jack stepped in front of the rest of the crew and raised his voice. "When I first come across the captain, I was a proper wreck, me. Hadn't held a berth in months on account of me drinking and that. D—d if I know what she saw in me, begging your pardon, but she picked me right up out of the gutter and gave me a chance. It was more than anyone had given me in a long time, I can tell you. Something told me this was the best shot I was ever going to get at getting meself back on course, and thanks to her I did. I will always be grateful for what she done." He faltered as if looking for what else to say but merely stepped back.

Dutch was next. "Suppose it won't come as a surprise to you, but I had a hard time of it growing up. Running around like one of the lads is all right when you're a kid, but once you start in to marriageable age, people start giving you the side-eye. I was working at a dockside tavern, having a bloody awful time of it. One day, in comes the captain and somehow...she saw me. I mean the real, proper me, what I had to hide at that blasted place. She told me she was looking for crew, and if I wanted to sign on as Dutch then, well, that's who I would be." She grinned, rubbing a hand over her close-cropped hair. "Well, I didn't even finish my shift! Next port, I got my hair cut properly and some new clothes, and that was that. Without her, who knows? I might still be at that bloody awful tavern."

And so it went. One after another, the crew came forward, each sharing a memory. I, of course, related how she found me aboard the *Cecilia* and how my life had changed as a result. As we went on, it seemed everyone had some variation of the same story. Captain Cunningham had seen something in us, perhaps something we were trying to hide, or even something we didn't know ourselves. She saw us all the same and gave us the chance to become something better.

As day turned to dusk, the flow of reminiscences continued. We made a campfire, and the stories continued on into the night. I remember well the stirring adventures retold round that fire. As I sit here in this cell, the memories of that night provide some comfort, however small. It was not a grand send-off for a captain so loved as she, but in truth, it was one she would have appreciated.

The next morning, a meeting of the full crew was held on the shore of the island. There was of course only one item on the agenda. Namely, what happens now? There were few enough in the way of options. With only one boat and no charts to speak of, it was clear the majority of us were going to be spending a fair amount of time on the island. Jansen said he could get us to a port through dead reckoning and, with any luck, scare up a ship to affect a rescue. That was going to be the sticking point, of course. We had precious little to barter with besides ourselves. Privately owned vessels would want paying, in advance no doubt. As for the authorities, well...better to stay where we were.

In fact it wasn't so bad. There were fish and fruit aplenty, and a stream that kept up a small but adequate supply of drinkable water. We could hold out there for a good while, and indeed more than one of the crew had been in a like position before. Still, no one much relished the idea of spending out their days in the middle of nowhere, however pleasant the exile. Quite what to do about it was a matter of no little contention. Eventually, the meeting broke up with no plan in mind. We all went off to think and discuss and see what we could come up with.

Later in the evening, as the cooking fires were lit, I went to tell James and the other officers what was on my mind. A great deal of discussion and argumentation back and forth occurred. In the end, they had to own that no better ideas seemed to be forthcoming. If worse came to worse, it would only be me who bore the consequences of failure.

The next morning myself, Dutch, Anna, and Black Jack rowed out away from the island into the open sea. We did not go too far, I being of the opinion that if it would work anywhere, then anywhere would suffice. With the help of the others, I lowered myself over the boat and into the water. After maneuvering myself behind it, I disrobed and passed my clothes up to Anna, who wrung them out and set them to dry.

"All right," said Dutch. "So now what happens?"

I had done it once, but not on purpose. I held on to the back of the boat, legs idly paddling in the warm Caribbean sea, and cast my mind back to the night of the terrible storm. Had it only been two years ago? I remembered the plunge, the moment of certainty that I was about to die, and then…

Of course.

I gave the others a quick smile. "One moment. Let me try something." I let go and dove into the depths, continuing until the rowboat was a dim shape above me. Nothing changed. I realized that I had instinctually held my breath before taking the dive. I forced myself to blow the air out of my lungs and allowed a sizable portion of seawater to take its place.

The effect was immediate. I began to choke and thrash about, my every instinct urging me back to the surface. It took all the discipline I had to fight it. I writhed beneath the waves, fists clenched, sending out a prayer to G—d that this would work.

I felt the old familiar sensation of the pendent that rested against my chest. Once again, it married itself to my skin, and I felt the warmth spread through me. I forced myself to relax.

Scallywag!

I took a long, deep breath of the ocean water, felt it circulate through my body and out my newly restored gills. I flicked my tail a couple of times and laughed as it caught the sunlight filtering in from the waves above. The amulet was still warm to the touch. I prodded at it curiously, but it seemed bonded quite firmly to my skin. Probably best not to mess about with it.

I swam back up to where the boat lay. Grinning, I took hold of the keel and kicked my tail up, making it breach the surface of the water. I heard Anna let out a little yelp. Laughing, I allowed myself to resurface and waved at the others. "It worked!"

Black Jack smirked. "Did it, now? We hadn't noticed." His face turned serious. "I wish we had more of those things. I don't much fancy sending you off by yourself, Molly-girl."

"I know. But this is how things are. If this works, who knows? Maybe I'll get them to give us more."

He laughed. "Now that would be a real turn-up, eh? Buncha mermaid pyrates comin' up out of the sea an' that." His face turned thoughtful. "Actually, that's not the worst idea. Look, if you find them—"

"Then she can get our crew off that bloody island." Anna was in no mood for nonsense, and in truth, one could not blame her. She handed over a satchel, which I carefully slung over my shoulder. "There's some fruits for you, and a little hardtack, in case you don't fancy raw fish. And Jansen's done a map showing his best reckoning of our location."

"One more thing, me girl." Black Jack handed over a long strip of leather from which hung a carefully made sheath. I took it in my hands, looking it over. "This is your belt? But why—" a gleam of light caught my attention at the top of the sheath. "Is that…Jack, is that your knife?"

He nodded. "Reckon you'll need it more than I." He lay a hand on my shoulder. "You be careful down there, eh? There's things in the sea that…well, I don't hardly need to tell you."

I nodded. "I'll be careful, my friend. We just have to trust in Providence." I made ready to dive, then noticed a look on Anna's face. "Something wrong?"

"Oh, no. No. It's just…well, what's it like?"

It took me a moment to understand what she meant. "You mean being a mermaid? Well, it's…different. It's like having one leg but lots of knees. Also, you can feel the saltwater come in and out of you. Very strange feeling, that I can tell you!"

She smiled and looked wistful. "I should like to try it sometime," she said quietly.

Dutch smiled. "You'd make a d—n fine one in my opinion."

I laughed with the others. "Tell you what. If we get through this mess, I'll let you have a go."

"All right," she said. "I'll hold you to it, mind."

"Deal." I pushed myself off from the boat, saluted my comrades, and dove beneath the waves. As I felt my body adjust itself once again to the depths, my stomach knotted. I had put on a brave face for the others, but the fact of the matter was that I was alone in a hostile world. I was looking for a people I had only glimpsed once, years ago. And they might very well be disinclined to help. What other option was there? I had to take the chance, and that was all.

My mind went back to Jansen, and the things he had told me when I would watch him plotting out the ship's course. "You may use every sign at your disposal to guide you, but the plain truth is sometimes you *will* be lost. When that happens, the indecision can swallow you whole. Don't let it. Always remember, when you don't know where to go, you can always go forward."

I took a deep breath, feeling the briny water churn through my torso. Then I pointed myself forward.

Chapter Twenty-Three

Proceeding was easier said than done. I very quickly realized that if I were to get anywhere, I would need to learn how to propel myself competently through the water. Thus, while my friends were rowing their way back to shore, I was busily swimming about in circles only a few fathoms below. I would prefer not to say just how long I took to gain some sort of competence in my new form, nor how many times I wound up upside-down or veering off in the wrong direction. It is just as well that they departed when they did.

I eventually discovered that my main fault was in trying to swim as if I had two legs together: it seems that trying to move both at the same time was paradoxically sending me off-true. I forced myself to stop thinking in terms of legs and forced myself to imagine my tail coming out behind me. It is somewhat difficult to explain as I sit here on land once again, but it felt rather like a completely different part of the body, not just my legs fused together. This improved things tremendously, and I was able to maneuver myself competently in short order.

That being settled, I took a moment to take in my surroundings. Reader, how shall I describe what I saw? Beneath the churning emptiness of the waves was an entire world. Of course, having grown up by the sea myself, I had spent some time exploring the shore and the tide pools, discovering the creatures that dwelt therein. Those had been but the barest tastes, wherein I had been safely tethered to the land. Now I was surrounded on all sides by the open sea, the land a distant thing. As I swam about, I came to realize that we who ride the waves truly know little of what lies beneath. We have our speculations and our legends—it is a poor sort of sailor who cannot tell you of at least one mysterious creature he has sighted breaching the waves—but what we know is lamentably small. I can tell you, it is an entire other world.

And such a world! Strange multicolored flowers carpeted the sea floor, with many-legged creatures scuttling about, around, and within them. Curious rock formations covered in colorful blossoms waved lazily in the current. And everywhere were the denizens of the sea. Fish swam separately and in schools, crabs, shellfish, even a couple of turtles swam by, giving me not so much as a glance. And this too was a revelation. As I proceeded along the depths, I realized that none of the creatures were fleeing from me or seemed in any way disturbed by my presence.

The reader may recall my earlier mention of my brothers' love of hunting in the woods outside our town. I myself did not care for such pastimes, but as the eldest, it often fell to my lot to fetch them home for supper. As I walked through the woods, calling for my brothers, I often noticed how the animals would run and hide once aware of my presence. They had learned through hard experience not to linger when humans were near. Truth be told, I cannot blame them. We do seem to come with our own in-set cruelty, so that even our young are dangerous. Father Byrne, back home, said this was because the animals knew that G—d had given us dominion over all the creatures of the world, and they fled out of pious respect for His plan. But I have always suspected they just understand that our kind is dangerous to be around.

Down beneath the waters, they have no such fear. I tell you, a person may stay still in one spot and watch all manner of creatures swim by without the slightest concern as to one's presence. To be surrounded and thus accepted by so many of nature's children at once is an experience I have never felt anywhere else. Reader, if I could give you but one moment experiencing what I felt down there, I could deem no greater gift worth giving. Even now, thinking back to the treasure I & my crew have amassed over the years, I would happily trade it all to be back in the sea, swimming among those beautiful creatures.

I picked a direction roughly away from the island and struck out, keeping close to the ocean floor. As I moved into the deeper waters, the world darkened around me, the water turning a deep blue. Happily, my eyes were able to adjust to this new circumstance, and I was able to keep going with little difficulty. That being said, anything beyond my immediate surroundings was only vague shadows, and I began to feel I might well be in danger. Happily, I remembered Black Jack's knife and removed it from its sheath, ready for use should the occasion demand.

As I swam on, the enormity of the task I had set myself began to intrude upon my consciousness. The plan was to seek out some of the merpeople like the one I had glimpsed before. Surely if there was one, there would be others?

I was alone with neither stars nor compass to guide me, nor any idea where they may be found. For that matter, what if they turned out to be hostile? The thought had not occurred to me before, but down here in the strange depths, it seemed all too likely. Quite a mess indeed if I were to find them, only to have them attack me on sight. Old sailors' tales came back to me of sirens who sang sweetly to lure ships to their doom. In my mind, I heard their singing turn to merry laughter as ship after ship foundered on unseen rocks and sank beneath the waves, never to be seen again. Thus it was that, as the shape of the wreck loomed up before me, it was quite a fright.

Even at a distance, the sharp angles and unnatural juttings were clearly out of place. My mind tried to make sense of the unfamiliar shapes and conjured up some grotesque images indeed before the thing resolved itself. There was the prow, there the mainmast broken in half, the tattered remains of the sails billowing in the currents like the movements of some disconsolate beast. I allowed myself a moment to settle my heart, then curiosity overcame fear. I needed to investigate.

It was a Dutch trader, an older one by the looks of it. A large gaping hole in the side of the hull told the tale right enough. Someone had set off the powder in the hold. Every sailor has heard cautionary tales of ships destroyed by a moment's carelessness. Of course, one didn't generally get to see the results up close and live to tell the tale. I swam in through the splintered wound and began to explore.

I was down in the cargo deck from what I could tell, though there was precious little left of any cargo. Most of what remained was overrun with barnacles and other such creatures. I noticed some particular activity aft. As I got closer, colors and movement resolved themselves in a veritable oasis. Sea creatures of all manner and description were clustered together in this one corner. I puzzled at this for a moment, moving in as close as I dared.

Quite a lot of splintered wood was in this place, which I quickly recognized as the remains of old barrels. I carefully plucked away a piece of what must have been a lid and turned it over. Underneath was a black, sticky substance crawling with small creatures I could not identify. I realized with a start that the ship must have been carrying a consignment of molasses. Upon the ship's sinking, it had spilled out everywhere, attracting the thriving little colony I saw before me (not at all dissimilar to how our own people flocked to the West Indies to set up sugar plantations).

I moved upward to the next deck and found myself in the crew's quarters, which were...well...occupied, if you take my meaning. A half dozen, maybe more. Very little was left of them, to be sure, but one could easily see that their last moments had been horrific. To die in such a way, unshriven and decaying below the waves! Every sailor knows in their heart that they, too, could well meet that fate one day. I crossed myself reflexively, then went away from that place. Best not to disturb them.

Back outside, I swam up to the main deck. The door to the captain's quarters hung open, showing only darkness inside. I hesitated, then eased my way in, looking out for any sign of danger. It was rather plain as such places go, though I suspected it must have looked nice enough before. The captain's remains were sprawled on the floor where he had tried to run for it. In his arms, he held the disintegrating remains of the log and a locket covered in corrosion. The locket was open and held close to his face.

In the dim light, I squinted and saw the cameo of a woman and a little child. I felt grief tighten around me, imagining the last seconds of the captain's life. Trapped, with the waves crashing in and no hope of survival, all he could do was gaze upon this tiny picture of his loved ones and know that they would not meet again on any earthly shore. I wiped my eyes—can one cry underwater?—and took my leave. This wasn't just a wreck. It was a sacred place. As I departed, I pulled the door of his cabin closed. It was not easy, the wood being splintered and warped, but I managed to get it sufficiently to ensure he would not be further disturbed.

With a pensive and reflective mood, I set out once again. Honestly, I ought to have been paying rather more attention to my surroundings, but my exploration of the wreck had turned my thoughts back to the rest of the crew, to our captain and that horrible moment still so fresh in my mind. I even found my thoughts going back across the ocean, to my own family. With a pang of guilt, I realized it had been an awfully long time since I'd written them or sent any money. I resolved that, if ever we got back to land, I would remedy that at once. Thus occupied as I was, I feel it is at least understandable that I did not see the creature until it was right on top of me.

Long as a rowboat, a head like an arrow, and an array of limbs trailing out behind it, the horrible creature was right out of an old seaman's tale. Those limbs seemed both hands and feet, and animated with a dexterity most unlike anything I had ever seen. Its eyes were curiously slitted, rather like a goat's. Withal it was a most disturbing creature. Resting on a nearby rock, its coloring was such that it was nearly invisible until I accidentally jostled it, whereupon it immediately turned a livid pink and lashed out at me with its limbs.

Scallywag!

More out of instinct than anything, I slashed at it with my knife, a shot made more out of fear than any deliberation, and only managed to graze against the unwholesome, rubbery hide of the creature. This caused it to come violently about and fetch me a wallop with its head. This frightened me more than hurt me, and I brought the knife down again, coming quite near to its eye.

It shied away, moving back quickly and giving me a moment to think. Whatever its skin was made of, it was a fair bet that its eyes were much like any others. At least in terms of delicacy, at any rate. I steeled myself, readied my knife, and watched the thing carefully.

It was not long in trying again. It lunged forward, trying once again to assault me, but this time I was prepared. As it came, I slipped neatly to one side and jabbed the blade right at its eye as it passed. I didn't get a good look at the result, but the sudden, violent reaction of the beast told me I had struck home.

Not waiting around for the thing to seek revenge, I turned and swam away as fast as I could. Alas, I was still not entirely familiar with my new form, whereas the monster was a very swift swimmer indeed. I chanced a glance backward and saw it coming after me, closing the distance with remarkable alacrity. I had struck home right enough, but it was clear that the creature was determined to avenge itself upon me, one eye or not. I looked about hurriedly for some way to shake the d—d thing. Back to the shipwreck? No, it would only come in after me. Hide? Unlikely. Outswimming the thing was clearly out, at least in open waters...

I dove, heading once again toward the sea floor and the strange little world that covered it. There wasn't much, but some batches of coral and seaweed broke up the going enough to slow anyone. My tail, it turned out, was quite adept at taking sharp turns and maneuvering swiftly around obstacles. Also, of course, I wasn't handicapped by the loss of an eye. More than once, it seemed to me, I heard my pursuer thump heavily against some obstacle or other, delaying its pursuit.

Presently, I came to a place where the sea floor dropped away. Ahead, I saw nothing but blue darkness. Nowhere to hide, and G—d only knew what was hiding in the depths. I looked about for any other route, but there were none. Circling back, of course, was out of the question. The creature had lost some ground in the pursuit, but would no doubt gain it back as soon as it got clear. Seeing no alternative, I aimed myself toward the darkness and headed down.

K. L. Mitchell

The gloom of the place was all-encompassing. As alive as the areas I had left behind had been, this place was utterly dead. Few fish were here (not a good sign, I thought to myself), nor any plants or other things to speak of. All I could do was keep swimming, hoping that I might find some place in the darkness to conceal myself, if only long enough to get the jump on the thing. It was a dismal prospect, but none other occurred to me in my flight.

I kept close to the cliffside, keeping an eye out for hiding places. There seemed to be an opening below, perhaps a natural cave. I steered toward it, hoping against hope it would turn out to be unoccupied. Just as I reached it, a movement caught my attention. I turned just in time to see a mass of rope come hurtling out of the darkness. In a trice, I was netted and pulled into the dark of the cave.

Chapter Twenty-Four

IF I WAS SURPRISED BY this turn of events, then my captors were no less so. I heard their cries as they pulled the net close. There was a shouted command, and then a cool blue light that put me in mind of moonlit nights back home. Three faces looked down at me, eyes wide. One of them, a somewhat heavyset fellow, leaned forward and addressed me.

"Sister," he said, "what are you doing here? You know the pit is dangerous!"

In fact that is not what he said at all. The sounds he made were a sort of musical gurgling, quite unlike any other language I've ever heard. Yet somehow, I was able to also hear a second voice, as one whispering in my ear, and knew that it was a full and correct translation. Later, when I had leisure to consider, I concluded that the amulet must have allowed us to understand each other. At the moment, I was too preoccupied with confusion and panic to give the matter sober consideration.

The three mermen—for such indeed they were—were clad only in a rough hide belt that held various pouches for carrying things. The one who had addressed me was holding a short black staff topped with a glowing blue crystal that provided what little light there was. The other two, both younger and leaner, helped me out of the net. They were all of a robust complexion, with light brown skin not dissimilar to that found on their surface cousins. Each sported a fishtail that glistened like silver and emeralds.

I do not recall precisely what I said. I believe I babbled something about the ship and the captain and going for help. I daresay it cannot have been too coherent, but they at least understood that I was a surface dweller. This was worrying, as it seemed one of our kind had not appeared in their waters in this guise in quite a long time. They had a quick discussion a little further away in the cave where I could not hear, then returned and said I must go with them. They were fishermen, they explained, and had come to this place because large game was often to be had here. It was very fortunate that I had been caught by them, they explained, as the depths contained things that made the *ik'ua* (their name for the creature that had been pursuing me) seem quite harmless. In any case, if I truly was from the surface, they would need to take me to someone who could make some sort of decision about me, this being quite beyond their experience.

It transpired that the leader, Li'iuk, was a hunter. He was training his sons, Deru and Glossut, to follow in his footsteps (or rather, in his wake). He seemed oddly incurious as to who I was or where I had come from, choosing instead to chat amicably about his life and family. "Our family has been hunting in the pit for ages, snaring just about any creature you could name. I won't say we're the best, but I can't think of anybody better. Easier now that I got the boys to help me out. Usually my brother, Kiyo, comes with us, but he has business in the town."

"I see, sort of a family tradition?"

"Tradition, ya. We've been hunters ever since we moved down below. Longer, even. Fathers, sons, even the occasional daughter. My grandmama, she once killed a king shark by herself with only her knife. Pretty much everyone in the family has some part in hunting. Except for this one." He reached over and mussed the hair of the one named Deru. "Wants to go off and become a scribe, he does! Well, he's got the brains for it. From his mother, no doubt, hah!"

Seeing a possible opening, I interjected. "Since you came down below, you say? Dear me! How long ago was that?"

"Ah, let me see..." He screwed up his face in concentration, looking for all the world like my Papa when he had to do sums. "I believe...ah, it is too many. Hundreds of years, though, yes."

"Hundreds, you say? My word! And why did you all come down?"

I realized (admittedly rather late) that I had perhaps taken my enquiries too far. "I'm not sure I should talk about that. I mean, no disrespect to you, but if you are from up above, well...it's not really my decision to make, ya?"

I assured him that I quite understood and meant no offense by my questions. Deru, who up to that point had been particularly quiet, asked how a surface dweller had come to find herself in the pit and in the shape in which I now found myself. Picking my words with some care, I said that I was a sailor who had found the amulet on an abandoned island and had discovered its power quite by accident when I fell overboard. I added that I was now seeking assistance for my fellows who had been shipwrecked. The words were close enough to the truth without bringing in any details that might work against me. The boy seemed somewhat dubious concerning how I found the amulet but did not voice his doubts.

Scallywag!

The cave turned out to be a system of tunnels in the rock. Beacons made of the same blue crystal as the fisherman's torch marked the way, though it was clear that my escorts knew the way perfectly well. The journey back was not terribly long, somewhat less than an hour. The leisurely pace was welcome after my rush to escape the sea-beast. Along the way, Li'iuk did most of the talking, discoursing upon his family and some of the great hunts in which they had participated. It seemed to me he was avoiding any discussion of his people in general or their history, and I made a point not to press him on these subjects.

The tunnels had seemed to lead deeper into the sea, yet we emerged into an area almost as light as though we were just below the surface. Colorful sea-plants spread out on all sides of this large valley leading down to the city below. The buildings were most unusual, resembling nothing so much as giant shells, each uniquely ornate and shining with iridescent hues. I later learned that they were not so much built as cultivated. The merpeople had perfected the art of causing shells to grow to their desired size and shape, even with interior walls, windows, and so on. Many hundreds of such places were laid out before us. They appeared to be in no particular arrangement (there being no need of streets in such a place), but the overall effect, far from being cluttered, was one of perfect harmony.

Beyond the residences (for such they were), larger buildings and the occasional open area could be espied. These public areas were home to the marketplaces, artisans, and other such necessities of civilization. The city itself was populated with hundreds (if not thousands) of merpeople, swimming above, around, and through the different buildings as their business took them. Further, the valley was populated with life of all kinds. Fish of every size and color drifted lazily over the city, or grazed in the seabeds below. The effect was beyond anything I could ever have imagined. I can only apologize that my poor pen cannot truly convey the awe of that place. With no exaggeration, Reader, I tell you I was stunned into silence by the sheer beauty I saw.

Li'iuk must have noticed the effect the view had on me, for he stopped and watched me with an indulgent smile. "She a lovely place, ya?"

It was all I could do to nod my head. "It is magnificent."

He beamed. "Sure, it is a nice place to come home to. I tell you, we come home nights, when the lights are out, and it's just..." He trailed off and smiled.

"I've never seen anything like it," I said.

"Well, it's pretty nice for a fishing village, true. But if you think this is impressive, you should see the capitol."

"This is just a village?"

"Well, a big one, I won't deny. Though I wouldn't call it a city by any means." This of a place in which my hometown would have been lost.

As we approached the residences, he took us on a slight diversion. "Got to let the wife know what is happening, ya? Won't take long."

We arrived at a lovely, well-kempt home in the conch style, whereupon he excused himself and swam inside, leaving me with his two sons. I think we floated there for no more than a couple of minutes, though the awkwardness of the situation seemed to stretch it out rather longer. Presently, the father emerged, his wife behind him. She was a most handsome woman of middle age, her silvery hair tied up behind her head in an intricate braid. Like her husband and sons, she wore no clothing except some jewelry around her wrists and neck. The expression on her face seemed somewhat dubious, but as she swam up to us, she bowed her head courteously to me.

"Welcome to our home. I apologize for my husband's lack of hospitality. Do allow me to invite you to share our evening meal and the shelter of our home."

I returned her nod and thanked her for her generous offer but explained that I was on a mission of some importance and could not tarry. To her credit, she did a quite passable job of hiding her relief, only stating that she understood and hoped I should call again when I was on less urgent business. These formalities concluded, we resumed our journey.

As we swam toward the middle of the town, we were joined by others heading in the same general direction. From time to time one would exchange greetings with my escort, but overall very little attention was paid to us. As we went along, I noticed that the travelers organized themselves into a sort of informal shoal, very much like the fish that swam around us. There were perhaps one or two dozen of us from one moment to the next, and in all that time, they moved with grace and ease, moving in and out of the group without the slightest difficulty. I confess I felt somewhat clumsy compared to the rest, but I stayed close to our little group and managed not to collide with anybody.

Presently, we broke off and headed toward a larger structure, clearly some kind of government building. I know not how it is so, but somehow one can always tell. I expect, if one day we travel to the moon and explore the wonders there, one will immediately be able to spot the place where the moon-men go to pay their taxes. No matter what fantastical shape such structures may take, somehow one just knows.

Inside was somewhat plain but still rather elegant, with various merfolk darting back and forth on one errand or another. My guide had a word with someone at the front, and we were asked to wait. A few minutes later, we were ushered into a large chamber at the center of the structure. Inside were clusters of merfolk. Some spoke in hushed voices, some waited with slates of polished mother-of-pearl. Some few with sashes around their waists moved from group to group and seemed to be generally in charge of keeping things moving. One of these greeted us at the entrance and ushered us to the back of the room.

Five merpeople sat in scallop chairs, watching the activity in the rest of the room. These were mounted on the inside of what appeared to be a giant oyster, the top shell opened out behind them. We were ushered forward, and the red-sashed merman announced us as "Li'iuk of the clan Eowa and sons, also one guest from Above." This caused a murmur of sensation from those listening, which did nothing to alleviate my discomfort. My escorts bowed before the five. In my fumbling nervousness, I essayed a curtsey. Realizing I was not in any way equipped to carry one off at present, I turned it into a presentable, if not entirely graceful, bow.

In the center of the group was an older woman, evidently the one in charge. She raised a hand and beckoned me forward. "Speak, stranger," she said, "and tell us what business brings you here."

I explained to them about my shipwrecked comrades, and how I was seeking to get somewhere where I could send help for them. They listened quietly without interruption until I was done. If they had doubts about my story, they did not express them. When I was done, the old woman fixed me with a long look. "And for this, you have come to seek us out?"

"Actually, ma'am, I had hoped to find my way to one of our settlements up above and arrange for a rescue." It seemed like the safest tack to take.

"I see. Fair enough. But it doesn't explain where you got that amulet. I was not aware that they were still in circulation on the surface."

"Oh no, madam, they are not," I said. "I found this one on an abandoned island."

One of the others leaned forward. He was not quite so old as the woman, but quite thin with a fringe of hair around his balding head. "What island was this, then?"

I told them of the abandoned place we had found, and the sights that greeted us within. As I told the story, the listeners grew increasingly agitated, and even the five seemed, if not alarmed, then thoroughly surprised. When I finished explaining how I had discovered the amulet's ability by falling overboard, they finally broke the silence.

"That island," said the balding one. "Do you know the history of it? Do you have any understanding of what happened there?"

I shook my head. "At first we thought it was one tribe making war on another, but it was...different. Like an extermination."

He nodded solemnly. "Very like an extermination," he said. "The figure you saw on the throne. It was still impaled, was it? Still six spears in it?"

"Yes, sir."

There was, if not a complete release of the tension in the room, then certainly a lessening. "I see. Thank you." The older woman turned to the others. "Anyone else, questions?"

A brief pause ensued that no one sought to fill. "Very well." She turned to me. "Wait here." She knocked twice on the back of her scallop-seat, and the large oyster shell closed itself slowly over them until they were entirely hidden from sight. I leaned close to Li'iuk. "Here, what's going on?" I whispered.

"They're deciding what to do," he whispered back. "That's so they can converse in private. Don't worry. They don't generally take too long."

That was not what I was worrying about, but I didn't say so.

In fact, it wasn't much more than a minute later when the shell opened again. The merwoman floated up from her seat and addressed me. "Stranger, we are willing to accept your explanation but fear there is little we can do to be of assistance to you. We have labored mightily since coming down here to avoid all contact with the ones who live Above. You must understand your presence is...complicated. For this reason, it is our decision that you are to be taken to the capitol with all due dispatch. Li'iuk, thank you for your help. You and your sons may leave."

The last I saw of them was a trio of red-sashes escorting them politely, but firmly, out of the chamber. Two others arrived on either side of me, and I was taken away from that place.

Chapter Twenty-Five

I EXPECT WE ALL have, at one time or another, experienced the sensation of waking up in a strange place and the momentary disorientation that it brings. One lies there, drowsy and half-awake, then suddenly the unfamiliar setting jolts one awake, while the mind races to reconstruct its memories. It was just such an awakening I experienced several hours later upon finding myself in a darkened place, stretched out upon a marvelously comfortable bed.

The memories of the previous day returned with speed, though I had to lie a moment to determine whether or not they were just a particularly vivid dream. As I looked about, the darkness resolved into dim yet familiar shapes. I was in the fore of a large cone-shaped shell on a bed of soft moss with a delicately woven sleeping net holding me in place. The cabin (if I may call it that) was small and sparsely appointed but quite comfortable for all that. I noted a curtain for privacy and a small hole for making one's toilet (it being considered most impolite to do so indoors). I recalled the carriage shell, a kind of underwater palanquin drawn by dolphins fore and aft, that brought me to the capitol of the merpeople, along with a clerk and a brace of guards. They said that the guards were for our protection, though I noticed they did not say from what.

It had been somewhat late in the afternoon, by my best reckoning, when we boarded the thing. The size of a small schooner, the vessel had a few small cabins and a common area open to the sea. My escorts and I watched as the dolphins were hitched in place and given their instructions. I made a joke about how I thought that they would use seahorses, which was met with looks of confusion. The clerk, a rather serious young man named Shuu, explained to me that seahorses lacked either the size or intelligence for such a task.

I didn't attempt any jokes after that.

Still, the journey had proven quite pleasant. Dinner had been some variety of fish unfamiliar to me, uncooked but prepared with some strange yet delicious herbs. The bed in the cabin proved enormously comfortable indeed, which was just as well. Given the day I'd had, I was more than ready to retire.

Some conversation occurred between myself and the clerk in the evening. Shuu was polite but somewhat formal. The guards didn't seem in a sociable mood and kept to themselves the whole time. But then, I've never known guards to be great conversationalists.

Having completed my morning ablutions (there was no soap, but a pumice-like stone one could rub on one's skin), I exited the cabin to find I was just in time for breakfast. More fish of course, along with a curious jellylike roe. This latter was a bit salty for my taste, but I had some to be polite. The clerk said that we should be arriving at the capitol before very long and I would be taken directly to an audience with the king.

The rest of the journey consisted of him giving me very detailed instructions on the etiquette of addressing royalty. Readers with ambitions in that direction might do well to consider the sheer volume of etiquette involved, to say nothing of the number of ways that things may go wrong. I shall spare you the details. However, for the ambitious reader, I believe I may summarize the salient points.

- Do not speak, approach, touch, or think anything unless told to do so.
- End everything you say with "Your Majesty."
- When in doubt, bow.

By the time we were approaching the capitol, I had undergone a considerable amount of lecturing on the finer points of these rules, with the result that I was quite thoroughly unnerved. Nevertheless, on the clerk's recommendation, we trooped up to the open space at the top so that we could see the city as we arrived.

The wonder that the fisherman's village instilled upon me only partially prepared me for the sight of the capitol of the merpeople. It was like six of those same villages all in a circle, with a grander city right in the middle. This was the capitol proper, a cascade of milky-white shells connected by a series of large, transparent tunnels, through which streamed a constant traffic of merfolk. They were everywhere, swimming in and out of the various sections of the city, or riding in a variety of vehicles. The small ones were farm carts by the look of them, generally with one or two large fish hauling them along. Open-topped ones carried many people at once, hauled by teams of dolphins not unlike ours. As we approached the city, a shadow passed over us. I looked up in time to see a whale, and upon its back an ornate structure, all red and gold like the elephant howdahs they have in the East Indies. Even the clerk, used as he was to the ways of the good and fine, was visibly impressed.

"Who does that belong to?" I asked, but he merely shook his head. "I have no idea," he said, "but they must be very important indeed."

As the behemoth made its stately way toward one of the more opulent areas of the city, we turned our attention to our destination. It was then that I first caught sight of the palace.

The magnificent structure, all in mother-of-pearl, stood in the very center of the town, cultivated in an order of magnitude with more skill and grace than I had hitherto seen. Great spires with twisting tops surrounded on all sides the main structure, a titanic sphere that tapered to a delicate point, the whole covered bottom to top in delicate filigree. Every surface of the palace caught the light and reflected different colors, as the light shifted through the play of the water. The never-ending display would have set even the hardest heart into rapture.

I don't know how long I remained there, just staring in awe. Finally, I was taken out of my reverie by the sound of one of the guards calling instructions to the dolphin team. They banked to the right and began to descend toward the seafloor. Shuu had been watching me this whole time and smiled. "It is rather good, isn't it? I've only been a few times myself, but it never ceases to impress."

I managed to nod. "It's the most amazing thing I have ever seen."

This remark clearly pleased him. "They started cultivating the palace when we first came down here. I hear it took almost fifty years to achieve this magnificent state. My great-grandfather says he can recall when the structure was not much larger than our town hall, if you can believe that."

"Amazing." I shook my head, overwhelmed by it all. I even managed to forget the urgency of my errand, if only for a few moments.

By this time, we were coming in close to the castle proper. Our team brought us into a tunnel that had been hollowed out into the ground. This led into a great open space that was full of merfolk and various modes of transportation, all with at least one sea creature to carry them. It was clear, even to a stranger such as myself, that these were particularly fine conveyances, akin to what one might see with a nobleman or wealthy merchant. Like their above-ground counterparts, the carriages were generally ornate, with bits of embellishments and filigree all about. We came to rest in an unoccupied area, whereupon several merfolk rushed forward to escort us from the shell and see to the dolphins.

We were escorted through myriad hallways and chambers until we arrived at an opulent waiting room. This was where petitioners waited to be allowed into the king's presence. I must say, the sheer number of people present was somewhat unnerving. Most were affluent and decked with fine jewelry, though some were of a plainer appearance. My clerk went off to have a word with the officials in charge. After a surprisingly short time, he returned to inform us that we had been bumped up (as he put it) on the list and would be before His Majesty soon.

I will admit that I was somewhat relieved that we would not be sitting there all day. Nevertheless, my stomach was in knots as we waited. Shuu, noting my nerves, tried to reassure me. "Don't worry. The king is no tyrant, I assure you. In any case, I shall do most of the talking. Just remember what I told you, when in doubt—"

"I know, bow."

He chuckled. "A fast learner. You should do well." A brace of guards approached, each wearing a red sash like their counterparts back at the fishing village, though these were considerably more ornate. One moved forward and bowed.

"His Majesty will see you now."

I suppose I must have been expecting something rather like the council room in the village, though obviously on a grander scale. The reality was frankly beyond anything I could have imagined, as if someone had sought to replicate the grandeur of the sea indoors. The interior walls were covered with intricately detailed murals showing a majestic spread of ocean, filled with sea life of all kinds bathed by sunbeams. By some trick of art, they had managed to make it appear as if the light was shifting with the movement of waves up above. From time to time, a painted fish scale would catch the light and gleam. The illusion was aided by shoals of creatures who swam about freely in the upper reaches of the chamber, including (of all things) a pair of whales and their calf.

The rest was laid out like a pleasure garden, complete with a variety of topiaries, and sea flowers, and corals grown into intricate shapes and festooned with astounding beauty. In the center of it all, a magnificent pagoda, open on all four sides, held the court proper. And what a court it was! A few dozen all told were present, between the various functionaries, messengers, ladies-in-waiting, lords of this and that, and heaven only knows what else. And at the very center of it all, the king himself.

Scallywag!

The king reclined on his titanic shell throne, a masterpiece of gold and what looked for all the world like red velvet. It was not quite as large as the shell which the five council members had used for privacy, but more than enough room for company. Indeed, a few mermaids flanked either side of him, holding refreshments or fans, or just looking ornamental.

The king was a portly fellow, larger than the other mercreatures around us. His tail was black and sleek. When it caught the light, there was no hint of scales but instead a uniform, glossy slickness, like tar. His black hair was sculpted into an intricately woven structure that must have taken ages to complete. He looked to be about middle age by my reckoning, with a meticulously trimmed mustache and a face that arrested one's attention. There was a quality about him—something in the eyes, perhaps, or the set of the jaw—but if you saw him walking down the street back home, you would immediately know he was a person of considerable importance and yield the way to him almost unthinkingly. His face bespoke absolute authority.

The two functionaries who had escorted us to the throne room brought us to a smallish pavilion before the main structure and made signs for us to stay. One floated forward and announced, "King Ulanu Bas Yalanakan, Beloved of the Sea Goddess, Ruler of the Blue Waters, we present the petitioner Molly Donnelly McCormick, who has come from the surface world to beg aid of the mighty An'ui!"

This caused a sensation. I do not know if the reader has ever been in a room with several conversations going on at once, and suddenly the room becomes silent. A most disorienting sensation, particularly when one is the reason for the silence occurring! Nevertheless, I pulled myself together and bowed like I had been taught. I heard the susurration in the room begin anew, though now in an altogether more animated mode.

"You may rise." When I looked up, the king was regarding me with a languid eye. His facial expression had not noticeably changed, yet I felt certain that I had his full attention. He nodded to an attendant, who raised an arm to me. "You may speak."

"Your Majesty, I—"

"*You!*"

And there she was. The same moon-white hair was now done up in an ornate style and affixed with rather more silver jewelry than I remembered. Still, I had no doubt in my mind. This was the same mergirl I had seen on the day of that fateful storm. She left the cluster of other girls who had been lounging to one side of the throne and floated tentatively in my direction.

The king arched an eyebrow in mild surprise. "Itaska, you know this person?"

She turned back to him and bowed. "Apologies, father. I believe I do know them, though I only saw them once and that briefly." She turned back to me. "That is, if I am not mistaken?"

I nodded. "The storm, yes. I fell overboard. I thought I was done for, but then the amulet...and you came along and...well, yes." I smiled, remembering to add a quick bow. "I do remember you very well."

She returned the smile in a way that made me feel quite warm and almost forget I was supposed to be petitioning the king. "As do I. It is good to see you survived."

A soft chuckling noise came from the king, who had leaned forward the better to watch the exchange. "Well, now. This is an interesting thing, yes." He signaled to an attendant. "How many more petitioners today?"

"Twenty-two, Your Majesty."

"Ah, well. We cannot keep them waiting. Escort our surface friend and her party to the guest areas." He leaned back. "I think this matter is better taken up in private."

Chapter Twenty-Six

IT WAS RATHER SOME time before our audience with His Majesty was granted. I suppose it is no surprise that a king's schedule is a very busy one indeed. In any case, it was well into the afternoon before we were escorted into the private residence of the royal family. The king was relaxing in a comfortable room, on an array of cushions, with his various wives and children fanned out on either side of him. A mermaid in the corner was playing something pleasant but unobtrusive on a lyre, and servants were present to ensure everyone had refreshments to hand. The atmosphere was certainly more relaxed than in the throne room. Shuu had explained to me that being invited to a private audience like this was a considerable honor. In theory, this was an informal audience, in so much as there is any such thing as a truly informal audience with someone who could have you put to death.

He listened patiently while I narrated the history of my finding the amulet, my accidental discovery of its powers (and meeting his daughter Itaska in the process), and how the men from the British West Indies Company had forced us to retrieve that conch from the ghost ship, only to betray us afterward. There was something of a sensation in the room when I explained about the shell. King Ulana seemed particularly interested and had me give every detail I could about what transpired on the ship. When I finished, he sat for a long moment, regarding me with a deep, penetrating gaze. It felt like I was a puzzle, and he was taking me apart and turning over each piece in his mind. At last, after a seemingly interminable amount of time, he spoke.

"The conch," he said. "Do you know any more about it? Than what you have said already, I mean?"

I searched my mind, trying to dredge up any little morsel I hadn't mentioned. "There was…let me see…yes, when we were on the ship, the ghost crew. They wanted us to join them. They called it the Horn of…Aza…something?"

"Azatot."

"That, yes. Thank you, Your Majesty. They said something about playing my part and all would be made right. Search me what that was all about."

"This voice you mentioned. It didn't tell you the nature of the horn?"

"Not as such, Your Majesty, no. It showed me some images, which I believe to be of its history, but I confess I didn't understand much. Only that it was very important."

He nodded. "Well, that is true enough, yes." He drummed his fingers on his fishtail, gazing at me for another long moment. "Well. I think we may be able to help each other, Molly of the tribe McCormick. There are ships above that are…" he waved a hand vaguely. "Lost. Abandoned. Fit for use, though without crew anymore. I can have my people find one for you and your fellows. In return, you must do me a favor as well. Or rather, two."

I bowed. "I am at your service, Your Majesty."

"Very well. The second task, I think, is best left for after you have completed the first. So then, to explain what is required, I must first tell you something of our history. We are the An'ui, children of Yalanakan who rules the sea. Many, many generations gone we were like you, walking on land and knowing nothing of the mysteries of the Blue Waters. One day, a hero called J'ya had a vision from Yalanakan herself. She told him our people had been chosen for a special purpose and that she was going to take us into her bosom, the very Blue Waters themselves, where we would live in joy and contentment forever.

"She gave him the first amulet, that which allowed him to live below, and with it the secret of how to make more. Individuals, families, then whole tribes followed him below, many returning to the land to fetch their loved ones and tell them of the glories of the sea. Some few of our people did not come, of course, but remained on our little island and continued to trade with the other islands around.

"Unfortunately, not all of them were peaceful. It soon became apparent that our numbers were dwindling—on land, at any rate. Another tribe, whose name I shall not speak, decided this provided an opportunity for them. One night, they swept over our old home and carried away every man, woman, and child.

"It did not take long for us to discover what had happened. We tracked them to their home, the selfsame island upon which you found your amulet. There we found they had struck a bargain with…" He hesitated. "Well, I trust you noticed the curious shape of the place, yes?"

"Like a giant bowl, Your Majesty?"

"Indeed so. It was once the peak of a mighty volcano, long dead but with entrances penetrating the depths. No doubt you saw the one in the temple. There are…things down there. They live far below, even below the surface of the sea. These people, in their arrogance, had allied with them. They received unholy powers by which they might enslave all others around them. In exchange, they provided sacrifices and…other things."

"Other things, Your Majesty?"

"I will not speak of them. Know only that a great battle took place, in which we were joined by most of the neighboring peoples. In time, we did vanquish them, though in the process we lost many of our own. We put a seal on the place, destroyed everything we could, and from that time, the island was forbidden to all.

"Once the battle was done, we desired not to resurrect the memories of the surface world. We spent much of our time building our new homes here. Thus, no attention was paid to our history for a very long time. Two generations ago, one of our greatest scholars discovered that some of our precious records, indeed, the entire written history of our people, may yet exist.

"It seems that, when the first attack happened, some of our scholars sought to hide the records so they would not be taken away. One of them survived the attack and went on to join us in the great battle against those fiends. According to the account given by his fellow soldier, that scholar was fatally wounded. Before he died, he revealed the location to this soldier and made him promise to tell others.

"Sadly, this knowledge was not acted upon and eventually fell by the wayside. Naturally, upon its rediscovery, a great desire was borne in us to retrieve these most precious histories. Unfortunately, this has proved to be impossible."

"Why is that?"

"The gift of the amulet is more than you know. You have noticed none of our people are wearing amulets, yes? This is because every child conceived under their influence would receive the gift from birth. As would their children and so on. The difficulty, however, is that there is no changing back. Indeed, for us, there is no back. We simply are." He swept his arms around the room. "By the time our people understood this truth, no one was left of that original first generation, and we had long cut off contact with the surfacers."

"I understand. And you wish me to fetch these histories for you?"

"Precisely. I propose that my guards will escort you to the site of our old island. You go onto the land, thence to the hiding place described in the soldier's account, retrieve the histories, and bring them back to us.

You do this, and it will be a great boon to our people, for which you will have our eternal gratitude. And of course, we will find you a nice ship." He smiled. "I will even have it delivered to your crew, if you like."

I bowed again. "Your Majesty is most generous," I said. "Is there any danger I should be aware of?"

"Difficult to say. Those of the neighboring islands know our history and leave it alone. It is too small for anyone else to take an interest. That being said, one never knows what creatures have taken up residence since our time. A natural cave is located underneath the island, with an entrance near the center of the town. We will ensure you have proper directions. I'm sure a map can be arranged. No doubt the place is not what it once was, but you should be able to find your way around."

"I see. Anything else I should know?"

"Well, the records are believed to be quite extensive, so we don't know how many there will be. It may take more than one trip. Hard to say."

"Do you think they will be all right after all these years, if you don't mind me asking?"

The king laughed. "It will be well. The skins and inks they used are made to last for hundreds of generations. Even taking them down here should not have any effect."

"Well," I said, remembering to bow again, "it all sounds very straightforward, Your Majesty. I would be happy to perform this task for you."

He smiled. "Excellent." He raised a hand, and two servants appeared by my side. "You shall be our guest at the palace tonight, then set off in the morning. This is acceptable?"

"Very much so, Your Majesty."

"Good." He rubbed his hands together in anticipation. "This will be a fine thing indeed. With any luck, you should be back in time for supper. In and out, easy as anything."

I should have known right then it wouldn't be as easy as all that.

Later that evening, having dined on some superbly prepared delicacies (heavy may be the head that wears the crown, but it does have its compensations), I was relaxing in the guest quarters provided to me within the palace. My escorts had already departed for home, their duty done. I found myself somewhat at a loose end. A balcony was in my room, and I was relaxing there, watching the busy life of the sea all around me. I contemplated the things that had happened over the day and the mission the morrow would bring.

This turned my thoughts toward my friends and shipmates, still stuck on that island, like as not. If something had happened to them, there was no way for me to even know, let alone intervene. My mind briefly flashed before me scenarios of horror, returning in triumph only to find them all gone, or worse...dead. I shook such intrusive thoughts from my consciousness and reminded myself that the crew was sea-wise and highly competent. Several had knowledge of foraging, &c. I was quite settled in my mind that they were more than capable of taking care of themselves, though my heart and gut remained distinctly unconvinced.

It was while I was in this pensive state of mind that a knock came at my door. One of the red-sashed servants bowed and informed me that I had been granted an audience with Princess Itaska, and would I kindly follow him. I was surprised, to say the least. Of course, when royalty calls, one responds promptly. We went along naturally curving corridors, all bathed in pearlescent light and graceful beyond description. Eventually, I was ushered into a small but daintily appointed receiving room and instructed to wait. I felt quite self-conscious and wished I'd had the opportunity to brush my hair out, however one went about doing that underwater.

Presently, her highness was announced, and she glided in all grace and serenity. For a moment it seemed she was propelled forward without any sort of movement upon her part. Closer observation revealed the slightest undulation of her tailfins. For myself, who still needed practice in stopping before rebounding off nearby walls, her movement was as impressive as it was beautiful. Her hair was freed from its elaborate construct and now hung in back of her, constrained by a series of bejeweled clasps. She was clad (inasmuch as any of her people ever were) in a few simple bracelets and other accoutrements, with pearls being the defining feature. I had almost grown accustomed to the nakedness of the merpeople, but seeing her again was...bewitching. I could well believe the stories of sirens luring unfortunate sailors to their deaths.

The red-sashed merman moved forward and bowed, and I recovered myself enough to do likewise. "Your Highness," he announced, "I present Molly McCormick."

"Rise." The attendant did so, whereupon the princess gestured to a nearby couch. "Please, have a seat." She gave a hand signal that told her entourage and the attendant to vacate the room. One elderly merwoman remained, sitting in the corner with her gaze fixed on the two of us. The princess smiled. "My duenna," she explained. "Pay her no mind. She is merely here to make sure nothing untoward happens."

I nodded and moved to the couch. "Yes, Your Highness." I seated myself and tried to untense. "How may I help you?"

She smiled, sitting across from me. "You may dispense with the formalities. Just call me Itaska." She curled up in her seat, a large half-sphere that looked like a giant pearl hollowed out and lined with pillows. "I thought we might talk a bit. I've always rather wondered about you since that day, you know. I've only ever heard of the surface world secondhand, and generally from generations long past. I would like you to tell me of life on the surface, what it is like where you grew up, all that sort of thing." She stopped, giggling at her eagerness. "I'm sorry. I'm not asking for your life story, honestly. But whatever you would be willing to share, I would appreciate."

So I told her of Ireland, of the lush green countryside and the village where I was born and raised. I spoke of my family and the little shop we had. She laughed as I described how I used to go tromping through the woods to drag my little brothers back home and listened rapt as I described the port and the ships and crew of all nations that came through the place.

Inevitably, she asked why I had come out to sea in the first place. I was hesitant, as the reader may imagine. She being a princess and all, it seemed to me the best thing was to tell her the truth. I told her of Mr. Hennessy, and the bargain my parents had made with him. When I told her how I had run away instead of marrying him, she nodded, her eyes downcast.

"Alas, this I can well understand. It is a comfortable enough life being a princess, but part of it is that you will eventually be married off to someone to seal some alliance or other. I'll likely wind up with one of the noble families or the son of some rich merchant. I wish I could get away from it, you know. It would be so...*freeing*, you see? But I am a princess, and that means I have a duty." She shrugged and trailed off, looking quite melancholy.

I searched my mind for some word of comfort, but I could think of nothing to say. After a long moment of silence, she collected herself and rose. "Well, I have kept you long enough. You have a long journey ahead of you in the morrow, so I shall wish you the fairest currents in your endeavour."

I rose as well. "Thank you, Your Highness."

She rang a small bell by her side. The attendant from before materialized at my side as if by magic. "Thank you for indulging my curiosity, Miss McCormick," the princess said. "Perhaps when you return, we might…talk more?"

I bowed low. "I would like that very much."

She smiled, just a little. "So would I." With that, she turned to leave, duenna in tow.

Chapter Twenty-Seven

WE SET OUT EARLY in the morning, insofar as I could tell. Day and night tended to blend somewhat in the depths, but as the chariot with myself and two guards departed, the city had the air of a town getting ready for the day. The dolphins who pulled us were nimble and swift, and we soon left the city behind. I was traveling light, bearing only my knife and a satchel with the map, some supplies, and a bit of shimmering green cloth I could use for a toga when I got to the island. The reader will smile, but though I had gotten rather accustomed to being unclothed below the sea, the idea of walking around in that state on land was quite out of the question.

The journey took a couple of hours by my reckoning, the most of which were spent in silence. The younger of the two guards, being somewhat curious, asked a few questions about the world above the waves. These conversational attempts did not last very long, as they were both obviously uncomfortable with the thought of our destination. It seemed the land was as mysterious and unnerving for them as the depths of the sea for my own people. I remember smiling at the guards and telling them to cheer up. They weren't the ones having to go ashore, but this seemed cold comfort at best.

The deep blue around us softly brightened, and shafts of sunlight filtered through the waves. I felt a thrill of excitement as we came into shallower waters, even as my escorts became increasingly unnerved. We arrived at a small cove nearly overgrown with coral, the waves rippling no more than ten feet above us. The guards set anchor while I prepared myself. Donning the garment and readying my knife, I swam up toward the surface.

There was a moment of sickness as I breached the surface of the water. The transformation back was not a smooth one. I was still coughing up seawater as I staggered onto the beach, where I promptly collapsed. So used had I gotten to the natural buoyancy of the sea that, once ashore, it felt like I was carrying a great weight upon my back, and my legs seemed to have forgotten how to walk.

The map was simple but quite adequate to lead me from the bay to what was left of the village. Nature had done her work. Years of accumulated growth encroached on the path, and stone circles were all

Scallywag!

that remained of the huts. The village had almost been completely engulfed by the surrounding woods. This made the going a bit harder than I had anticipated, but eventually I managed to climb over and around until I arrived at my destination.

A wide open space showed where the center of the town must have once stood. The trees here were younger, nature's conquest of the spot not yet complete. A creek, now little more than a trickle, meandered through the area. Long ago, it seemed, they had routed it into a canal, though with time and neglect, it was little more than a ditch. Still, I was able to follow it upstream to the small cave mouth from which the water emerged. I had to crawl in on my hands and knees. Happily, once I got round the first bend, the space opened up so that I could walk, even if at a crouch.

The palace had thoughtfully provided me with a sort of lanthorn, which was a glassy jar containing a luminous jellyfish. It's eerie blue light cast around the cave as I held it aloft and followed the stream back to its source. I could not help but imagine those poor scholars scrambling through the dark, hauling the scrolls through that tiny entrance, and all the while listening for the sounds of attack.

I had gone perhaps two hundred feet into the cave when I heard a noise. Something ahead snorted in a raspy, husky manner. I put down my things and prepared my knife, creeping forward as silently as I was able.

There was another turn up ahead. Whatever was making the noise seemed to be right around the corner. I dropped to a crouch and inched forward, knife at the ready, until I got to the bend in the tunnel. Behind me, the lamp cast a dim blue light upon the far wall. I kept to the side as best I could. Even so, the movement of my shadow against the wall must have been apparent. Still, whatever creature it was carried on as before, snuffling to itself in a manner unconcerned, insofar as I was able to tell.

I risked a peek around the corner. Carved into the back wall of the cave, just above where a stream of water came out through the cracks, was a small hutch filled with what appeared to be rolled-up scraps of leather. Between myself and these, a large white creature lay worrying at some sort of small animal corpse. It was shaped like a lizard, though larger than any I'd ever seen. Indeed, it was like a mastiff in size, and all muscle. As I watched, it turned its head just enough for me to catch a glimpse of an eye. Milky white it was, with no sign of a pupil whatever. I recalled tales I'd heard of creatures that lived forever in the dark, and grew pale and blind, only being able to hunt by sound and by smell.

The import of this last point had only just enough time to impress itself upon me before the creature reared up, sniffing at the air. Emitting a low, throaty growl, it swung its head to and fro. I cursed my ill luck but knew the thing would have to be dealt with. I held as still as I could and tightened my grip around the knife.

The white beast came snuffling forward, nose in the air and its muzzle barely open, just enough to reveal two rows of very sharp teeth. I held my breath as it got closer still. When I saw its muscles tense, I braced myself and said a silent prayer to St. Hubert.

The beast leapt, and I thrust my dagger forward to meet it. The blade struck home right at the throat, causing red blood to burst forth across the white flesh. The thing raked its foreclaws at me, the left one catching my cheek and giving me the scar I wear to this day. Screaming, I pitched the creature to one side until it came off my knife. Before it could recover itself, I leapt upon its back and began to stab at it again and again.

The creature thrashed wildly about in its attempts to dislodge me, but I wrapped my legs around its torso and hung on tight. It raked at my legs with its hind-claws, but it was apparent that the greater part of its strength and power were to the fore. I had no alternative but to hang on and keep at the thing until either it fell or I did. I managed to get my other arm crooked around the beast's neck and brought my legs forward as much as I could. The damnable thing was still clawing at them while it thrashed about but could do little more than scratch.

I stabbed the beast again and again, hanging on hard as it tried to throw me off. Its leathery hide was tough and took my blade only reluctantly, so that I had to settle for just breaking the skin. The creature soon sported a few dozen narrow slits from which blood trickled black in the sapphire light. By now the creature was growing desperate and began throwing itself against the cave walls in an effort to dislodge me. I managed to hold on, for all it bumped and scraped me about.

It seemed to me the thing was starting to tire, but then so was I, and quickly. I could feel my strength flagging as the fight wore on, and my legs, now numb, were beginning to lose their grip. One way or another, the fight was soon to end.

I made to bring the knife once more to its throat, but timed it poorly, for the creature was just coming down from another jump. It hit my blade crossways, and the handle, now covered in gore, slipped out of my grasp.

I snatched at it in midair but was too late. It clattered to the ground out of reach. I screamed in rage, whereupon the beast bellowed as if in pain and staggered to one side. I was correct in thinking its hearing and smell were most sensitive. Loud noises were probably especially hurtful. I could not spy anything that one would call an ear, but nevertheless I put my mouth as close to where I assumed it would be and let forth the loudest, most high-pitched scream I could muster.

    The effect was immediate. The beast spasmed, flailing away from the sound and sending a foreclaw up in an attempt to bat me away. Happily, the creature was not equipped with the flexibility to reach back that far, it being dependent upon attacking prey from the front. I was able to easily dodge the claw and send another scream at its opposite side. The beast, quite out of sorts by this point, lashed out with its foreleg, hitting the nearby wall and causing it to stumble and land hard on its side.

    I managed to hang on, despite having the wind knocked quite out of me. The beast was struggling to right itself, and I searched around wildly for anything that might turn the advantage. My knife was still where it had hit the ground a few feet away. For a moment, I considered jumping for it. That would have meant dismounting from the beast and trusting my speed, something about which I felt no confidence in my present condition. Besides, my leg was still pinned under the creature. I wasn't going anywhere until the beast was upright.

    Just out of my reach, I espied a fist-sized rock among the rubble of the cave floor. It was a little away from the water and had not been subjected to the wearing down of those stones in the stream itself. By shifting my body weight suddenly, I spoiled the creature's attempt to right itself. It fell close enough that I was able to grasp the jagged rock.

    I brought it down hard upon the creature's head, not really caring where it landed, thinking to club the thing insensible if nothing else. What I was not expecting was for it to fall back, screeching and flailing about in agony. My blow had fallen right onto one of its dead eyes. The end of the rock tapered to a rough point, not enough to serve as any sort of blade, but certainly enough to pierce the tender eye-stuff. Moving quickly, I brought the stone down upon the other eye as well.

    The animal's movements became erratic, its attack attempts halfhearted. I could feel the thing breathing raggedly beneath me and determined to press my advantage. I brought the stone down upon the creature's head again and again. My arms, bloody and bruised as they were, were sore to the point of insensibility, but I pushed myself to carry on. It tried once more to knock me off but could not gather the necessary momentum. At last, it staggered to one side and collapsed.

The bloodied beast lay there on the cavern floor, panting, its legs raking aimlessly against the air. I moved to disentangle myself but found the d—d thing had my leg pinned down. I had to press my other foot against its back and rock it back and forth, inching my leg out a little more each time. When at last my foot came free, I allowed myself a short moment of rest before scrambling to my feet and looking about for my knife. I was rather the worse for wear as I staggered around the prone creature, but managed to retrieve the blade and wipe the handle off on my considerably deteriorated tunic.

Behind me, the creature lay where it had fallen, its breathing increasingly erratic. For a moment I thought to leave it thus, but t'would not be honorable to take my prize and leave the beast to slowly expire in the dark. I approached the creature, moving slowly and keeping my eyes open for any last attempt it may make upon me. It only lay there, its chest rising and falling as it slowly bled out.

It must have sensed my presence, for it turned its head to face mine. How it managed to do so I could not say, but somehow, I understood it was no mere chance. The creature moved its foreleg with some difficulty, resting a claw against a small hollow in its throat. It opened its mouth, a pool of blood and saliva spilling out onto the cave floor and mixing with the stream as I closed in...

My escorts were understandably more than a little perturbed when at last I returned, all blood and bruises and dragging behind me the sack of scrolls. As soon as I hit the water, they guided me back to the chariot and steered me to the back to rest. I was so worn down from pain and exhaustion that I didn't even notice when I transformed back into mermaid form. One of the guards took out a jar of salve, which she industriously applied to my wounds, while the other retrieved the sack and gave its contents a careful inspection. I was not, in my present state, in any condition to answer their myriad questions, so I just told them that the cave had been occupied and left it at that. Happily, they did not press for details, and I was allowed to rest as we made the journey back.

The salve did a remarkably quick job on my wounds, closing them up and stopping the bleeding, but did little to alleviate the pain. I spent the majority of the trip trying to rest but unable to stop thinking of the creature in the cave. It had offered no resistance as I moved in to give the killing blow. The spot it had indicated took my blade easily, and the blood had flowed freely from the expiring beast.

Reader, I have told no one this before. As I pulled away the knife, it raised its head to my ear and murmured something. The sound was nothing I could understand, heaven only knows where it came from, but I will swear before my G—d and Poseidon both, *those were no mere animal sounds, but words of an unknown tongue.*

Chapter Twenty-Eight

IT WAS IN A rather worse-for-wear state that I arrived back at the capitol that evening. The two guards escorted me to the royal residence where I had some time to refresh and compose myself before being summoned into His Majesty's presence. I had done the best I could with myself, but I have no doubt that those present could tell what a time I'd had of it, even if the guards had not reported as such. Itaska let out a little gasp upon seeing me, which (if I am honest) gave me the tiniest bit of pleasure that she would be affected so. It is probably not to my credit, but I am set to write the truth here, and so I shall. I even flashed her the briefest little smile before approaching the king and bowing before him.

    He was reclining in the same seat as in our previous meeting, but now a table had been brought for him, and the recovered scrolls spread out. He looked up from one as I approached and returned my bow with a gracious nod. "Ah, our surface born adventurer returns! Very well done! I was just reading of the first treaty between our people and some neighboring islands during the reign of Ukyumuk the Second. A most fascinating account." He rubbed his hands together with glee. "Oh, yes. A fine treasure indeed! But I understand it was not so easily taken?"

    I proceeded to relate the tale of the creature I had encountered in the cave and the fight that ensued. It was somewhat embarrassing, being put on the spot and all. The king asked for the particulars. I told him of the creature's size, its teeth, and what eventually amounted to a blow-by-blow recitation of the entire ordeal. I have never been of a boastful nature, and standing there relating the matter in such detail was rather off-putting, if I may be honest. The one compensation was seeing the effect my tale had upon the princess. She was thoroughly absorbed by my narrative. She clung to the arm of her duenna and did not let go until the tale was finished.

    The king nodded solemnly. "Well, I must say, it is a remarkable job you have done. I would also apologize for the situation in which you found yourself. Please understand that we had no idea the hiding place would be occupied, let alone by such a creature as you describe. The fact that you were still able to retrieve the scrolls and return to us in triumph enhances your glory even further.

Scallywag!

"Now then, I have sent my scouts to the places where we know certain abandoned ships are to be found. It shall, in all likelihood, be some time before they return. While we wait, you will be our honored guest. The pleasures of the palace are yours to enjoy, and I shall instruct the court surgeon to ensure that your recovery goes as swiftly and painlessly as possible." He smiled. "By the time our scouts have done their work, I daresay you will be fit and ready."

The days that followed were most pleasant. The castle and coral gardens were idyllic, and many are the hours I spent in the latter while I healed and afterward. Would that I could describe it to you, reader, without sounding faerie-mazed. Imagine a beautiful garden with all manner of colorful plants, some flat and some made of snakelike tubes. The seabed is rich with them, but in the palace garden they have been placed with care and an aesthetic sense. Ribbons of color guide the eye, converging on carefully arranged sights to please the eye and heart.

Very often, these would be large rock formations, sometimes carved to cunning shapes, but always covered top to bottom in fine-colored coral, as skillfully applied as any artist with his paint. I recall, particularly, a bust of an early queen whose name I never quite got. Her hair had been done in long, thin traces of seaweed. The bust had been placed in such a way that the natural currents set the 'hair' billowing out to a most captivating effect. Murals also were done entirely in living coral, depicting scenes from the An'ui history, both above and below.

"The interesting thing about them is they are not plants, but animals." The princess was accompanying me in a stroll—well, a swim—round the gardens. She had taken to doing so on a daily basis. Naturally, I was glad of her company. She would speak of her world and ask all about mine. I fancy I acquitted myself well, unused as I was to bantering with royalty. As time went on and I recovered more fully, we tended to tarry together all the longer.

On this day, we were observing a sculpture of Yalanakan, patron goddess of the An'ui. She bore somewhat of a resemblance to her worshippers, though considerably grander, with a tail that put one more in mind of an eel than your standard sea fish. She had fins upon her cheekbones, and her hair was portrayed in a cascade of blue coral. Whoever had sculpted her gave her a most regal bearing and a profile that, from the side, seemed to convey imperial haughtiness. But when viewed head-on she had a decidedly maternal aspect. We had stopped to admire the sculpture, and Itaska was telling me about the artist's technique.

"An animal?" I asked. "Get away!"

"It's true!" She smiled. "At least, this is what our scholars say."

I peered closer at the brightly colored growth. "It looks like a plant to me."

She laughed. "And to me as well. But those who are knowledgeable in such things say otherwise, and I am not of a mind to contradict them." She reached out a delicate finger and lightly brushed a patch of tiny crimson growths. "Actually, some of our old legends have rather interesting things to say about coral. They say that each individual piece is a simple animal by itself but that together they form a greater creature. The reef, you know. It is like..." her brow furrowed. "What do you call them? Little surface creatures? They live in holes in the ground."

"Rabbits?"

"No, no. Tiny. Like this." She held her fingers apart. "They crawl about and take food back to their home. Apparently, there's hundreds of them to a colony, and most spend their lives going to and fro, serving the nest."

"Wait," I said. "Are we discussing ants?"

"Ants...yes, I think that's what they're called. We had them on the island, so they tell me. Did you happen to see them?"

"I was a little occupied. But you were saying?"

"Well, it seems that our philosophers believe that each ant is a tiny part of the hive—if that is the correct term—and thus that the hive must be another, greater being. And they think the same is true of the coral. Some reefs have been around for hundreds of years and grow out across the ocean floor farther than any An'ui may swim. It is said that they must remember the Old Ocean, and the things that swam in her before. Even Yalanakan, in one of her revelations to J'ya, speaks of creatures so ancient that only the great reefs remember them. Is it not fascinating?"

I laughed. "Well, it's certainly an unusual idea, I must admit."

Itaska squeezed my arm. "Well, I think it is very romantic."

Our promenades had (inevitably, I suppose) attracted the attention of the court and set tongues wagging. I had become conscious of rather more persons loitering about the gardens over the course of the last several days. I pretended not to notice them. To their credit, most pretended to enjoy the scenery. But it was very hard to ignore the fact that we were becoming fodder for the palace gossip mill, which Itaska assured me was as active as that found in any small community. Truth be told, I was beginning to worry. I hadn't really gotten a full understanding of the mores of the merpeople, but I felt instinctively that a surface dweller courting their princess would not be a popular person in certain quarters.

As we stood admiring the intricate sculpture, I plucked up the courage to make my misgivings known. "Oh, I shouldn't worry about that." Itaska gave my arm a reassuring squeeze. "You are very much in favor, just at the moment, having returned the scrolls and all. Life at court is an endless parade of people jockeying for position. Anyone who has enough sense to get here in the first place will know that trying to undercut you would be an unwise move indeed."

I laughed. "Well, I hope that doesn't change. I just…well, you know how people gossip. And of course we're both…" I trailed off, waving a hand vaguely between the two of us.

She tilted her head toward me. "Yes?"

"Well, I mean to say. After all, you're a lady and so am I, right?"

"I don't think I quite see what you're driving at."

"I mean that people would probably object to you courting another woman. Let alone a surface dweller. That's probably two taboos in a row, and that's not even adding in that I'm a commoner."

Light dawned. Itaska threw back her head and laughed. "Oh, I see. Do women not seek out each other's companionship in the surface world?"

"Well, not as a general rule, no. I mean it happens, but generally in secret."

"I see. My. That is…odd. Why is that, if you don't mind me asking?"

I shrugged. "To do with religion, I suppose. You know, man must take unto him a wife and all that."

"Ah. Well, if it helps, that isn't really an issue here. We just think one should be with whoever brings you joy." She smiled at me and gave my arm another squeeze. I found myself gazing deep into her eyes, entirely bewitched. It was almost as if they shone a light of their own. It seemed as if the entire world went silent, colors and sounds fading into the background.

I do not recall whether she moved to me or me to her, only that one moment we were apart and then we were not. Her lips, how sweet they were against mine. Her hair, stirred by the currents, brushed feather-light against my shoulders, and her skin…if I close my eyes, I can still feel the divine softness of her body against mine. It might have been but a moment, but that moment felt like an age of bliss, an early taste of paradise.

When we separated, I found myself quite at a loss for words. She managed to recover before I did and gifted me a coquettish smile. "So, Miss Surface Born, tell me, does this bring you joy?"

Somehow, I managed to nod.

"Very glad to hear it." She slipped her hand into mine. "Now come along. I want to show you the Folly."

The days that followed were blissful indeed. A princess does not have an overabundance of free time, but what she had she increasingly spent in my company. Some older women of the court kindly took me under their wing and advised me on appropriate behavior for courting a high royal. It felt so strange, yet liberating, to go along with her, everyone knowing the nature of things between us but no one seeming to mind. Truth be told, this was the most alien thing I had encountered since my journey began.

As splendid as my days were, my nights were rather less so. It was then, lying alone in the dark, I'd see the faces of my friends and shipmates floating up at me. Here I was, basking in the very lap of luxury, while they were stuck foraging on that island, assuming they were still alive at all. Of course, I would remind myself that there was nothing I could do for them until a ship had been retrieved, whereupon I would set off at once, rescue the lot of them, and all would be well again. Except.

I didn't want to go.

That is, I wanted to rescue them, of that let there be no doubt. Whatever one may think of pyrates, loyalty to one's crew is paramount. Even if I had no desire to do so, I would still have been duty-bound to assist them. The fact that they were my dearest friends made it even more imperative. But the world below the waves was so wonderous and the company of her grace so agreeable that I was loath to part. I desired two separate things, each of which would negate the other. I tried to tell myself how grand it would be to have my friends back, and what fine adventures we might have, but I could not bear to think of the inevitable parting that must needs precede it.

Scallywag!

It was in very much this mood that I received the news that a couple of suitable ships had been located and were being brought for my inspection. It had taken about a fortnight to find them and get them back to the capitol, the ships being hauled along by whales beneath the surface. (I did wonder if any ships saw these two go by, and what they may have made of it.) I was escorted to the surface, where the two ships lay in wait.

The first was little more than a fishing smack, able to hold a dozen at most, and with a couple of rather old cannons in case one wanted to lay siege to a bit of driftwood. The other...the other one was a magnificent galleon, Portuguese to my eye, fairly bristling with cannon, not excessively adorned but certainly built to a high standard. The reader shall think me foolish, but in truth, I could not tear my eyes away from her.

A rope was procured and secured to the rail with a grappling hook. I hauled myself out of the water (nearly losing my grip as my body reverted to its regular form) and climbed up to give it a proper inspection. Overall, the ship was in excellent trim. There wasn't much in the way of cargo. It seemed the vessel had been stripped clean of anything useful that could be easily carried away. Here and there were signs of struggle, tell-tale marks of dagger-point in the wood, more than a few puddles of dried blood, even the captain's door had clearly been forced. She had a history, this one, but overall she was in good trim. With a little work, she'd be as fine a ship as ever a buccaneer crewed.

When I dove back into the water, the king was waiting with his retinue. "Well, now," he said, "I hope one of these ships meets with your approval?"

I bowed. "Yes, sire. The galleon will do nicely, though I could hardly crew it myself."

He laughed. "You needn't worry about that. We'll have it towed to the fishing village where you were first discovered. I believe it is not far from the island you mentioned?"

"Yes, Your Majesty, very close."

"Splendid. I'll give the order to have it taken there at once. And will you be ready to follow it in the morning?" It was not a question.

"Yes, Your Majesty."

"Very good! We shall have a farewell feast for you this evening, then you and I shall discuss future plans. As I recall, there was a second favor that I wished to ask of you, yes? I think it is time we discussed that particular matter."

I assented.

"Then we shall see you at dinner." He turned and, with his retinue, headed back to the castle, leaving me to ponder my future.

That night I lay in my bed, quite unable to sleep. The feast had been most generous. By rights, I should have been pleasantly sleepy from having a full stomach, but I could not stop myself thinking of the day to come. All of the mixed feelings and conflicts I had harbored over the time of my convalescence returned tenfold. Excitement, fear, regret, and I daresay a good few other emotions competed for place in my mind. Eventually, I was compelled to give up on sleep altogether.

Leaning against the balcony rail in this pensive mood, I gazed out at the underwater world for what I was certain would be the last time, as the princess floated into my view.

I should not have been too startled. I had spent enough time around her people to know that they regarded up and down as just ordinary directions like any other, but something about the way she gracefully drifted down to my balcony gave the moment a rather unreal aspect. I recovered enough to remember myself, and bowed, inviting her inside.

"I hope you do not mind my visiting." She smiled. "I only came to wish you luck. I know something of what Papa told you this evening, and...well, it shall be quite the challenge. I want you to know that I truly believe, if anyone may accomplish this, it will be you."

I laughed. "Very kind of you, Princess, and I do wish I shared your confidence. For what it is worth, though, I shall not be alone."

"Even so. Papa says that the difference between an army and a mob is a capable general in charge. You know he thinks very highly of you."

"Does he?"

"Oh yes." She moved closer. "As, in fact, do I." She took my hand and glided into the room with myself in tow. "You know, I have read that in the old days, when a warrior was going off on a perilous mission, their lady would send them off to battle with a favor, like one of her handkerchiefs or similar." With that she shed one of her bracelets, a lovely silver thing decorated in multicolored coral. I expect it's locked away somewhere here in the prison with the rest of my belongings, if someone hasn't already pinched it. I remember turning it over in my hands, being overwhelmed by the magnanimity of the gift.

"There was another thing," she said. "Sometimes, the lady would…she would be afraid of not seeing them again, you understand? The lady would think to herself that she may never have such an opportunity again." She blushed, and for a moment, the world went still.

"Miss McCormick, she of the surface world, friend of the An'ui, I wonder if you would give me the honor of your company this night?" Her body was so close, not quite touching but still I swore I felt the warmth of it so close to mine. Right then, after a night of conflict within myself and so many factions fighting to be heard, they were all swept away with one absolute and beautiful certainty.

"Your Highness, I would be honored."

I will draw a veil over the rest of the night. Suffice to say, the memory of that night is a treasure, than which no greater could be imagined. Even as I sit in this cage of stone, the last light fading from this lone window, the memory of our first and last night together keeps me warm and serene, and helps to stave off the fear and loneliness that I believe would otherwise quite overwhelm me.

Chapter Twenty-Nine

THE PRISON CHAPLAIN (HE of whom I have spoken before) has informed me that the governor is scheduled to arrive in about a week. Generally, this is the time when he signs off on execution orders, &c, which tend to be discharged without delay. As such, I shall skip the greater part of my adventures and go directly to the circumstances that brought me here.

I wish you, reader, could have seen the looks on my crewmates' faces when the new ship entered the bay being towed by a brace of whales and yours truly standing at the very tip of the bowsprit, hanging on to the forestay with one hand and waving with the other. I must have made an incongruous sight, dressed once again in one of the simple green shifts from the merpeople. Happily, Black Jack and the others had kept my clothes safe, and soon I was feeling very much my old self again.

The crew had spent the intervening time making themselves comfortable. By the time I arrived, they even had a small garden started. Of course, now that we had a ship again, all hands turned to getting her seaworthy. Inside a fortnight we had her ready to sail. By night, as we had our dinner by the fire, the crew would ask me a thousand questions about the merpeople and the world beneath the sea. I told them as much as I could, and while I cannot say how much of it they believed, it was certain that they were more than sufficiently impressed.

I remember well the night before we set sail. After much discussion, we had decided to rechristen our new ship the *Cunning*, it being a not unsuitable name for a buccaneer ship such as ours, and a sort of private tribute to our late Captain Cunningham besides. We had no wine, but a bottle of rum recovered from the wreckage of the *Bonnie Mary* served just as well, and more fitting too, in my mind.

Afterward, we had a fine dinner, making excellent use of the bounty of the island and surrounding sea. Health was drunk to the ship, to myself, to the late and lamented captain, and to the merpeople who had been so generous with their help.

As the evening went on, many of the crew found themselves in a sentimental mood. Various members of the crew shared this or that memory of their time aboard the *Bonnie Mary*. It seemed everyone had some fond memory or another. It was universally agreed that she was a fine ship, and Cunningham a very fine captain.

Scallywag!

"Talking of captains," Black Jack stood and addressed the rest of us. "You will have, no doubt, reflected on the fact that we must needs select a new one from among our number. I now call upon Quartermaster Heinz to take nominations."

Heinz stood slowly, his old knees giving him trouble. "Aye. Well. Floor's open to nominations." A handful of the crew rose to their feet. He pointed to the nearest one. "Go ahead, Sam."

"I nominate Black Jack."

"Black Jack, do you accept?"

Black Jack, who had sat back down, made a face. "Me, captain? Bugger that!"

"As you like it. Who else?"

Next named was Mate James, who accepted the nomination, though without any evident enthusiasm. Someone nominated Maggie, who replied that he'd better hope she didn't win, or he'd be in dead trouble. After the laughter settled, Heinz looked around at the group and asked if there were any nominations left. Dutch stood, pointed directly at me, and loudly proclaimed, "I nominate Molly, without whom we wouldn't have a ship or a hope in hell!"

This raised quite a cheer. I was quite taken aback, truth be told. When Heinz asked if I would accept, it took me a moment to get my head round the question. "Me? I mean, me? I...I...Look, it's dead flattering, but what do I know about captaining?"

"What d'ye know?" Black Jack was back on his feet, looking at me. "Girlie, y'went off by yerself, at great personal risk, not knowin' if you'd find anything but the inside of a shark, just for the chance of saving the rest of us. And ya did and all! H—ll, I was listenin' when you were talkin' all about the kingdom they got down there. Sounded like you had a pretty sweet arrangement. Coulda stayed there. But ya didn't! You came back and with this bloody brilliant ship to boot. Ya got guts, girl. And honor. Anyone who would go to those lengths to save their stranded crewmates is sure enough captain material in my book." He turned his attention to the others. "What say you?"

The cheer was almost deafening. In the face of it, I could hardly refuse. The vote, when it came, was like a typhoon. Even Mate James put his hand up for me, much to my surprise. In retrospect it is obvious he hadn't particularly wanted the job and was only too happy to let someone else have it. There followed a jubilant celebration wherein I was duly invested with the title of captain, with Heinz reading out an oath while I knelt before him. I swore to abide by the oath to the best of my ability, whereupon he took a sword and, with great ceremony, brought it down on each shoulder in turn, then offered it to me handle first. "With this sword," he said, "we give you our loyalty and our trust. Taking this sword in hand, you will accept that trust and strive ever to be worthy of it. Do you accept?"

I nodded and took the sword in hand.

"Then rise, Captain."

There was great cheering and much tossing of hats into the air, as I turned to face the crew—my crew—once again. I smiled and generally tried to look like I knew what I was about and was not overwhelmed by the weight I felt settling on my shoulders.

Black Jack cupped his hands over his mouth. "Speech!" He bellowed. "Speech!"

The cry was taken up with alarming speed. Suddenly the entire crew was shouting for my acceptance address. As I looked out at them, my crew, my friends, my family really, I felt that I would do whatever I could to do right by them, no matter what. I suddenly knew what I had to say.

I saw a large stone nearby, not quite the height of a man. I scrambled up it and held up an arm. Aside for a couple of final cheers I was greeted with a full and attentive silence. Feeling all eyes on me, I nevertheless cleared my throat and began.

"My friends, it is honored I am that you have bestowed this title upon me. To think that this selfsame crew, which took in a frightened child and taught her the ways of the sea, should now judge me fit to lead them is a most singular privilege indeed. I do not know how good of a captain I will prove to be, but I can promise you two things. That I will do the best by you as it is within my power to do, and that there is no crew on the seas I'd rather be with."

This elicited another cheer. I held up my hand again. "But there is something you must know. The ship you see waiting for us there"—I gestured toward the shore—"comes with a duty attached. When the An'ui, the merpeople, provided the ship, it was with the understanding that we would help them in a great task of vital importance. I pray your patience, my friends, as I tell you of these things."

I then told them the story of the merpeople, how they fled from the land and became guardians of the ancient conch we had discovered. Of their consternation when its hiding place returned to the surface. And what the king had told me before I left. "Their goddess came in a vision to their priests and told them that it must return to the surface for a while, as an important duty was to be done. Their king believes that I have a part to play in this, though what role it might be he could not say. But in fairness, I must tell you this.

"Therefore, my friends, I offer you a choice. The burden of which I speak is mine, but none else's. I would not force you to take it on with me. Understand that if you stay, we may find ourselves involved in something most dire. Jansen reckons he can get us to a proper port within the week. If at that time you do not wish to continue, you may leave, and no harm done. But if you stay, we shall be undertaking rather more than our usual business. I will not ask for your answer now, only that you take your time and think on it."

In the silence that followed, I tried to read the faces spread out before me. Nobody spoke, only looked at each other. Mate James joined me on the rock and put his hand on my shoulder. "You don't understand," he said quietly. "You're captain now. You've sworn yourself to us. Well, that goes both ways. Your burdens are ours now, you see? We've got your back just like you have ours."

I looked out at the crowd again, and I could see it. There was not a man-jack among them who did not look utterly resolute. Where I led, I suddenly knew with absolute certainty, there they would follow. It was both a gratifying and terrifying thought.

"Very well," I said. "I thank you one and all. Now, if there is no further business, I suggest we call it a night. Make ready to break camp, for tomorrow we set sail again!" The crew cheered one final time, and the evening broke up as they went about their business.

The next morning broke as clear and blue as ever you could want. A few wisps of cloud meandered across the sky, and a fair wind proposed to send us on our way. It didn't take us long to get used to the new vessel, and with Jansen's skill at reckoning, he was able to get us to a port town inside of five days. There we were able to sell off whatever bits and pieces were leftover on the ship (as well as some flotsam the crew had retrieved from the *Bonnie Mary* wreckage in my absence) to reprovision her. It wasn't a lot, but it was enough for us to get started.

The next few months were spent getting back up to snuff. New letters of marque had to be acquired, suitable targets located, and so on. It was often tedious, unpleasant work, but we soon found ourselves back to our old strength. Better, really. The new ship was rather larger and better appointed. Once we got the cannons, &c, in working order, we could take on ships that would have previously been out of our league.

During this time, in addition to the normal day-to-day of a privateer, we also kept an ear out for any activity of the West Indies Company. There was surprisingly little going on as far as we could reckon, rather a dearth of any scuttlebutt regarding Lord Armstrong or any unusual activity to speak of. I almost began to wonder if they had not simply desired the thing for itself, just another bauble to put with the rest the bloody English have pinched from every corner of the globe.

As we went about our business, it was occasionally our lot to come upon some strange and marvelous secret of the sea. How I wish I could regale you, reader, with what we found at Skull Rock, or the discovery of the *Aurora*, an actual living ship. Time, alas, is not on my side. In the unlikely circumstance that I should somehow escape the hangman's noose, perhaps I shall have the opportunity to complete these chronicles. At the present, I must proceed to the crux of my narrative.

The first clue we received was by way of a tale overheard in a tavern in Port Royal. One of the sailors there had just come in on a freighter and said that just before they crossed over from the Atlantic to the Caribbean, they had come upon some most unusual wreckage. It appeared that a ship had been not just wrecked, but utterly destroyed. A swath of flotsam was all in one place, enough to make up a good-sized ship. At first, they thought it must have been an explosion, but they found no sign of burnt wood or the like. Nor, according to the sailor, were there any bodies. A ship of such size would have had a large crew, he reckoned, and given how close the bits were, whatever happened had been fairly recent.

According to Paulo and the others who were in the pub at the time, the man's audience spent a fair amount of time speculating on what may have been the cause but were unable to come to any satisfactory conclusion. I myself found it a most puzzling mystery at the time, though I did not realize its import until later.

Some weeks later, another rumor came to our ears. There were some mysterious goings on around San Andrés, a tiny island far to the west and outside the normal trading routes. Nobody seemed to know what was going on, but a lot of West India Company ships were around, and they were being very unwelcoming to anyone who even came near those waters. I decided we ought to go and have a look.

We were in Santiago de Cuba at the time, practically the other side of the Caribbean. Rather than plot a direct course, we worked our way along the Cuban coast, then crossed over to Nizuc. From here, we worked our way down the coast until we reached a pair of minuscule islands just off the coast that Jansen happened to know about. We weren't far west of San Andrés, so we were able to set up camp on the smaller of the two islands, from whence we could carry out our investigation. We started simple, just rowing out at night 'til we were fairly close to the island and able to see whether anything caught our eye.

After the third such expedition, our scouting party returned in a state of much excitement. They had been getting progressively closer to the island, trying to work out the minimum safe distance from which they could observe. The moon was full, giving a particularly good silhouette of the island. It was mostly flat, with an odd sort of hill near the middle. Something was going on, right enough, but even with the spyglass, all they could see were lights moving about. Occasionally, they heard the echo of a shout but little else to disturb the silence.

Then, a little before midnight, they heard an uproar. The shouting carried across the waves. More lights danced around the island, converging on the middle. Afterward, our scouts said that there had been a tremendous splashing sound, which one described as being like someone dropped the very Rock of Gibraltar. This by itself was more than sufficiently alarming. What truly sent them back to camp as fast as they could row was when the island's hill lurched out of position and disappeared.

Chapter Thirty

UNDERSTANDABLY, WE WERE ALL quite taken aback by the news. The reader, of course, may find a disappearing hill difficult to believe, but I may say that the party on that particular mission were all reliable persons who could be trusted to mind their duty and report what they saw. Of course, if one has gotten this far in my epistle, I suppose there is not much you are unwilling to at least regard as possible.

    In any case, we resolved to get a closer look the next night. The mysterious hill did not return. I gave orders that the island be surveilled during daylight as well, staying at a distance and making use of the spyglass. On the third such day, word came back that a large mass similar to the former hill could just be discerned, albeit a bit closer to the southern end of the island. Upon receiving this news, I resolved to have a look at the thing myself that very night. Taking with me Black Jack and Dutch, we rowed across, determined to strike land. The moon was on the wane, but there was still plenty of light for us to get across.

    We pulled up in a particularly dark area in the southernmost part of the island and proceeded to work our way closer to where the lights had been, always listening for patrols. Happily, the Company had set up on the eastern side of the island, so we had most of the wild part to ourselves. Mind, sneaking through a forest in pitch darkness is not exactly easy. One never knows what one is about to put one's foot on. Or in.

    All told, I daresay it took the better part of an hour to get across to the other side of the island. They had set up a small inlet as a harbor where several ships were anchored while a fair few were out on patrol even at this time of night. As we watched from our hiding place, a number of guards and others could be seen moving about. We watched the guards for a while, getting an idea of their rounds and how long it took between them. A few guards were stationed around the perimeter, right where the woods had been cut away. After a brief discussion, we decided to move in close to one of these areas and see if we could pick up any information when the patrols came round. One was fairly close to where we were, so we moved in, getting as close as we dared while keeping absolute silence.

    The guard was stocky, leaning against a tree and staring out to sea. His lanthorn was next to him, spilling an eerie light over the area. He puffed reflectively on a tobacco pipe as he stood his watch. The minutes ticked by. I had to change position twice, each time a slow and painstaking process that left me barely more comfortable than before.

At long last we heard the tell-tale crunch of boots through undergrowth. One thing about the Company, they didn't put a lot of store by stealth. A patrol of three guards approached, an officer and two torch-bearers. Our guard saluted.

"Sir. Nothing to report, sir."

I felt the blood drain from my face. *That voice...*

"All right. Carry on."

"Yes, sir."

The three men trooped off, leaving the guard alone. I thought fast. If I were right, then things could suddenly become a lot easier or a lot more complicated. Of course, if I was wrong...

I decided to chance it. I whispered some hasty orders to Black Jack and Dutch, then crept off to the side. The foliage was thick, making it very difficult to get close, but I found a gap which allowed me to crawl around just enough to get a look at the guard.

He had put his pipe away when the patrol came through and was currently trying to relight it. He had hung the lanthorn off a nearby branch, so the light shone full in his face. I was right.

The guard was muttering to himself, trying to light his pipe, but his flint wouldn't strike. As I watched him, an idea came to me. In hindsight, it likely wasn't the smartest move, but the idea tickled me so much I really couldn't stop myself. I inched my hand down to my belt pouch. My own flint & tinderbox were quite reliable, and I always kept them close at hand. I slipped them out as quietly as I could and got ready.

He was still fumbling with the tinder box when I moved. As he struck his flint, I struck my own, matching the movements so that the sound of his would disguise mine. One, two, three strikes, and still his tinder was unlit. Mine, however, was coming up nicely. Cupping my hand, I blew on it gently to bring the flame to life.

The guard poked around in his tinder box and turned the flint around a couple of times. It was old and well-worn. No doubt that was the problem. Suppressing a smile, I moved behind him and brought my glowing tinder box into his line of vision.

"Light, Sean?" I whispered.

He nearly fell back in surprise, poor lad. He scrambled for his lanthorn and his musket, then spent an anxious second or two fumbling about with them before getting himself in order. He held the light up to my face and turned pale.

"Molly?"

What followed was not, if I am frank, one of my better moments. Mind you, it was rather gratifying how quickly my comrades came running when they heard my brother strike me. I daresay Dutch would have run him right through had I not hastened to intervene and explain.

"Your brother? Really?" Dutch looked him up and down, her expression unreadable.

"Yeah, her brother. Really." Sean glared at me. "Surprised she remembers my name and all."

"Now, now, Sean. There's no need for that."

"Isn't there, then? D'yer friends here know why you came out here? Proper left us in the lurch, you did! Me an' Mike, we had to get work to make ends meet. Da nearly lost the shop! And of course poor Mum was beside herself with worry about you. Not that you cared."

"The hell I didn't! Anyway, I sent money back. It did get there?"

"Oh, aye. Eventually." He looked me up and down, his face marked in distaste. "Probably filthy lucre and all, by the looks of ya. A bloody pyrate, I can't believe it. And you want to know the worst part?"

"Well, I'm sure you're going to tell me, so—"

"Six months." He held up his fingers. "Six. Bloody. Months. That's how long old man Hennessy lived after you ran off. Barely half a year! You could have been a fine lady, had your pick of whoever you liked. But no, you just had to bugger off and leave us for the other side of the bloody world."

"Look here," I said. "I don't care if it was six months or six bloody days. There was no way I was marrying that old coot. Not for anything."

"Not even us? Your family?"

I shook my head. "No, Sean. Not even for you."

He sagged a little. "Never would have thought it of you. I mean, you were always the responsible one, always looking after me an' Mike, helping mind the store and all that. And now here you are, some kind of what, a pyrate?"

"Privateer, if you must know. All legitimate, of course."

He rolled his eyes. "Oh. Well, that's all right, then. 'Sblood, Mol. How could you?"

"Look," I sighed. "I didn't want to. I hated it, truth be told. But...well, if I didn't leave, then I was being pushed into marrying the old man whether I wanted it or not. It was like I was being...sold off or something. Leaving...well, I just didn't see any other way."

Sean rubbed his temples. "Bloody hell," he murmured. "I just...I can't believe this. Look, what in fact are you doing here?"

"Well, as a matter of fact, there's been rumors that the West India Company has been up to something, so we thought we'd better have a look around. For that matter, why are you here?"

He shrugged. "Had to do something, didn't I? Mike has taken over the store, so I reckoned I'd see the world. The money's decent, and you do quite well for yourself if you don't mind...keeping your mouth shut and doing as you're told."

"Aye, I just bet. They have a reputation in these waters, you ken. There are some things even pyrates don't do."

"Well, I would rather have been a gentleman of leisure, but somebody ruined that opportunity, didn't they?"

"All right, all right." Black Jack inserted himself between us. "Entertaining as this all is, may I remind you we are in the middle of something, and I think I see torches coming this way."

"Bugger!" Sean looked around wildly. For a moment, he hesitated, then waved a hand at us. "Get down, back in the undergrowth. Don't make a sound." He got himself together just as the patrol came round again.

We listened in silence as the others approached. "All right, Sean. Any news?"

"Sir, no, sir."

"All right. Stanley will be along in a bit to relieve you."

"Yes, sir. Thank you, sir."

We waited in the undergrowth until the sound of boots was no longer audible, then Sean cleared his throat. "All clear."

I hurried out from my hiding place and smiled. "Thanks, our Sean. For a moment, I was worried you might give us away."

"What, really?"

"Well, not seriously."

"Ah." He looked around, then moved closer. "I'll tell you what, though, there is definitely something altogether nasty going on around here. They won't tell us nothing, but the rumors..." he shook his head. "You wouldn't believe me if I told you."

I couldn't help but smile. "Sean. Mate. If you had any *idea* what I've been through since I came here, believe me, you would not talk such rot."

Black Jack chuckled. "Listen to the Cap'n. She knows what she's talking about!"

"Captain?" He stepped back, looking me over. "You're a captain now?"

I grinned sheepishly. "Aye well, what can I say? I've been busy."

He let out a low whistle. "I guess. Anyhow, look, there's a beach near the southern tip of the island. I'll be getting off guard duty in a little bit. Meet me down there and I'll tell you what I know."

I clapped a hand on his shoulder. "Good man."

"Just..." he hesitated. "Just be careful, okay? If you get caught, I can't do a thing for you."

"I understand. Don't worry about us. We're dead good at keeping our heads down."

"Okay. You'd probably better go. See you in a bit."

We slipped back into the woods and began to wend our way south. Once we'd got some distance, I turned and had one last look. Sean was standing alone in the lamplight, his face unreadable. All this time, and it was still hard to believe. I shook my head, then turned and carried on.

How long we waited I could not say with certainty, save that it cannot have been more than an hour. It was a pleasant stretch of beach, empty save for the remains of a campfire and a few bits of log pulled around it in a rough semi-circle. Presumably, the spot was a favorite for the company men in their off hours, but at this time of night there was no fear of interruption. Nevertheless, we secreted ourselves in the nearby tree line until Sean appeared. He hurried out to the middle of the beach, looking about for us. I gave him a quick whistle, and we emerged from our hiding places.

"Sblood," he muttered. "About gave me a start! You made it, then. Good."

I smiled and nodded toward the logs. "Shall we?"

"All right." We made ourselves comfortable and waited for Sean to begin. He was not eager to do so, it was clear, but we gave him a moment to set himself to the task, and with a deep breath, he began.

Scallywag!

"Ah, I guess it started a couple months ago? Several ships got orders to drop what they were doing and come out here. They'd set up this little base of operations, like just new. Everything was barely complete. We even had to bunk up on our ships because they hadn't finished our quarters yet. Anyway, no one would say what was going on, only that this was an extremely important operation and that we were to provide security and assist in any other duties that may come up. You know how they talk.

"It didn't take long for the rumors to start. There was talk of a new weapon, something terrifying, unnatural. But there wasn't any sign of anything being built. I thought there'd be some massive thing under construction, you know, with scaffolding all round it and whatnot, but there's nothing like that. Then some of the lads said they'd been sent to tow a skiff out away from the island. They had to go a long way off, and this other ship was full of important Company officers and whatnot. They were to release the skiff and return here. Before they got back to the island, there was this horrific noise, and a few seconds later, here comes this bastard of a wave, right out of nowhere. A little later, the ship with the Company officers came back. The men asked if someone needed to go retrieve the skiff, and they were told no, it was gone, and not to worry about it.

"They did it a few more times then, y'see, with bigger boats, and even used one of the older three-masters they had. Even we on land heard the noise when that one got it. And it was worse the next day."

"Why? What happened then?"

"Bits started washing up on shore." Sean looked ill. "That'd been a full-size ship, you ken, but there wasn't one piece bigger'n a man. It was all"—he waved his hands—"like someone had torn up a piece of paper, you see? Like that.

"Anyway, that's when the rumors got really wild. People started seeing a big mound out a little way from the island, but only in the dark, like. And sometimes it would move around, if you watched it careful. People were saying that His Lordship, he'd made a pact with the devil, who'd sent him some g—dawful creature to do his bidding.

"It got so everyone had seen the thing, whatever it was, even if only a glimpse. Then another mate of mine had to go out on one of the officer's ships when they did another of their tests. He saw the whole thing."

"Aye?" Black Jack leaned forward. "What did he see, then?"

"It was a monster." Sean's voice dropped to a hush, as if he barely dared speaking the words. "A monster big enough to take on an entire fleet!"

Chapter Thirty-One

IT WAS A QUIET journey back to our crew, each of us wrapped in our own thoughts. In truth, I had rather expected the news to be something of the kind. That did not make its confirmation any easier to think about. I had spoken of my suspicions to a few trusted persons (including the two who accompanied me on this particular expedition), but now I saw the time had come wherein I would have to tell the rest of the crew all that I knew.

To that end, I called a general meeting in the morning with the object of explaining the situation as it stood. As soon as everyone was gathered, I asked for their attention, and began.

"My friends, you will perhaps remember that when I accepted the very great honor of being your captain, I mentioned how I had been given a task to perform as a condition of receiving our fine new ship. As you will recall, we were forced by the West India Company to obtain a certain item for them. The price for our ship is to retrieve that relic before they can make use of its power to wreak havoc upon the world. Today, I regret to say, it appears they have already learned to harness its power. Therefore, I must share with you now the history told to me by the king of the merpeople himself.

"There is a great beast, the Stelladax—that which we call the Leviathan—which was once gifted to the An'ui as a mighty protector, able to overcome any threat that may come along. According to tradition, Stelladax was a gift from Yalanakan, their patron goddess. The conch shell is how they controlled the great beast. With the protection of the Stelladax, the An'ui prospered, growing rich and powerful.

"Unfortunately, they also grew greedy and began to use their protector to attack other peoples and subjugate them to their will. This, of course, angered their goddess. She locked the conch away so they couldn't use it anymore, then she took them down under the sea, where they would be safe.

"Well, it seems the story of what happened is still very much alive and well among the other tribes. Somehow or other, word of the conch must have come to the ears of Lord Armstrong and his lot. And, of course, nothing will do but they've got to pinch it and turn the monster to their own ends. So it's our job to take it from them and destroy the d—d thing once and for all.

"Now, it seems they're still in the testing stages, so this is our time to strike. I vote we lay low today and keep watch. We have a man on the inside, fortunately, and we'll go over tonight and see if he knows where it's being kept. With any luck, we can snatch the thing right out from under them before things go to the bad. Any questions?"

The rest of the day was spent in preparation. Those of us to be on the scouting party got some rest, while others prepared their weapons and made sure everything was in good working order. When night came, myself, Black Jack, and Dutch rowed across to the island, once again, and made our way to the other side. However, when we arrived, we were in for a surprise.

The island seemed unusually quiet as we crept toward the spot where Sean had been standing guard. We kept low and stayed watchful, but we detected no sign of him or anyone else. We emerged from the woods and found no light to be seen. No patrols, no nothing. I felt my stomach knot up. Something had clearly gone wrong.

"They've left," said Dutch. "I don't believe it."

I frowned. "Neither do I. Come on." We crept closer to the makeshift facilities that inhabited the eastern side of the island. Sure enough, the place was empty. Not a soul to be found. The only lights to be seen were on the distant Company ships as they sailed away.

"D—n! D—n and blast!" I will admit I lost my composure. No doubt they had set sail as soon as night fell. I glared out at the departing ships, almost as if I could force them to return through sheer will. "I can't believe they did that."

"I can't believe Sean wouldn't tell us they were shipping out," Dutch grumbled.

"Well, like as not he didn't know. He would have said something, I feel sure."

Black Jack nodded. "Must've sprung it on 'em today. They like to pull things like that. Shame. I only wish he'd had time to leave us a message or something."

"Maybe he did." I tapped my foot, thinking. "Think we can find the spot where he was standing guard last night?"

"Yeah, should be no problem. It was at the edge of the forest, right near a couple of rubber trees."

Scallywag!

"Right. Let's find it. But first..."

"Aye, Captain?"

"Does anyone have a lanthorn? Under the circumstances, I don't think we need to crawl around in the dark anymore."

We didn't have one, but we were able to improvise some torches that were enough to get us around. We found the spot without too much trouble, but there was no sign of anything he might have left behind.

"Of course," said Black Jack, "he wasn't the only one guarding this spot. Probably too dangerous to leave something."

I grimaced. "True enough, I reckon. Well, it was a thought."

Dutch spoke up. "There's the beach though."

"The beach? Oh, aye. Well, I suppose it's worth a go. Since we're already here and all. Shall we?"

The way to the beach was clear enough, so we were able to hurry with relative speed, making allowances for the dark. Preying on our minds was the fact that the Company ships were getting away. If Sean hadn't left us any kind of message, we were losing valuable time.

The beach was just as we had left it the night before, with the long-dead campfire still lying forlorn and abandoned. I raised my torch up to get a better view. "Right. Now, he wouldn't have left it out in the open, but I daresay he wouldn't have been *too* clever about it, so...*ah!* The logs. Check under 'em."

Sure enough, Dutch found a folded-up piece of paper with *Molly* in Sean's unsteady handwriting. Black Jack held my torch for me as I read.

Mol -

Something's up. They've got everyone running about getting ready to depart. They won't say what's happening, only we're meant to leave as soon as everything is on the boats. Rumor is we're having a go at the Spaniards, and I reckon that means they're satisfied with whatever it is they've been trying with this bl—y monster of theirs. I've got to go with 'em of course, but a lot of the crew are not liking this, figure it ain't natural. I don't know if anyone can do anything about it, but you seemed to know a little about it last night, so I thought maybe I would tell you. If there's anything you can do, please do it. This sort of thing doesn't belong in human hands.

Sean

PS: I'll be on the Anatola *if you catch us up. Try not to sink me.*

There was a moment, as we all digested the contents of the letter. The grim consequences of someone like Lord Armstrong having an actual Leviathan at his beck and call needed hardly to be elaborated upon. My mind raced, trying to determine the best course of action.

"By the Virgin," murmured Black Jack. "This is too much. What do we do about this, Captain?"

"Aye, Cap." Dutch turned her face toward me, looking as worried as I'd ever seen her. "What do we do?"

I felt a change in the wind. These two had been my friends from the beginning, and in all that time, I had always been just "Mol" to them. Even after we got the new ship and were busy reestablishing ourselves, I had always felt myself to be first among equals. But now they were calling me Captain and asking for orders. In a moment, I understood that this was what being a captain really meant. It meant being the one the rest looked to when things got bad. When you're crew, life is simple. The captain gives the orders, and you follow 'em. You may grumble a bit, or even put up a fight, but in the end it wasn't you as had to make the big decisions. The world suddenly became a much more complicated place.

After a moment's thought, I folded the note back up and put it in my pocket. "Right. The first thing we do, we head back to the others and get ready to sail. We've got a long trip ahead of us, I fancy." We headed back to our skiff. With any luck, this would give me some time to think about what the hell I was supposed to do.

We departed with the dawn, reasoning that even if we could catch the fleet up (unlikely), we would almost certainly not survive the experience. Therefore, a bit of strategizing was needed. We headed to safe harbors where pyrates were known to congregate and started putting out the word. Most pyrate companies are sufficient unto themselves. When things get bad enough that all of pyratedom is under threat of extinction, most are smart enough to see sense and come to parlay. Thus it was that several of us gathered on a remote island, which had often been used for such gatherings as brought pyrate captains together. A great deal of discussion and debate ensued over the three days that we were gathered. An accord was reached, and a plan agreed upon.

We set to work making ready. Those in a position to observe the following weeks may have noticed some rather unusual behavior on the part of the pyrates around the Caribbean. Most of them seemed to go to ground, appearing only sporadically on the high seas. From time to time, one ship or another would poke its head out (as it were) and lead the authorities on a merry chase, but nothing ever came of these.

Meanwhile, yours truly was running herself ragged making preparations and dealing with the other pyrate captains. There is no more arrogant, onery, or independent bunch to be found. It's like someone took a bunch of cats and gave them swords. I had to see to supplies, making sure we could last long enough to set our plan into motion. On top of which, I had to make all the other special arrangements that only I could. These, as one may guess, took up some considerable time, but happily everything was arranged to our satisfaction.

In the meantime, my crew was getting ready for the final attack. I remember well the night I gathered them round and explained the nature of what we had in mind. It had not been best received, especially since we'd only got a new ship and all, but the necessity of the plan was understood. Once it was finalized, they set to work with a will.

In the meantime, reports were beginning to come in of unusual doings in the sea north and east of the Caribbe. Strange shapes were sighted, and stranger wreckage. It seemed that the gentlemen of the West India Company had chosen this remote area for their base of operations, it being relatively out of the way of general traffic, yet convenient for intercepting ships coming into the area. Clearly, it was only a matter of time before they began to move to bolder, more public acts. We had little time indeed.

At last, all the preparations were done. We put the word out that the West India Company had a new and terrible weapon, and that all the pyrates had joined together to stop them. We named a time (one fortnight hence), and a place (that selfsame island at which we had been betrayed) where all who wished to stand with us were to gather. Soon the word was going through every dockside tavern, every ship's mess, anywhere sailors were known to congregate. I daresay that within the week, there wasn't a tar on the Caribbean seas who didn't know of the upcoming gathering.

The West India Company knew about it too.

We made sure of that, right enough.

Chapter Thirty-Two

TWO WEEKS LATER, I stood on the bowsprit of the *Cunning*, scanning the horizon with my glass. Word was the West India Company was headed this way double quick, no doubt with their new toy in tow. Everything had been prepared, every detail that could be checked had been, and more than once besides. There comes a point in any Great Undertaking when one has done all the preparation and can only wait for the thing to commence. One inevitably finds oneself retreading the same ground over and over in one's mind, looking for anything one might have missed. It does not do for a captain to fret, so I kept my demeanour calm and my eye on the horizon.

It wasn't quite midmorning when I first spotted the approaching ships. They were too far away to see clearly, but as the distance closed, they resolved into a veritable forest of masts approaching us. There was no more waiting to be done. The mountain was coming to Mohammed, and no mistake.

We had brought the *Cunning* into the bay and turned it round, facing the open sea. I glanced back behind me. The guns we had moved up on deck were braced and ready, each manned by a small and dedicated crew. There was no chatter, no idling among them, only the pin-sharp attention of my most trusted crew.

Black Jack, who held charge of the forward port gun, caught my eye. "Any sign of 'em, Captain?"

I nodded. "Just clapped eyes on 'em now. Everyone stand ready."

I watched as the Company fleet approached. The wait was excruciating, but we had to time it right. Go off too early, and the whole thing would be for naught. I scanned the oncoming fleet with my spyglass again. If I squinted, I could fancy I saw an unusual rippling of the waves going out in front of the lead ship.

As the fleet approached, I brought my arm up. Behind me, the gun crews made ready.

The lead ship was the same one upon which myself and the others had been imprisoned. They came into range, and I brought my sword down. Behind me, the cannons roared in unison, sending a volley toward the intruders. At the same time, the ship lurched beneath my feet and moved forward toward the fray.

Behind me, the gun crews moved with swiftness to fire off another volley, and another. We were quickly approaching the mouth of the bay, tapering strips of land on either side of us. I kept an eye on our progress. As the bow reached the last point of land, I turned away and swung back onto the deck.

"Go!" The gun crews dropped what they were doing and dove over the side, swimming to shore and retreating into the wooded areas. The rest of the crew were already manning gun posts along the coast. As I ran, I could hear the distant roar as they began their assault. I ran pell-mell aftward, shedding my coat and hat as I went. Underneath, I was clad only in a rough linen blouse and skirt, and my sword belt. The belt weighed heavily, laden as it was with several pouches I had prepared for the occasion. At the far end of the main deck, Black Jack waited for me. I threw him my coat and hat as I went past. "You're in charge 'til I get back."

He nodded grimly. "Aye, Captain." With that, he jumped over the side after the others.

My bare feet thumped against the decking. I scrambled up to the poop deck, sheathing my sword as I went. Below me, the now-empty vessel continued forward. At the very aft of the ship, a single torch burned, its flame flickering in the wind. I held on to the aft rail and waited for what I knew was coming.

I didn't have long to wait.

I could see the shape of the creature rising up out of the water. It came faster than anything that size had any right to move. No time to spare, I grabbed the torch and threw it onto the deck, where a chain of oil-soaked sheets led down into the hull. The makeshift fuse caught quickly, thank goodness. I vaulted over the railing and leapt into the blue waters below.

Down I plunged, only just missing one of the two whales that were propelling the *Cunning* from behind. I took hold of the harness on the nearest one and forced myself to expel the air from my lungs. The transition did not seem to get any easier with practice, but at least I was accustomed to it. I felt the water rushing through my gills, and saw the blurry underwater world resolve into crystal clear sharpness. As soon as it was done, I gave the whale a quick pat. It veered away from the ship, the other one doing likewise in the opposite direction.

Distance, that was the thing. The whales were two of King Ulanu's finest, swift and capable beasts who were well-accustomed to the battlefield. I felt the current rush against me, as we surged away from the ship as fast as possible. In my mind, I tried to picture the flame traveling down through the empty interior of the ship, past the galley, through the infirmary to the gunport and the barrels of powder and shot that had been squeezed in 'til it was fairly bursting.

I hesitated at first, then turned back to look. Down here, the creature was even larger than I had imagined. It was somewhat like a giant octopus, but with rather more tentacles, including smaller ones that branched off from the main ones. The head (I suppose one would have to regard it as such) was vaguely conical, easily the size of a frigate by itself, with long vertical slits placed regularly around it, which I judged to be the thing's eyes. It had already closed with the *Cunning,* wrapping its tentacles around her hull. I gripped the whale's harness and waited.

The sound of the explosion was somewhat muffled by the water, but we felt the impact right enough. The whale faltered and frantically righted itself. I, myself, felt like I'd been hit by a typhoon. Fortunately, my grip on the harness held as the whale sped off.

The Leviathan, of course, was not so fortunate. It was wrapped right round the ship when the explosives went off and caught the full force of the explosion. By the time we wheeled back around toward the oncoming fleet, the behemoth was drifting down toward the sea floor, its tentacles hanging limp. Too much to hope that we'd killed the thing, of course, but our little gambit had put it out of commission and hopefully bought enough time for us to do what had to be done.

Still, it was a pity about the *Cunning*. She was a nice ship.

We surfaced a little way from the oncoming fleet and paused to see where things lay. The island in question was part of a small archipelago, with most of the islands being relatively small, big enough to hold two or three villages at most. Fortunately, they were more than adequately sized for concealing a goodly number of ships.

On the sound of the explosion, our comrades came out of their hiding places, moving quickly to flank the Company's fleet. There were precious few ladies & gentlemen of commerce who had not, in the course of their business, come up against the Company on more than one occasion. Our call to arms had attracted a great many responses. A good thirty ships came sweeping out of their hiding places, closing with the Company ships as fast as the wind would carry them, cannons already blazing.

Meanwhile, my whale had brought us back up to the surface. I tugged myself up the harness a bit and willed myself back into human form. With my legs back under me, I scrambled up onto the whale's back and surveyed the scene. We were off to a good start. I shielded my eyes with my free hand and searched the oncoming ships for what I knew must be out there.

It took a moment before I saw it. Indeed, for a bare moment I thought they might not have come at all. At last I spotted the capitol ship, cowering all the way in the back with a phalanx of gunboats around it. Bl—y cowards, I thought to myself. I ought to have known. I felt the bile rise within me. Somewhere on that ship, Lord Armstrong and the rest were sitting back and watching other men fight. Well, this day, the fight would come to them.

Too many ships lay between myself and my goal to take a direct route. Nothing for it, then, but to clear the way. About a dozen ships of various sizes were approaching this side of the conflagration. I managed to spot the *Dahlia*, a galleon under the captaincy of Gerald Sorrowe, popularly known as The Second Son. He was closing with the Company fleet, guns ablaze, eager as always to be first to the fray. I pointed the ship out to my trusty steed (if I may call it such), and we closed with the *Dahlia* as fast as we could.

Coming up alongside her, I ran forward toward the head of the whale, clutching hold of my skirts. I leapt over the blowhole, just as it let loose a spray that sent me flying up in the air to land (albeit awkwardly) on the deck.

A couple of his crew who were not engaged in firing upon the enemy helped me to my feet. I recovered myself, turned to Captain Sorrowe on the quarterdeck, and bowed with what dignity I could muster. "Permission to come aboard, Captain!"

He laughed and held his arms out in a gesture of resignation. "After that entrance, how could I refuse?"

I smiled back and pointed toward the distant capitol ship. "Look here, how close can you get me to that?"

The captain shielded his eyes and studied the situation. The *Dahlia* was a fine ship, its captain having come from landed gentry, and as such, it could bully its way through conventional warships. But the ones hanging back were altogether another story. "I can get you close," he said, "but I don't reckon we can get through that wall."

Scallywag!

I bowed again. "I understand, sir. Just get me close as you can, and I thank'ee."

The captain turned and barked some orders to his crew. I felt the ship shift direction beneath my feet and watched as the mate ran aft to the poop. He hoisted a green flag off the stern and fired two shots in the air. Behind us, some of the ships that saw the signal began to fall in line, joining our assault.

The initial resistance had been somewhat less than expected. No doubt, the Company ships were expecting their precious Leviathan to do most of the heavy work. As our makeshift fleet closed in around them and the import of the situation imposed itself upon them, they wasted little time in mobilizing their retaliation. The air was thick with cannon shot, the roar of the guns drowning out all other noise. The *Dhalia* plowed forward, now part of a wall of ships determined to pierce the heart of the Company fleet through sheer, brute force. I joined the captain on the quarterdeck, watching the progress with a wary eye.

The Company ships were well-equipped and their crews well-trained, but our group had all the momentum. A legion of rogues we were, battle-hardened and hungry for the fray.

As we approached the enemy ships, they turned in a desperate attempt to bring their cannons to bear upon us. Unfortunately for them, they had elected to come in a close formation, which quickly proved unwise. Each captain found himself desperately trying to maneuver around another. More than one ship found itself borne down upon by one of its fellows, and a few of the Company ships were lost in the initial panic for this very reason.

We pushed on into the very heart of the fleet. All guns blazed as we plowed through, and though we lost a few ships ourselves, I may say that we gave better than we got. It wasn't until we were right in the thick of it that things got rather too hot for comfort. A full-sized man-of-war with three tiers of cannon loomed into view, right in the middle of our path. Captain Sorrowe swore at the sight of it, and in truth, so did I. Signaling the captain to hold his ship back, I charged toward the guns as fast as I could.

Up ahead, the giant ship (christened the *Behemoth*, I could not help but notice) was already beginning her assault. The cannons roared, and the air suddenly became thick with iron death. I fumbled in one of the pouches attached to my sword belt until I arrived at the cannon nearest the giant enemy. "Here," I said to the gunner, "Do you think you could hit that thing from here?"

The grizzled old man squinted. "Not from here, ma'am," he said. "Would fall a mite short."

"How about if you used this?" I pulled out a small sphere of grayish stone, not quite so large as cannon shot and considerably lighter. "That might do it," he said, "tho' I can't see as how it would do much damage, beggin' your pardon."

"Never mind that," I said. "Just land it against the ship. Anywhere is fine."

He shrugged and took the ball, handing it off to his loader. It was ready in a trice, and the fuse was lit. I held my breath. Due to the size of the stones, I'd only managed to take three. I determined to only use them when necessary. If even one went to waste...

The cannon discharged, sending the stone sailing through the air right toward the behemoth. It seemed to me that I could see a faint trail of green liquid flowing in its wake. *Hold together*, I prayed silently, *hold together.*

The stone smashed against the lower hull, just below the gun emplacements. It shattered on impact, sending a spray of greenish fluid into the sea. Perfect.

The old gunner looked quizzically at me but said nothing. I kept my eyes locked on the expanding pool of green amongst the Caribbean blue. Any moment now...

I just had time to register the movement of several shapes in the water before the vessel lurched to one side as if buffeted by an unseen giant. It happened again, and again, each time with increasing violence. The gunship began to list, no doubt taking on water. In little more than a minute, the *Behemoth* was thoroughly crippled, desperately trying to limp away from the field of battle.

Behind me, Captain Sorrowe came running up in astonishment. "Good G—d," he gasped, "Whatever was that you shot at it?"

I smiled and removed the other two from my pouch. "Scent-bombs. A wee gift from the king of the merfolk. The whales will strike wherever you land 'em."

"King of the...?" He shook his head, laughing. "If it were anybody else...still, can't argue with the results, eh?"

I grinned. "Get me to that capitol ship, and you can have the other two and all."

Scallywag!

His eyes went wide. "G—d's truth?"

"G—d's truth."

He bowed shortly and turned. "Right, you lot! The way is clear! Let's get this lady where she's going!"

Chapter Thirty-Three

We had pushed through a good portion of the opposing fleet and were coming in close to our quarry. Someone must have noticed what we were up to, for we soon saw a flurry of frantic signals, and the capitol ship's escorts hastily arranged themselves into an impromptu wall of wood.

Captain Sorrowe surveyed the scene with me. "Bloody hell, that's some odd tactics there. If there was more of them or less of us, I'd say they were getting ready to flank us." He looked back at the other ships trailing behind us. We had lost a couple in the fracas, but still had a goodly number traveling with us, enough to mean that the half dozen ships blocking our way were in no position to outmaneuver us. And yet in formation they stayed, side by side, like soldiers marching to battle. "What are they playing at?"

"Silly buggers." I nodded in the direction of the capitol ship lurking behind the rest. "Some d—d fool has panicked and ordered them to block the way. Now they've got to avoid bumping into each other, and their guns are useless. Can't imagine what they're..." I trailed off, squinting at the oncoming ships. Something was not quite right.

"Is it just me," said Captain Sorrowe quietly, "or are the ones in the middle rather closer?"

They were. The ships had arranged themselves arrow-fashion, providing an effective cordon while at the same time freeing up their cannon. I should have known it was too good to be true. I drummed my fingers on the rail, trying desperately to think of a countermove. "How many ships do we have?"

"Looks like...eight, all told. Could be enough to take them out, though it might be tricky."

I didn't answer right away, my eyes locked on the two ships in front. A narrow gap appeared between them, though now they'd pulled ahead their captains had clearly taken it upon themselves to widen it a bit. It was hard to estimate the gap at this distance, but it could just be enough.

The captain studied my face. "Got an idea, then?"

"I think so...but getting it to the rest, that's going to be the tricky part."

Scallywag!

I glanced around the scene, silently cursing myself. One could plan and plan, and cover every detail, but something would always be unaccounted for. It was enough to make a girl cry, it really was. There was, of course, the use of large flags and a few simple signs to stop, follow, and so forth. But for anything beyond that, one was quite without recourse.

Glumly, I turned my eyes downward to the waves below. There was the Caribbean, sparkling and blue as always. For a moment, I toyed with the idea of changing to merform and delivering the instructions myself, but making the rounds of all eight ships and back again was quite out of the question. I found myself wishing I could dive down below the waves, back to Itaska's arms, and leave the whole surface world behind. But that was quite impossible. I had pledged my honor to this bit of business and was determined to see it through.

A bit of stray movement caught my eye. I peered harder at the waves. Once I realized what I was seeing, I could not help but smile.

"Captain," I said, "I'm going to need paper and ink. And empty bottles. Just as quick as we can."

A few minutes later, I hung from a rope over the side of the ship, handing out bottled messages and directions to a school of dolphins that had been swimming alongside. My amulet had been more than sufficient to catch their attention. With simple gestures, I was able to convey that they should take one bottle to each of the ships behind us and get someone's attention. This was less difficult than it may sound. The dolphin is a surprisingly intelligent beast, and they are often used down below for tasks that even the most clever dog would find perplexing. Indeed, by the time I got to the third, they had clearly got the idea. Each one grabbed a bottle and hurried to one of the ships without further prompting.

I watched the departing shapes with some anxiety, as the crew hauled me back up. Dolphins are quite intelligent, but humans are uncomfortably inconsistent in this area. It occurred to me (not for the first time) that a more elaborate signal system was needed to send messages between ships. Perhaps an expansion of the flag system, the set of flags already in place for the most common messages, then a second set for common words, and a third for letters. Each set would have a distinct shape, and each flag visually different from the others so as to allow easy discernment. Perhaps if I finish these memoirs before I am hanged, I may turn my attention to devising such a system.

Nevertheless, by the time I was hauled back on deck, the dolphins were already closing with their targets. Through the glass I watched them leap and cavort, bottles held delicately in their mouths, trying for the sailors' attention. It took a minute or so, but one by one, each ship sent down men on ropes to collect the bottles.

I have mentioned before that my literacy was something of a rarity among the fellowship of pyrates. As such, I had resorted to drawing out my plans in a rough diagram with elongated triangles serving as ships, and arrows showing what I had in mind. Your average pyrate captain may not be much for book learning, but it's a sorry one indeed who cannot read a chart.

The messages were received and acknowledged, generally by waving a flag or firing a pistol shot. Captain Sorrowe, who was watching the situation with me, rubbed his hands together. "Well. Looks like we're ready."

I eyed the oncoming ships. Not much longer and they would be in range. "I hope so."

"Right." He turned to his mate. "Nevis, sheets down but be ready to raise again on my mark." The mate nodded, and hurried off, barking orders. Above us, the sails were coming down. I could feel the momentum of the ship slow and dissipate, as we came to a near halt.

Ahead, the Company ships were slowing down as well. It seemed our sudden switch in tactics had not escaped their notice. Doubtless they were expecting us to attempt to swerve out of their way, or possibly even retreat. What they were not anticipating, I feel confident in saying, was our escort ships to come flying past us, four each to the port and starboard, barreling on full speed through the gap between the two leading ships. One after another they crisscrossed in front of us, heading straight into the gauntlet, guns blazing all the way. After the first half had gone through, Captain Sorrowe gave the orders to up sails and ahead full. As the last two ships came by, we fell in right in front of them.

The Company escort ships, now finding themselves in a gauntlet of their own, broke formation and fired wildly at the pyrate ships. Doubtless they had expected our lot to try to go around and had prepared their guns & tactics for that eventuality. Captain Cunningham once said to me that one must never meet the enemy on his own terms. Give him the fight he *isn't* prepared for.

As we sailed past the first two Company ships, a cheer went up from the two pyrate ships between us and them. They were in their element, harrying the Company ships no end while the latter scrambled to respond. One of the two ships seemed familiar to me, though I could not immediately place it. As we approached, I noticed the name painted across the stern, *Bahati*.

That rang a bell all right. Hadn't I been taught the word years before? It was the Swahili word for fortune. A suspicion formed in my mind. Sure enough, as we passed the ship, I saw that I was right. The *Bahati* was crewed entirely by Africans, firing round after round at the hapless Company ships. On the quarterdeck, watching over it all, was Captain Sanyang himself. I called out to him as we went past. He raised his hat in salute, and his crew gave a mighty cheer.

Up ahead, the way was clear. The capitol ship wallowed fat and slow before us. I turned to Captain Sorrowe. "Get us as close as you safely can. I'll do the rest. Once I'm off, feel free to get away as fast as you like."

He bowed. "As you wish, madam. And may I say, it has been a most singular honor."

A moment later we tacked to port, moving to sweep past and away before her guns could respond. The capitol ship tried to move to the offensive, but such vessels are not made for maneuverability. We curved in a graceful arc, letting loose a volley of cannon shot at the closest point before we began to veer away. I shook hands with Captain Sorrowe (handing over the scent-bombs as promised), bowed my thanks to the rest of the crew, and dove headfirst over the starboard rail into the blue sea.

I plunged beneath the waves, willing my body to transform for the second time that day. Looking back, I should have anticipated that doing it twice in so short a span of time would be somewhat rough on my constitution. (I have mentioned before, I believe, that it never got any easier or more pleasant.) As it was, I had to stay where I was for a moment and wait for the wave of nausea that washed over me to abate.

Once I was more or less myself again, I looked up in time to see the hull of the *Dahlia* cutting away at speed. Some cannonballs plunged into the waters after her, leaving a trail of bubbles in their wake.

No safe waters here. I turned, and swam toward my quarry, keeping low in case anyone should be looking over the side. She was a large ship, fat and riding low in the water. I began to work my way around the hull, looking for some sort of rope or purchase I might climb. When I reached the stern, I surfaced to take a closer look. No portals were here, only the windows for the senior officers' cabins far above. Still, I kept low as I examined the ship.

Someone had decided that what a capitol ship really needed was lots of filigree all around the place, and from top to bottom as well. Curlicues, running slats of exotic woods, and any amount of other flummery abounded until it looked like a floating cathedral. Even the rudder had some decoration in the way of wood carved to resemble stylized waves. A nice enough effect, but at the moment I was more interested in their usability as stepping stairs. I hoisted myself up to the closest one, hanging on tight as I hauled my lower half above the surface until I was perched, more or less, in place. I tightened my grip on the slick wood, closed my eyes, and tried to will myself once more to transform, albeit slowly.

Sadly, it was still a d—d ordeal switching back. Only my tight grip on the rudder kept me from dropping back into the sea. Making a promise to myself that I wouldn't swap back again that day if I could possibly help it, I gritted my teeth and set to.

The opinions of the Company and the Royal Navy notwithstanding, I maintain that it is of incalculable advantage for a captain to come up through the ranks of a common sailor. There are several reasons for this, most of which come down to the fact that the more one knows of the fundamental operations of the ship, the better and more informed decisions one can make. There is also, I would suggest, a practical side. My years of climbing the monkey lines stood me in good stead, as I worked my way up the rudder to the ship proper.

It was then something of a scramble to find purchase from which to climb, but at least I had got high enough that the going was dry, barring the occasional light spraying of mist. I worked my way to the hatches for the aftward guns and pressed my ear to the hull to discern any activity therein. It was rather difficult to tell, what with all the other noise going on and all. In the end, I decided it was best not to chance it.

Scallywag!

Up some more, I continued moving slowly and bracing myself every time we crested a wave lest the drop jostle me from my position. For those who don't have the knowing of ships, generally the great cabin, or officers' quarters, tends to protrude somewhat aft of the ship proper, supported by braces and such, not unlike a balcony. Above me, the great cabin jutted well out. Even if I could somehow climb up, it would take me right past their windows. Not that I expected anyone would be in their cabin in the middle of a battle. If anyone would, it would be His Lordship. Either way, there had to be a way up.

Glancing round, my eye lit upon a curious arrangement of ropes hanging down just below the great cabin. I followed them with my eyes until I saw a plank about halfway along. The rope went through a hole on one end and out another opposite, forming a sort of rudimentary seat. Of course! A ship like this needed constant maintenance, and no doubt the officers liked their cabin windows nice and clean. Which, naturally, meant that some poor sod had to lower himself down on the ropes and wipe them down. Generally one had other lines secured to the main ropes to keep from falling off. Even so, it's a desperately unpleasant job and generally given to crew members in disfavor.

Some iron eyelets had been bolted into the hull just below the protrusion for the officers' cabins. I made my way toward them. A quick test showed that they would indeed hold my weight, so I set to getting a hold of the ropeworks. Alas, even hanging on with one arm and stretching the other out as far as I could, I could only brush my fingers against the nearest rope, unable to seize hold.

Cursing to myself, I kicked a leg up and out, trying to catch the rope with my foot. The first time my heel struck it and sent it away, but the second time (by way of contorting myself) I was able to catch the rope and hook my foot over the loop. With my other foot braced against the hull, and still holding on to the eyelets, I endeavoured to get the rope to come down. Frustratingly, it refused to do so. Too well secured, no doubt. I stood this way a long moment, wondering quite what on earth to do, until it came to me a most desperate plan.

I took my other leg away from the ship and raised it to join the first upon the loop of rope. So now I was hanging on to a couple of iron eyelets in the hull of the ship, and my feet hooked on the rope by my ankles, with the rest of me hanging over empty space and giving a splendid view of where I would land if this didn't work. The sea I didn't mind so much, but I would likely hit the rudder on the way down, and I preferred not to do that.

I began to "walk" the rope toward me, moving first one leg then the other. Up the shins (a most uncomfortable experience), then the thighs, then up to my waist. And all this time, not to be indelicate, but my skirt was riding up as I maneuvered into position so that by the time I got the rope to my waist I was in a most unenviable position. Just as well no one did see me, as I might have died of embarrassment on the spot.

In any case, I managed to shift to my side and, moving first one hand then the other, wound up more or less upright and hanging on to the rope like a child on a swing. I felt a moment of vertigo as it swung away from the hull, but soon enough it settled just below the windows to the great cabin. I hauled myself up, so I was standing on the loop of rope, took a moment to adjust my skirt, and took stock of the situation.

There were two levels of windows, no doubt one for the captain and the other for His Lordship. Perhaps one cabin or the other might be empty enough that I could affect a stealthy entrance. A nearby pulley system allowed me to haul myself up to where I could listen by the lower window without being seen. A lot of activity was definitely going on in there. I could hear orders being shouted and people running in and out. I was about to pass on when I heard something intriguing.

"Lieutenant, any sign of the beast?"

"Nothing yet, sir."

"D—n and blast. Right. Take that thing back up to His Lordship's cabin, will you? It's just taking up space, now."

"Aye, sir."

That thing indeed! Well, I didn't need telling what they were referring to. Grabbing the pulley rope, I hauled myself to the upper set of windows and risked a peek.

It was a lord's cabin all right. Someone had done everything they could to make it look like a country estate rather than a ship at sea. I'd never seen such finery before. Mind, some pyrates love nothing more than to wrap themselves in the trappings of luxury, but they always come off as rather gaudy and overdone. This room…well, it was elegant. The walls were decorated in seafoam green with white trim, the bed a full-size canopy in carved oak with fine linens, and the cabin sported a vanity and even a writing desk. Impressive and no mistake.

I kept my eye on the door. Sure enough, the officer whose voice I'd heard below came through, carrying the conch in hand. He looked around, shrugged, and placed it on the desk before departing. I made myself count to ten before moving slowly out from my concealment, then commenced to test the windows. Not one would open. I cursed my ill luck. There was the object of my quest, right there, and no way to get to it.

Nothing for it, then.

I kicked away from the ship, judging my momentum. It was possibly enough, but I wanted to be sure. The next time the ship pitched upward over a wave, I kicked out again, swinging out as far as I could. I came swinging back just as the ship crested and pitched down again. I had just enough time to curl into a ball before I hit the window head-on and went sailing through.

The landing was bad, as you may imagine. I hit the deck hard and rolled a bit before finding my feet. I staggered forward to the desk, trying my best to avoid the shattered glass. There was a commotion outside. No doubt they heard my entry. I reached the conch just as the door burst open. I scooped it up in my hands and held it aloft, then...

...I was in the white place once more.

Ah, you have returned. It was the same voice I first heard upon finding the conch back on the old ghost ship. It did not sound at all surprised. *Very well. I believe you have a task to perform?*

I cleared my throat. "Yes. I bring a message from King Ulanu Bas Yalanakan, King of all the An'ui."

Then give it.

"In the name of the goddess Yalanakan, you are free."

The whiteness around me shattered, revealing a riot of ever-changing colors. I felt a strange sort of vertigo, as if I were standing still but the world was spinning around me. The colors dissolved into darkness, and the last thing I heard before the vision ended was the voice whispering its thanks.

I opened my eyes. The cabin was full of guards, all pointing their weapons at me. I hazarded a quick glance in the direction of the window, but that way was blocked as well. No matter. I smiled as Lord Armstrong entered the room. Looking him dead in the eye, I hurled the conch to the deck, where it broke into several pieces.

Chapter Thirty-Four

THERE REMAINS BUT LITTLE to tell.

Surrounded as I was, I had no chance of escape. I do believe Lord Armstrong would have struck me down then and there, had he been alone. Instead, he gave orders to have me taken down to the brig where I spent a most unpleasant week, the details of which I shall not here relate. I regret to say that one of the guards made an attempt at my virtue (such as it is), but I was able to repel him quite ably. I proceeded to explain to him in quite explicit terms that I was very likely to be hanged, and as such had nothing whatever to lose should it come to a *contretemps* between myself and him. He got the message, right enough, and I was able to spend the rest of the voyage in peace, at least on that account.

It wasn't long before I was conveyed to this prison, in which custody I have been ever since. I am, for the most part, content. While in the brig, I overheard some scuttlebutt from the crew to the effect that their secret weapon had done a runner. Apparently, His Lordship was beside himself with fury the whole way back. I had done what I promised to do, and while I am by no definition a saint, I may think that having given up one's life and freedom to honor a promise of such import has to count for something.

Indeed, it is only when I think of Itaska and her world below that I find the melancholy coming upon me. So kind and sweet as she was, and so idyllic the life below the waves. I had rather hoped to return to her once everything was settled and my old crew put to rights. Sometimes at night I dream of the garden, and I swear I can feel her hand in mine. What a d—nable thing it is, to wake up from that to these four walls of stone. The chaplain tells me that they have not been able to round up any of my old shipmates. This is well. I expect they never shall. Black Jack may not crave the leadership role, but he is a wily and intelligent old salt. I have no doubt the crew is in good hands.

In any case, the governor is meant to be here in two days' time. I, at least, have finished this ms. As such, I can rest. The chaplain has assured me he will keep it safe after I am...gone. I wish someone was here to give me last rites, but I suppose I must make do with my lot. He has kindly offered to do what he can for my soul, but I suspect there isn't much, it being in the state it's in and all.

As I write this, the amulet sits next to me on the wooden bunk that serves as my bed, chair, and writing desk. I managed to convince the chaplain that it was a holy medal given to me by my Mum, and the last thing I had to remember her by. I'm not entirely certain he believed me. In any case, I have been allowed to keep it. Sometimes at night I have held it close to feel its warmth and dream of the world below.

But tonight, I have resolved to take the thing and throw it out the window into the waters below. I have marked the tide lines on the shore and am fairly certain I can send it out far past the lowest point if I use the leather thong as a sling. Probably nothing will come of it, but when all is said and done, it belongs to the sea, and to the sea it must return. Besides, the idea of it falling into the hands of Lord Armstrong or one of his toadies quite makes my skin crawl.

Itaska, my love, may it find its way once again to you, and may you know, rogue that I am, I did what I did with a glad heart. I hope you will think fondly of me. When they come for me two days hence, I vow my last thought will be of you.

It is done.

Afterward

At a little after midnight on July the 6th, a great commotion was heard coming from one of the cells in the eastern wing. When the guards arrived, they found that a considerable portion of the outside wall had been forcibly removed, and that the pyrate prisoner, "Mad" Molly McCormick, had disappeared. Given that the damage was centered around the place where the window had been, it was hypothesized that a stout rope or chain had been secured around the bars, then pulled away by force. However, as there were no ships in the vicinity that could possibly have done the deed, the actual cause must needs remain a mystery.

I have read through Captain McCormick's narrative. While I find much of it highly dubious, not to say utterly outrageous, there is a consistency that rings uncomfortably true. And while I cannot speak to what happened on that night, it did seem to me that I saw the spouting of a whale near the island some time before. I remember this struck me as unusual, but as to its significance, I refuse to speculate. In any case, prior to her disappearance, I had given her my assurance that I would keep her memoir safe and as such have placed it with my private papers to return with me to London when my term here is completed.

Rev. Simon Lockwood
Chaplain, Ft. St. Ambrose
July 19th, 1680

Other Books by K. L. Mitchell

The Kalazad Trilogy: three comic fantasy novels in the picaresque tradition. Jobbing adventurer Revka and her centaur girlfriend Iyarra encounter a variety of challenges, including power-mad dukes, con artists, rogue librarians, storybook villains gone horribly wrong, and chaos in the Old West.

The Helen Highwater adventures: In this new series, Ex-pat American pilot Helen Highwater trots across the ancient world, hunting down ancient treasures and dangerous secrets with straight-laced historian Abigail Dawson by her side. So what happens when a freewheeling adventurer teams up with a serious scholar? Sparks fly.

About K. L. Mitchell

K. L. Mitchell was raised all over the south in a series of increasingly tiny towns until she finally joined the Air Force out of a desire for some culture. She's spent most of her professional life working on computers in one capacity or another, and occasionally manages to get them to actually work.

She's been writing for fun most of her life, and for publication since about 2011. She's written for multiple websites and local publications, and in 2013 was a recurring columnist for the *Kansas City Star*. She lives with a gray cat named Molly and would like to be an astronaut when she grows up.

Connect with Kelly

Email: k_l_mitchell@mail.com
Facebook: https://www.facebook.com/KLMitchellHere/

Note to Readers:

Thank you for reading a book from Desert Palm Press. We appreciate you as a reader and want to ensure you enjoy the reading process. We would like you to consider posting a review on your preferred media sites and/or your blog or website.

For more information on upcoming releases, author interviews, contests, giveaways and more, please sign up for our newsletter and visit us at Desert Palm Press: www.desertpalmpress.com and "Like" us on Facebook: Desert Palm Press.

Bright Blessings

www.ingramcontent.com/pod-product-compliance
Lightning Source LLC
LaVergne TN
LVHW041802060526
838201LV00046B/1101